CATCHING
Lucas Riley

PRAISE FOR
Catching Lucas Riley

"With characters that immediately 'catch' your heart, Farnsworth crafts a charming love story with the perfect mix of humor, surprise, and *ahhh*."

— JENNIFER MOORE
Author of *Becoming Lady Lockwood*

"Witty, creative, and unexpected, *Catching Lucas Riley* is a captivating read. Fans of romantic comedies and retellings will adore this book.

— RACHAEL RENEE ANDERSON
Author of *Divinely Designed* and *Luck of the Draw*

"So much fun! This lighthearted love story is full of funny scenes and sweet, romantic moments. And the ending was even better than I thought it would be. I highly recommend this thoroughly entertaining read!"

— HEIDI DOXEY
Author of *Liam Darcy, I Loathe You*

LAUREN WINDER FARNSWORTH

CATCHING
Lucas Riley

BONNEVILLE
BOOKS

AN IMPRINT OF CEDAR FORT, INC.
SPRINGVILLE, UTAH

ISBN 13: 978-1-4621-1791-8

Published by Bonneville Books, an imprint of Cedar Fort, Inc.
2373 W. 700 S., Springville, UT 84663
Distributed by Cedar Fort, Inc., www.cedarfort.com

LIBRARY OF CONGRESS CATALOGING-IN-PUBLICATION DATA

Names: Farnsworth, Lauren Winder, 1986- author.
Title: Catching Lucas Riley / Lauren Winder Farnsworth.
Description: Springville, UT : Bonneville Books, an imprint of Cedar Fort,
    Inc., [2016]
Identifiers: LCCN 2015040043 | ISBN 9781462117918 (softcover : acid-free
    paper)
Subjects: | GSAFD: Love stories. | Christian fiction.
Classification: LCC PS3606.A7262 C38 2016 | DDC 813/.6--dc23
LC record available at http://lccn.loc.gov/2015040043

Cover design by Michelle May Ledezma
Cover design © 2016 Cedar Fort, Inc.
Edited and typeset by Melissa J. Caldwell

Printed in the United States of America

10 9 8 7 6 5 4 3 2 1

Printed on acid-free paper

For Pete and Carie Winder, the most incredible parents a girl could ever have. Everything I am I owe to your endless sacrifice and love. I love you!

Also for Kristin, Brett, A. J., and Emily—I take back everything I ever said. I will never be able to adequately describe how grateful I am to be stuck eternally with all of you.

Also by
Lauren Winder Farnsworth

Keeping Kate

{ Chapter ONE }

"COME ON, GUYS! Hustle! Hustle!" Alex shouted, clapping her hands as she walked along the pool deck. Some of her Cache Valley High varsity swimmers shot her dirty looks as they pushed off from the wall, breathing desperately. She smiled to herself, knowing exactly how they felt. She had started swimming competitively at an early age and continued on through high school and college. Swimming was a difficult, demanding sport, but she loved it. Now, as a coach for the local high school team in Logan, Utah, Alex reveled in the opportunity to experience the fierce competition of the sport, with none of the physical pain.

"Come on, coach," Mark Peters complained from lane three. "We've been doing these sprints for twenty minutes now!"

"For every second you complain, I add one more," Alex warned, pointing threateningly at the set on the whiteboard.

"I'm going, I'm going," Mark said quickly, pulling his goggles over his eyes.

Alex chuckled as she turned and began walking the opposite way down the Cache Valley Recreation Center pool. Suddenly she froze as her eyes fell upon a vision of absolute perfection. Through the glass wall surrounding the pool area, Alex saw him smoothly sliding his card through the swiper, laughing at something the girl behind the front desk was saying. He was beautiful. He was inspiring. And he was oh so unattainable.

His name was Lucas Riley. He was the elders quorum president in Alex's LDS singles ward, so she'd had plenty of opportunities to ogle him. Tall and tanned, with adorable curly brown hair and light-green eyes, he looked like what a Greek god might aspire to. Though she doubted any of the gods could have actually succeeded.

Lucas was a wide receiver on the Utah State University football team. Recently the team had actually begun making a name for itself, and she liked to attribute all the progress to Lucas's efforts. Granted, he had no idea who she was or even that they sat in the same chapel every Sunday, but she just knew that if she were provided with the right moment, everything would fall into place. They'd be married with three kids in no time.

She watched him walk past the window with a couple of workout buddies from the ward. They headed up the stairs toward the weight room, never noticing her spellbound eyes fixed on them. When the gorgeous man was no longer in sight, she imagined him approaching the bench press. Then, single-handedly lifting the two hundred-pound plates and tossing one on each side of the bar, he would flash his dazzling smile, wink cheekily, and—

"Hey, coach!"

Crap.

She turned quickly, shaking her head in the process.

"Are we done or what?" Mark called. The twenty or so swimmers stared at her with hopeful eyes as she strode toward them across the deck.

"Five hundred cool-down, all of you, and then you can go," she conceded. Amidst the echoing cheers of her swimmers, she headed for her gym bag, the one that had "Eat My Wake! USU Swimming" stitched along the side. Yanking the strap over her shoulder and heading for the door, she considered staging a cool drive-by of the weight machines upstairs. But at the last minute, she veered left instead of right, moving toward the parking lot shimmering in the early August heat.

"Sunday," she assured herself. "I'll catch him on Sunday."

Never mind that she'd been promising herself that she would "catch him on Sunday" for the past three months. He had to notice her sometime, right?

* * * * *

"I'm telling you, if I see these one more time, you'll wonder where the rest of your pants went!"

Alex heard the war cry as she entered the apartment she shared with five other girls. She recognized the threat immediately as Kacey's, and she grinned and rolled her eyes.

"But I like those pants!" Rachel insisted, and Alex heard Jaclyn snicker. She walked into the kitchen in time to see Rachel dive for the ragged army pants, nearly face-planting into the closed pantry door as Kacey pulled them away easily. She held them high above her head, which at five feet and ten inches from the ground, was far above Rachel's reach.

"Might as well give up now, Rach," Alex said as she headed for the fridge. "Kacey declared war on those pants a long time ago, and while I admire your spirit in attempting to hang on to them, you probably should have known better."

"I don't see why she gets to mandate what I wear," Rachel grumped from the floor, running her fingers through her short brown hair.

"You should listen to her," Jaclyn pointed out, looking up from her biology homework. "No one in this apartment has had the kind of success with guys that Kacey has. Besides, she's only doing it for your own good. Admit it, Rach, the pants are hideous."

"But they're comfortable," Rachel complained as she climbed to her feet. "And it's not like I'm going to wear them on a date!"

"You'll never GET a date if you wear them," Kacey said, pointing at her. "Trust me, you'll thank me someday."

Rachel murmured something under her breath, just as the door opened to admit Sage and Meredith, who were coming from class.

The six girls in 26A were a mixed bunch. They ranged from five foot nothing to nearly six feet, had representation from every natural hair color, and included an education major, an engineering major, a theater major, an accounting major, and a pre-med. This was the girls' second year as roommates. They had been placed together by chance the prior year, and when none of them had managed to snag a husband the year before, they decided to give it another go as a team. They were all progressively a year apart in age. Rachel, at nineteen, was the youngest, followed by Sage, then Jaclyn, then Meredith, then Kacey, and finally, Alex, coming in at age twenty-four. She was the mother hen of the brood, although there wasn't much about her that resembled a mother. Or a hen.

Alex was tall, slim, and auburn-haired. Of the girls in her apartment, Alex was the only one with a completed degree. She had graduated two years earlier in dietetics and now worked at the local hospital in the maternity wing. Her jobs as swim coach and chronic advice-giver at the hospital had predisposed Alex to be outspoken and brutally honest. Her roommates bore bravely the burden that was Alex's mouth, but she had made herself more than one enemy outside the confines of the apartment over the years.

"Aha! The Return of the Army Pants. The saga lives on!" Sage crowed with her financial accounting textbook held high in the air as she viewed the scene before her. "I swear, this is the roommate sketch that will not die."

"She keeps finding ways to get them past me," Kacey muttered, stuffing the pants into a plastic grocery bag and knotting it tightly.

"Well, when you're three feet tall and fifteen pounds, you can do that." Meredith nodded, flipping her long, black hair behind her. She winked an exotic, almond-shaped eye at Rachel, who smiled faintly.

"So what's for eating?" Sage asked, moving toward the refrigerator. "My cost accounting professor used a wedding cake bakery as an example today, and I've been starving ever since."

"Speaking of weddings . . . ," hinted Jaclyn, with a significant look on her attractive, blonde pixie-cut-framed face. "Any glimpses of 'Mr. Untouchable' today, Alex?"

"Always," Alex sighed. "And I always manage to make a complete fool of myself when I see him. Seriously, I stop just short of drooling."

"Well, why stop there?" said Meredith, smiling. "After all, the man is a vision."

"And yet completely blind," Kacey commented bluntly. "After all, you'd have to be to not notice someone the size of Alex mooning over you."

"Excuse me?" Alex sputtered, spraying a mouthful of water over the countertop. "Someone the *size* of me? What am I, a red-haired *hippo*?!"

"Oh, calm down, I was simply referencing your height, you drama queen," Kacey said, waving a hand at Alex. "After all, at nearly six feet, with your hair and everything, it's not like you're not eye-catching."

"Yes, well, Lucas manages to miss me every time."

"Come on, Al," Meredith soothed. "There are plenty of fish in the sea. Why not just find another one? One who is as mesmerized with you as you are with him?"

"I want that fish," Alex said, with a hint of superiority in her tone. "He's a great catch. And I'm not such a bad fish myself. We could make beautiful, fishy music together."

Jaclyn snorted into her biology book but didn't look up.

"Fish sounds good . . . ," Sage commented as she rummaged through the fridge. "Do we have any of that salmon left?"

* * * * *

"This is painful," Meredith whispered to Alex as they sat in sacrament meeting the following Sunday. "Sometimes I think that skipping fast Sunday testimony meeting would be an effective plan for lowering my blood pressure. I should suggest it to my doctor as formal treatment plan."

Alex snorted. "Right. High blood pressure, you? I don't believe it."

"Well, it wouldn't be high if I didn't come to this meeting every month. I mean, I spend the entire hour cringing in sympathy or borrowed embarrassment."

"You're too kind," Alex said, smirking. "You should just learn to mock like the rest of us."

"Rude," Meredith whispered back.

"Shhhh!" Rachel glared with severity as she hissed down the bench at them. "The bishop is watching you!"

Alex glanced up at the stand, noticing Bishop King frowning at her. Whoops. She folded her hands in her lap and looked around, trying to ignore the crying brunette at the microphone. Meredith was right; this really was painful.

It wasn't that she didn't appreciate testimony meeting for what its purpose was supposed to be, but the problem was that too many singles ward testimonies turned into storytelling sessions or academy award speeches. This one was worse than most.

Alex allowed her eyes to wander around the chapel, searching for the curly head she thought she'd seen slip in just after the opening prayer. Finally, she found it, two rows up and to the left. Alex was thrilled to see that Lucas was not sitting with any girls today. In fact, he had sat next to Calvin Jones, a special needs young man who often sat alone. Alex felt her heart constrict. How could anyone not fall for Lucas Riley?

It took her several minutes to realize she was staring, very obviously and shamelessly, with a soppy look on her face. Looking around quickly to see if anyone had noticed, she glanced quickly up at the stand. Her eyes met the piercing blue gaze of Sealey Witchburn, the ward executive secretary. Meeting the eyes of the ward executive secretary was never a good idea, unless you were dying to be next Sunday's sacrament meeting fodder, but in Sealey's case, it was suicide.

Sealey was tall, blond, and extremely good looking, but no one ever noticed that part once they actually met him. The guy was the epitome of intimidating. He saw everything—noticed everything. He had his well-shaped finger placed directly on the pulse of the ward, and he was not afraid to use his mysteriously acquired knowledge for his own sadistic purposes.

Alex looked away quickly, afraid he would divine from her gaze all her deepest, darkest thoughts and wishes with regard to Lucas Riley. Few people knew Lucas as well as Sealey did—they were best friends and roommates, attended all the same ward council meetings, and even worked for the same company. She couldn't afford Sealey letting Lucas in on her secret. But she felt her heart sinking.

She knew she had been careless, staring so fixedly at her heart's desire—Sealey's knowing smirk had been enough to convince her of that. She should have been more aware of who was watching her. There was not a chance in the world that Sealey didn't now suspect how she felt about Lucas. What would stop him from revealing the secret? What would he demand of her as his price for keeping quiet? She shivered from the sixth row of the chapel, knowing that in order to preemptively save her dreams of one day catching Lucas Riley's eye, she would have to confront Sealey Witchburn.

* * * * *

"All right, what do you want?" Alex asked straightforwardly to Sealey's back after the meeting had ended.

"Why, Sister Foamer," Sealey said in his silky smooth voice as he turned to face her. "What an honor to be willingly approached by such . . . ah, grace." He eyed her thunderous expression with amusement. "And how are we this fine Sunday?"

"Stop messing with me, Witchburn," Alex retorted. "Just tell me what you want."

"Whatever do you mean?" He looked at her, wide-eyed and innocent, but his mouth curved into a wolfish smile.

"I mean it. I'm not in the mood. I don't want this splashed all over the ward, so either tell me what I have to do, or just swear right now to keep your mouth shut."

"Well, it's not like you're working all that hard to hide it," he pointed out, dropping his façade. "I wouldn't be surprised if everyone knew already."

"I'll take my chances," Alex said, sneering.

"Why are you so afraid of getting it out there, anyway?" he asked, raising an eyebrow. "He might actually stare back at you if he knew you liked him."

"I want to do it my way," she insisted. "I don't want to get all high school about this."

"Well, then," Sealey said, his manner suddenly almost businesslike. "In that case, I can help you."

"You can—what?" Alex said, thrown off by his change in tone.

"If you're wanting to be adult about your advance, then let me help you. Where are you going to find someone who knows him better than I do?"

He's got a point, Alex thought, but she stared distrustfully up at Sealey. "Why would you volunteer to help me? What's in it for you?"

"Just happy to see another young couple in the ward blissfully wed," Sealey responded angelically.

"Yeah, right." Alex rolled her eyes. "What is it really? Why are you willing to help me get Lucas's attention?"

"That's my business," Sealey said straightforwardly. "Just be grateful I'm in this giving mood today. Normally I might just have thrown you to the wolves. Otherwise known as apartment 34B."

Alex shuddered, thinking of the apartment of six girls who lived in her complex. They functioned as the ward information superhigh-way. Whether the information was verifiable or not was entirely another matter, and one they didn't concern themselves with.

"So let me get this straight," Alex said, narrowing her eyes up at Sealey. "You are going to help me get into Lucas's line of sight, and I don't have to do anything or say anything or give you anything in return?" Her tone plainly showcased her disbelief.

"I didn't say that," Sealey said. Alex grimaced and nodded her expectance of such a response. "As payment for my services, you have to do *everything* I say within the confines of our mission. I require your absolute and total trust. You tend to be a bit of an argumentative snot, Foamer, and to argue is to waste time and energy."

Alex opened her mouth to retort, but Sealey held up a hand. "Trust me, if you want Lucas to notice you, you need my help. You're better off just agreeing to my terms."

Alex closed her mouth, deflating. He was right. She knew that with-out his assistance, Lucas would be married to a perky little cheerleader before she had the chance to distract him.

"All right," Alex agreed, hesitantly. "But so help me, Witchburn, if you humiliate me or make me do something undignified, simply for your own enjoyment, I will make you very sorry."

"Well, you'll try, anyway," Sealey replied, supremely unconcerned. He turned and began walking toward the bishop's office. "Meet me in the gym after the mingle," he instructed over his shoulder. "Bring your game face, Foamer. We're heading into battle."

Alex watched him go, her stomach clenching queasily. What had she gotten herself into?

{ Chapter TWO }

"**WHAT HAVE YOU** gotten yourself into?" Meredith cried, her hands to her face. It was ten minutes later, and Alex sat in Sunday School with her roommates, waiting for class to start. "What were you thinking, going to *Sealey Witchburn* for help?"

"I didn't go to Sealey Witchburn for help!" defended Alex. "I went to Sealey Witchburn to prevent the entire ward learning my secret, and he *offered* to help. I accepted. There's a difference."

"But he's . . . he's . . . *evil*," Meredith whispered dramatically. "Didn't you hear what happened to Skye Matheson when she publicly called him out for refusing to support last year's stake date auction?"

"I know, but—" Alex started, but Jaclyn interrupted her.

"I didn't. What happened?" She chomped her gum in excited expectation.

"It *somehow* got around that she had once been engaged to that guy who got arrested last winter for chucking rocks at cars along Highway 89. Remember all those accidents? It was even suggested that he went all nutso because she had broken up with him. She ended up transferring to *Dixie State*," Meredith finished affectedly as though Dixie State College were where rumor legends went to die.

"Seriously? Skye was engaged to that homeless dude?" Jaclyn stage whispered as the Sunday School teacher got to his feet and cleared his throat loudly. "I didn't know that. Well, dang, I'd move too if something like that got around."

"You don't know for sure that Sealey said anything," Alex defended, somewhat weakly.

"But, Alex, really, who else would have known something like that?" Sage asked incredulously, ignoring the teacher as he glared openly at them. "He knows everything about everybody. It's downright *creepy*. And you're playing right into his hands!"

"Oh, relax," Kacey interrupted. "I think she was smart to go to Sealey. He's one of Lucas's best friends. Add that to the fact that he probably knows all of Lucas's darkest secrets, and Alex has got a valuable weapon in her hands."

"Right, like Sealey's going to turn on his best friend, just to help Alex." Jaclyn rolled her eyes. "If anything, he's going to turn on Alex and make her look like an idiot in front of Lucas, just for the entertainment value."

"Are you guys going to listen to anything today?" Rachel glared at each one in turn. "Why come to church if you're going to spend the whole time ignoring the stuff that actually matters?"

They all shut their mouths guiltily, recognizing Rachel's point as their collective conscience.

With the conversation finally halted, Alex ruminated on what she had done. How could she trust Sealey Witchburn? It was well known how dangerous he could be. Man alive, even his *name* sounded evil. Maybe she should just back out. Would he allow her to? What if he turned on her for attempting to break a deal with him? Oh, why couldn't she just have fallen for a guy who knew she existed?

* * * * *

Alex stood in the center of the church gym, scuffing the floor with her heel as she nervously waited for Sealey to show up. A thousand scenarios had run through her head in the past couple of hours, each one more unlikely than the last. By the time Sealey strolled through the door, she was ready to grab him by the collar and shout, "Let me out! Let me out, I beg you! I shouldn't have done it, I know, but I beg of you to *be merciful and free me!*" But one look at his face assured her she would never be successful. Sealey's expression was one of fixed determination.

"You ready for this, Foamer?" Sealey asked, his ice-blue eyes focused on her face. "You look queasy already, and I'm not a big fan of vomit on my shoes. I told you to bring your game."

"What does that even mean, anyway?" Alex asked, taking deep breaths and molding her face into nonchalance.

"It means that from now on, the only expression you're allowed to have on your face is one of complete confidence," Sealey answered. "No weakness allowed. Well, not unless I tell you that you can be weak. Some weakness is charming. Men typically don't want an Amazon."

"Was that a stab at my height?" she demanded, glaring at him.

"I seem to have touched a nerve," Sealey smirked. "Well, no need to burst a blood vessel. It was just an expression. All right . . . now where to start?"

"You're the expert; you tell me," Alex sighed.

"Well . . . typically the first step would be a full-scale, professional-grade makeover, but—and don't take this for more than it is—you're actually already pretty easy on the eyes, Foamer." His tone seemed to invite Alex to thank him for his observations.

She responded by raising an eyebrow scornfully.

Sealey ignored her and began circling her slowly, studying her from head to toe. "Yes, indeed," he muttered, his tone difficult to read. "Plenty of usable material here."

"When you've finished checking me out," Alex said sharply. "Could we maybe move on to something relevant? Like how I'm going to get Lucas to introduce himself to me?"

"If you don't think how you look is relevant to getting a guy to notice you, we've got bigger problems," Sealey responded, fixing his eyes studiously on her legs, a contemplative expression on his face.

"Right, well, I want him to more than just look at me," Alex demanded. "I want him to willingly talk to me."

"Oh, well, that's easy," Sealey said, finally focusing on her face. "We're going to force him to talk to you."

"Pardon?"

"We are going to manipulate the situation to where he has no choice but to talk to you," Sealey repeated. "Trust me, it's very simple."

"Okay . . . how?"

11

"The annual stake date auction," Sealey said, his eyebrows lowered, his voice ominous.

"The date auction?" Alex said in surprise. "But you hate the date auction!"

"As does every other individual with a certain level of respect for social and intellectual progress," Sealey replied. "Including Lucas Riley. But he's forced to participate as the elders quorum president. So . . . we make our move."

"I'm sorry . . . I don't get it," Alex complained. "How does the stake date auction help me? What are the chances that if I bid on a date with Lucas, I'll actually win it? Every girl in this stake wants to date him!"

"This is why you're so lucky you have me in your corner," Sealey replied, shrugging his shoulders. "I have far more influence than you give me credit for."

"So what do I need to do?" Alex asked hesitantly.

"Show up at the auction next week with five bucks in your pocket," Sealey said, heading for the door.

"Wait, that's it?" Alex cried desperately. "That won't be nearly enough for the highest bid!"

"What was my price for this venture?" Sealey thundered, his voice echoing throughout the cultural hall. "Total and absolute trust, Foamer! Date auction with five bucks!"

And he was gone.

* * * * *

"Will someone please explain to me what we're doing here?" Jaclyn complained as the six girls walked into the stake center cultural hall. Chairs were evenly spaced, all facing the stage at the far end of the room. "If I really wanted to find someone to date, I would not spend two hours looking for an opportunity to pay money to locate them."

"I admit, the concept is flawed," Alex said distractedly, looking around. No Sealey yet. No Lucas either. *So help me, if Sealey doesn't show up and leaves me to do this on my own . . .* Alex muttered in her head.

"The auction's for charity!" Rachel exclaimed, as if that explained everything.

"Jaclyn, you had every opportunity to be on the receiving end of the deal," Sage pointed out, ignoring Rachel. "All you had to do was enter yourself as a potential date. Then you wouldn't have had to pay anything."

"And have no say over who I spend an evening with? No thanks," Jaclyn said, looking at Sage incredulously. "Really, the only reason I'm here is to see what happens with Alex and Lucas. I'm morbidly curious."

"Aren't we all?" Alex muttered under her breath. She relaxed slightly as she saw Sealey enter the room. "Excuse me, girls," she said, pushing past them. "My, uh, consultant has arrived." She could feel five pairs of eyes following her as she approached Sealey Witchburn.

"So what's the plan?" she asked breathlessly. "What do I do?"

"Well, hello to you too," he said, with an eyebrow raised.

"I don't have the energy for niceties," Alex claimed, and her voice betrayed her panic. "What am I doing here?"

"You're going to bid," Sealey said simply, shrugging. "That's it."

"I'm going to bid?" Alex repeated, her voice nearly a screech. "That's your brilliant plan?!"

"Calm down, Foamer," Sealey hissed, looking around. "It's not that difficult, right? Raise your hand and bid five dollars. That's it. I've taken care of the rest."

For some reason that last statement made her more uncomfortable than ever. "What do you mean you've taken care of the rest?" she demanded. "What did you do?"

"Never you mind," Sealey said, moving past her. "Just do as I say. Do otherwise, and you're in breach of contract." He winked impertinently at her and walked away.

She rejoined her roommates, her expression indicating the dread she felt.

"Well? What did he say?" Kacey demanded. "What's the plan?"

"He just told me to bid," Alex said, hopelessly. "He said he took care of the rest, but I have no idea what that means."

"You know what I don't get?" said Meredith, running her fingers through her long hair and examining the ends. "Why doesn't he just introduce you to Lucas himself? I mean, they're best friends, aren't they? It's not like it would be hard to finagle a simple introduction."

"Oh, come on," Kacey said, rolling her eyes. "Isn't it obvious?

He's trying to make sure Alex makes a lasting impression! Just being introduced probably wouldn't do it. He wants to make sure Lucas *remembers* Alex."

Alex stared in horror at Kacey. What exactly had Sealey arranged that would ensure that Lucas remembered her? Was she about to be publicly humiliated and she didn't realize it? She trembled more than ever, trying to find the resolve she usually had by default.

"Welcome to stake FHE, everyone!" exclaimed a cute blonde from the stage. "Tonight, we're raising money for charity by auctioning off dates with some of our stake's most eligible bachelors and bachelorettes!" She flashed a white, toothy grin around at the room at large.

"Here's the deal. As soon as you see the man or woman of your dreams onstage, that's your cue to start bidding. There is no limit, but remember, you can only bid cash or canned goods. No IOUs will be accepted. Now let's get started!"

Cheesy game show music played over the sound system, and Bishop King, wearing a loud, checkered blazer, took the microphone.

"Brothers and sisters, welcome!" he said cheerily. "Tonight's main purpose is to support those members of our community who may be less fortunate, followed closely by our motivation to get as many of you married as possible." He grinned as a collective, good-natured groan echoed throughout the gym. "I am confident that at least one of you will find your eternal companion tonight," the bishop continued, smiling optimistically down at them. "So for that reason, don't hesitate to empty your pockets in the attempt. Now, for our first date auction participant!"

Alex watched numbly as various individuals strutted across the stage with their best catwalks, most of them dissolving into laughter in the process. The bidding was fierce, but friendly, and each participant was quickly claimed. Alex felt her heartbeat go into overdrive as Lucas Riley finally walked across the stage. He sauntered, cool and unconcerned, to the chair in the middle of the stage, smiling calmly at the breathless audience.

"And your name is?" Bishop King asked needlessly.

"Lucas Riley," Lucas answered smoothly into the microphone. He looked supremely unruffled, and Alex didn't doubt he was. After all, what did he have to worry about? He was the most eligible bachelor in the stake.

"All right, let's start the bidding at ten dollars!" Bishop King boomed into his microphone. Alex froze in horror. He had started the bidding at two dollars for every other participant! Why was he getting exorbitant *now*? He must be trying to milk the "golden boy" potential for all it was worth.

Alex looked around in panic. Sealey had told her to bring five dollars and no more! The bidding was starting at twice what she had! She looked around frantically for Sealey, needing his instruction. But something stopped her panicked search.

The room was dead silent. Nobody was bidding. Her eyes swept the gym, looking for the untold number of females that were sure to want to date Lucas Riley for so small a sum as ten dollars. Nobody moved. Alex noticed several girls moving uncomfortably in their chairs and looking around furtively. What was going on?

"Okay, fine," Bishop King said crossly. "We'll start at seven dollars."

Silence. Alex's roommates looked at each other in shock. This was unprecedented! Never in Stake Date Auction history had the starting bid amount been reduced for a date entry! Bids typically came in fast and furious, even for the less-desirable options.

"Seriously, ladies?" The bishop looked incredulous now. Alex glanced up at Lucas, noticing how red his face looked. In fact, he looked downright mortified. She had never seen him so off-center. Her heart ached for him. She looked around again for Sealey, finally spotting him leaning against the far wall, a crooked smile on his face. He was enjoying this! He caught her eye and, noticing her panicked expression, shook his head.

Not yet, he mouthed at her. Her eyes shot back to Lucas, his face almost purple with humiliation now.

"All right, starting the bidding at five dollars, then!" Bishop King said, the disbelief clearly ringing in his voice. "Five dollars is a *steal*, girls, for this young man! You couldn't find better than Lucas Riley. He's the catch of all catches! I promise you . . ." At each attempt at persuasion, Lucas looked like he wished he could burrow further and further into the ground.

Finally, Alex couldn't take it anymore.

"Five dollars!" she cried.

"Five dollars!" Bishop King called in relief. "Five dollars going once, five dollars going twice, *dated* for five dollars!" The last part was spoken so fast that it took Alex several seconds to process it.

As the realization dawned, Alex registered that nearly every female eye in the room was fixed on her. Some of them were smirking, but many of them looked truly concerned. Alex was sure this was a result of whatever Sealey had done to keep the female population at large from bidding on Lucas Riley, so she wasn't terribly alarmed. She'd find out sooner or later which taboo rule she had broken.

Finally, her eyes met those of her prize. For the first time in living memory, Lucas Riley's green eyes met Alex Foamer's brown ones, and he smiled in willful acknowledgement.

Sealey Witchburn was a wizard.

★ ★ ★ ★ ★

"I don't believe it!" crowed Sage, drumming her fingers on the steering wheel as she drove. "I can't believe it worked! What Sealey Witchburn must have done to keep an entire stake of girls silent when presented with a specimen like Lucas Riley, I have no idea, but it must have been a doozy!"

"He told the girls in 34B that Lucas had a psychotic redhead stalking him and she would go ballistic on any girl who bid on him at the date auction," Kacey replied, flipping through an institute brochure in the front seat. "I heard one of them talking about it after the closing prayer. Obviously, with their skills, a tidbit like that spread throughout the stake inside of a week."

"So now everyone's going to think that Alex is the psychotic stalker!" Rachel exclaimed, looking sympathetically over at her.

"Or that she was the one person brave enough to stand up to the psychotic stalker," Meredith pointed out, resting a reassuring hand on Alex's arm. "And maybe they'll just think it's a coincidence that they both have red hair."

Alex was barely listening. She stared out the window, reeling over the idea that she was secured at least one date with Lucas Riley. She had never actually believed she would get this far. One date was really all she needed to get her foot in the door. It took her several moments before she realized her phone was vibrating in her hand.

"Hello?" she said vacantly, not bothering to check the number.

"Hi, Alex?"

She knew the voice immediately, but she was totally unprepared for it. She felt her blood instantly carbonate as her hand tightened convulsively on the phone.

She nodded stupidly for a moment, before remembering he couldn't see her. "Yes?" she finally squeaked, trying not to hyperventilate. Her roommates' eyes were fixed on her.

Somehow, in all her fantasies of dating Lucas Riley and kissing Lucas Riley and marrying Lucas Riley, she had never imagined herself *talking to* Lucas Riley. Her mind was a fury of white-hot panic.

"This is Lucas Riley," he said. "My friend Sealey told me your name and gave me your number. I just wanted to thank you for bailing me out back there. I really appreciate the save."

She blinked frantically out the window, her phone clutched in her hand, willing her mouth to move and coherency to issue from it. "No problem," she finally peeped. She took a deep breath, remembering Sealey's demand that she be the picture of confidence at all times. "I live to save. I mean, serve. I mean—"

She heard her roommates snickering around her and she longed to kick each one of them, in turn, squarely in the shins. She could practically hear the smile in Lucas's voice when he responded.

"Well, in return for the rescue, I insist you let me take you out, instead of vice versa. It's the least I can do."

"Well, if you insist," Alex agreed, much too quickly. She could almost hear the imagined smack of Sealey's hand hitting his forehead at her eager response. *Play it cool, play it cool,* she lectured herself. "I mean, if that's what you want, who am I to complain?" Alex corrected, molding her voice into as much honey as she could muster.

"Great!" Lucas replied, his voice enthusiastic. "When are you available? A girl like you probably has all kinds of guys after her, so I'm happy to wait my turn."

Alex attempted to process this comment. Was that an effort to flatter her, or an effort to push off the date as long as possible? Oh, men were infuriating! Forcing her pulse to slow, she endeavored to think like Sealey. *Don't be too available . . . he won't want something no one else wants. Make him think that you are in high demand . . .*

"Well, I am booked this weekend and next," she lied easily. "But I could probably swing something the week after that. What about you?"

"Three weeks from now it is, then," he replied, and she could see him flashing his gleaming white teeth in her mind's eye. "How about that Friday night?"

"Perfect. I'll pencil you in," Alex said, finally getting the hang of the silky smooth tones.

"Sounds like a date to me," Lucas said. "I'll see you then. Have a great night, Alex." He hung up.

Alex sat motionless in her seat, the phone cradled in both hands, the trauma of the moment finally settling around her. Her roommates gazed at her silently, looks ranging from fear to scorn to amusement on their faces.

Kacey opened her mouth, her head craned around to stare into the backseat, but Alex held up a hand. "Don't ask," she said. "I am in no fit state to discuss it at this moment."

Kacey rolled her eyes and shrugged. Alex jumped a mile when her phone began to vibrate again in her hands. "Oh no! It's him again!" she exclaimed when she saw an unfamiliar number flash on the screen. "I've already exhausted my stores of conversation for the evening! Somebody else answer it!"

"Oh, for crying out loud," said Kacey, reaching around and grabbing the phone from Alex's hand.

"Hello?" she said boldly into the phone. She listened for a second and then pushed the phone at Alex again. "It's not Lucas."

"Oh," said Alex, sighing in relief. "Who is it?"

"It's Sealey," Kacey replied, a smirk on her face.

Alex doubted that was any better than the original assumption, but the difference was, she had *plenty* to say to Sealey.

"Well, hello, you dirty, rotten—" she started to say.

"Not bad, Foamer," he rode right over her insults. "Rough start, but by the end you had him eating out of your hand."

"How on earth do *you* know how the conversation went?" she demanded.

"Luke made the call on speaker from the car, and I was with him," Sealey said matter-of-factly. "How else would I know?"

"How do I know how you discover your diabolical secrets?" Alex retorted. Now that the date auction ordeal was over, she felt the irritation at the level of helplessness she'd endured all evening and had every intention of expressing it. "All I know is, you didn't bother to actually prepare me for exactly what I was going to be doing tonight, did you?"

"I told you to bid. All you did was bid," Sealey pointed out.

"Yes, after spending a full thirty seconds in cardiac arrest!" Alex screeched. Rachel put her hands over her ears and Jaclyn winced irritably at her.

"I couldn't give you all the details beforehand," Sealey said calmly. "If I did, the whole thing would've looked too scripted and Lucas would be onto us. You're not *trusting* me, Foamer. And I did get results, did I not?"

"Yeah," Alex muttered.

"Then stop your yammering and just be grateful. Now, I'll be over at your house after work tomorrow to work out our next steps."

"The date's not for three weeks!" Alex exclaimed, her eye twitching at the thought of Sealey in her apartment. "What could we possibly have to discuss?"

"You really don't want any contact with Lucas until your date? You really think that's the best plan of action?"

"But—"

"Foamer, if you want this thing to go anywhere, he has to already be interested in you by the time you go out," Sealey said, his voice clearly exasperated.

"Why?" she almost wailed.

Sealey groaned, and she imagined him holding his head in his hands. "Because," he finally responded, his voice fatigued. "The only reason he asked you out is because he felt obligated. However, in a perfect world, he would have asked you out because he was actually interested in you. Therefore, in order for this date to start out on the right foot, he has to be interested in you before it starts. Otherwise, you'll be spending the entire date trying to get him interested, and believe me, two hours will not accomplish a task that daunting."

Alex glared silently out the window at the passing scenery.

"*Capisci?*" Sealey prompted. "I'll be over at your place by 5:30 p.m."

"I have swim practice till six," Alex informed him. "Come over at seven."

"Fine," Sealey agreed. "See you then."

He hung up abruptly, and Alex's phone fell into her lap. On one hand, Sealey had already proven his usefulness and his expertise. But on the other, she had never met anyone whose company was so fraught with conflicting emotion. Being near Sealey Witchburn was frankly exhausting, but he'd gotten her this far. She trusted him enough to actually admit that she needed him now.

Sighing, she allowed her head to rest against the cool window, even as the car pulled up to the apartment building and her roommates began exiting the vehicle. She prayed the anxiety was worth it.

{ Chapter THREE }

ALEX SAT WITH legs jiggling spastically on the couch, simultaneously anticipating and dreading the sound of the doorbell. On
one hand, she was helpless and hopeless without Sealey, but on the
other, he was Sealey. 'Nuff said.

"I'd honestly consider making a break for it if I didn't feel so sorry
for you," Meredith said sympathetically as she folded herself sinuously
to the floor in the family room. She began her yoga stretches, her long,
dark hair sliding like water across her back. "Just don't expect me to say
anything."

"Thanks for hanging around," Alex replied, her brown eyes creased
with worry. The rest of her roommates had vacated the premises at the
news that Sealey was expected. "I really don't understand why he has
this effect on me. I'm not usually a timid person, am I?"

Meredith snorted. "Uh, no," she replied with a significant look. "I
remain convinced, to this day, that the only reason you're still unmar-
ried is because men fear you. You're beautiful, intelligent, athletic, and
a spiritual giant. Your only flaw is your willingness to open your mouth.
You know, so widely and so often . . ." Meredith's voice trailed off, and
she focused on her downward dog as Alex's look of flattery changed to
one of irritation.

"I'm not that bad!" she said defensively, throwing a couch pillow
directly through Meredith's graceful formation, making no contact
whatsoever. She reached for another, determined to improve her aim.

Just then, the doorbell rang. The sound echoed ominously through the apartment as Meredith and Alex looked at each other, wide-eyed.

"Do I have to?" Meredith whined, still in her downward dog pose, as Alex rose to answer the door. "Can't I just offer moral support from my bedroom? Do I really have to witness—"

"Good evening, ladies," came Sealey's voice as Alex opened the door to admit him. "Meredith, what a stunning exhibition." He raised an eyebrow at her, a smile twitching at the corners of his mouth. Meredith's face flamed and she removed her rear end from its position of prominence.

Alex gave her a sympathetic yet pleading look. *Don't leave me*, she mouthed at her roommate. Meredith glared at her rebelliously but nodded her agreement, rolling her eyes.

"Where are we setting up?" Sealey asked, turning to look at Alex. She wiped her face clean of all supplication and met his eyes.

"Setting up?" she repeated in confusion. "What could you possibly have to set up? Don't tell me you've put together a PowerPoint presentation."

"Sadly, I didn't think of that," Sealey replied, his brow actually scrunching in dismay. He marched toward the kitchen, and Alex noticed for the first time the shoulder bag he carried. A bag that looked depressively heavy.

"Just how much time is this going to take?" Alex asked, feeling the exhaustion sink into her tight shoulders.

"Depends on how quickly you catch on," Sealey replied. He swung the bag onto the table, where it made a formidable *thump*, and pushed up the sleeves of his tan sweater. "No complaints, Foamer. You're swinging for the fence, so now you have to put in the prep time to actually score the run."

"Please don't start with the corny sports analogies. I can't take it," Alex said, sinking into a kitchen chair.

"Lesson Number One: You want to impress a guy, especially a guy like Lucas Riley, brush up on your sports chatter, analogies included," Sealey said pointedly. "And I hear chatter is something you're particularly gifted at, Foamer, so let's put it to good use."

Alex shot Meredith a look that dared her to say something. Meredith smirked at her but continued silently on with her yoga in the living room.

"Lesson Number Two," Sealey continued, pulling a number of file folders out of his bag. "Brush *down* on the *rest* of your chatter."

Alex looked at him, eyebrow raised. "Excuse me?"

"Look, I hate to break it to you, but men don't have endless tolerance for prattle," Sealey said, continuing to pull things out his bag. "I know you think your mind is a treasure trove of brilliance yet untapped, but I promise you, he won't agree."

Alex gave him an affronted look.

"Now don't go getting all offended on me," he replied, noticing her expression. "I'm sure you're as brilliant as you think you are, but if you try to convince him of that, simply by telling him so, all you'll do is make him wish he'd never heard of Alex Foamer."

"I don't—" Alex began, but Sealey cut her off.

"When it comes to conversation, less is more," he emphasized. "Don't tell him all about you, show him! Let him get to know you through observation."

"Get to know me—what?" Alex screeched. "Look, I know it's stupid to spend a first date talking endlessly about myself, but how is he supposed to get to know me if I don't talk about myself at all?"

"I didn't say that. Just limit yourself," Sealey responded. "If he asks you a question about yourself, give him a general answer. Allow yourself to be mysterious to him. Allow him to come to his own conclusions about your favorite color, your perfume of preference, your skill set, and yes, even your character."

"Okay . . . ," Alex said, mulling over his words in her mind.

"If you tell him everything about you in a single date, what reason does he have to dig further? You want to intrigue him, to tantalize him, to leave him wanting more."

Alex looked at Sealey with an expression of disgust. "Remind me what you do for a living again? You sound like you're quoting some cheesy online magazine."

"Advertising," Sealey said simply.

"Oh, well that explains it," Alex muttered.

Sealey rolled his eyes. "Trust me, okay? If a guy figures you out too easily, he completely loses interest. It's unfortunate, but it's true. It's all about the chase."

"Well, technically, I'm the one doing the chasing," Alex said mournfully.

"But he doesn't have to know that," Sealey pointed out. "It's imperative that he believes he's chasing you."

"I know, I know," Alex muttered.

Sealey glared at her. "You know, I'm not really liking your attitude, Foamer," he said, irritated. "After all I've done for you thus far, the least you could do is be pleasant. After all, it's not like *I've* gotten anything out of this deal."

Alex sighed. He was right. He really had been helpful, and she'd been nothing but cynical and snotty throughout the entire process. "Sorry," she said, sitting up straighter in her chair and molding her face into a more pleasant expression. "How's this?"

"Better," he conceded. "Now, we need to stage some drive-bys within the next couple of weeks. Enough that Lucas is reminded of your existence, but not so many that he suspects you're stalking him."

Alex nodded in agreement. Sounded like a reasonable plan to her. "He comes to the gym where my swim team works out every day. Walks right by the pool area." She tried to keep her voice from sounding too dreamy as she said it.

"That will work for a once-a-week contact point," Sealey agreed, nodding as he shuffled through the file folders, apparently looking for something. "I have his client schedule here somewhere."

"His what schedule?" Alex asked, eyebrow raised.

"He works for my company, remember?" Sealey prompted, glancing at her.

"Your company?" she asked, her eyebrows rising even further.

"Yes, Foamer, *my company*," Sealey responded, his voice annoyed. "Trident Advertising."

"Wait a second, you *own* that company?" Alex clarified, attempting to keep her voice somewhere below a screech.

"Don't sound so surprised," Sealey said, finally appearing to have found what he was looking for. He pulled the piece of paper toward him and studied it thoughtfully, his hand on his chin. "It looks like he has meetings all over the valley in the next couple of weeks. We should easily be able to set up a couple random run-ins without it looking too suspicious."

Alex was still staring at him. "How old are you?" she questioned.

Sealey glanced up from the paper, his irritation evident. "How old am—what does that matter?"

"You seem awfully young to have your own company," she said, trying to mask how impressed she was.

"It's a small market," he said dismissively. "This is Logan, Utah, Foamer, in case you hadn't noticed. Not exactly a thriving metropolis."

Alex shrugged, but inside she marveled at this new tidbit she had discovered. She'd have to mentally nibble on it later.

An hour later, Alex had a list of dates, times, and locations where she was expected to be. The plan was unbelievably detailed, even to the point of Sealey telling her which door to enter and where to stand or pace, and whether to look concerned, disinterested, or ecstatic. Alex wouldn't have been surprised if he had insisted on seeing her closet so he could tell her what to wear.

"And what do I do when he walks up to me and asks why I'm so panicky?" Alex asked, raising her eyebrows.

"That's the part where you lie through your teeth about the great traumatic event you're suffering through," Sealey responded, shoving folders back into his shoulder bag. "Besides, you're giving Lucas more credit than he deserves for his level of concern. Most likely, he'll see you, remember who you are, but not even bother to approach you. He's a guy, remember?"

Alex couldn't imagine Lucas seeing a damsel in distress and not running to her aid. He was a knight in shining armor, after all.

"And that's good," Sealey continued, not noticing Alex's distracted expression as she dreamed of Lucas on a white horse, his armor gleaming in the sun. "We don't want him to approach you and talk to you every time he sees you. He'd get sick of you before he ever went out with you."

"This whole thing seems awfully risky," Meredith commented from the living room couch, where she sat with an electrical engineering textbook open on her lap. "What if you're wrong and he does approach her every time?"

"He won't," Sealey assured them. "First of all, he'll be with other people most of the time, many of them clients, and he wouldn't dream of making such a horrible impression. Second, you're overestimating Foamer's powers of attraction."

Alex opened her mouth to protest, but Sealey held up a hand. It felt like he did that a lot—the sight was overwhelmingly familiar. Maybe she did open her mouth more often than necessary.

"I don't want to hear it," Sealey said, his hand still in the air. "It's not like you're a hag, Foamer, but the sounds that issue from your mouth are not exactly a siren call, you know."

Again with the mention of her mouth. She'd never been so self-conscious about her candor.

"All right, we good?" Sealey asked, zipping up his bag. "Do you feel confident? Or at least non-queasy?"

"Yeah . . . ," Alex responded, her tone much less certain than she proclaimed.

"Let me just offer you one more piece of advice," Sealey said, looking at her seriously. "And that advice is, don't overdo it. I'm probably doing myself a disservice by saying this, but you're a pretty remarkable physical specimen all by yourself, Foamer. The more effort you put into enhancing that, the more high maintenance you're going to look. Take it from someone who knows, Luke is not interested in high-maintenance."

Alex was torn between flattery and confusion. "Are you saying I shouldn't wear makeup or anything?"

Sealey sighed. "Has anyone ever explained to you the concept of subtlety?" He rubbed a hand over his face. "I suggest avoiding one thing, and you immediately jump to the opposite extreme. I said *don't overdo it.* You're naturally non-gag-worthy enough that you could probably get away with no makeup, so maybe employ that strategy at the pool while you're coaching your team. Lucas wouldn't be surprised at all to see you go *au naturale* at the gym. But, if you're running into him at a nicer restaurant, he would probably expect to see the girl of his dreams make a bit more of an effort. Make sense?"

"Yes," Alex said firmly. She was embarrassed that a guy was lecturing her on when and where and how to utilize her Maybelline products. However, she didn't miss Sealey's continued reference to her looks. She was surprised that he was even capable of noticing that a girl was pretty. He seemed like too much of a shark to perceive things like that.

"Okay, then," Sealey said, slinging his bag onto his shoulder. "Well, good luck. I'll connect with you before your first drive-by, but if I hear anything of interest in the meantime, I'll pass it on."

"Cool," Meredith commented again from the living room. "It's like having your own personal spy camping out in Lucas's apartment, Alex."

Sealey rolled his eyes as he headed for the door. "Let's not get carried away," he muttered, reaching for the doorknob.

Alex followed him out, needing to ask him one more question, but not wanting Meredith to overhear.

"Hey," she said, catching him by the arm before he headed for his car. "Can I ask you something?"

"Sure," he said noncommittally, pushing a hand through his blond hair.

"Why are you doing this?" she asked. She purposely kept her voice soft and nonaggressive, knowing he wouldn't respond well to her usual form of address. "Why are you willing to expend so much time and effort to help me? I've never really gotten the feeling that you liked me all that much, so I'm confused as to why you would do this for me, without making any kind of demand."

"I thought I told you that I had my reasons," Sealey said, but his voice wasn't harsh or irritated. He sounded more uncertain than anything.

"You did, but I thought that just meant you were going to wait to go in for the kill," she responded. "Like you wanted me to get in so deep I couldn't get out before you revealed what you wanted from me."

Sealey whistled. "You really don't have a very high opinion of me, do you, Foamer?" he said, one eyebrow cocked.

"I just hear a lot of frankly brutal things about you," Alex responded. "It seems like you typically play hardball. You haven't been fully conforming to that stereotype thus far, and it's making me nervous."

Sealey sighed. "Well, we wouldn't want that," he said, with an edge of sarcasm. "Have a seat." He gestured to the steps in front of the apartment building.

Surprised at his capitulation, Alex sat down on the cement steps, leaning back on her hands. She tried to keep her anticipation hidden, afraid that if he noticed it, he'd take back his willingness to be so forth-coming. She let her head fall back, long auburn hair sliding from her shoulders down to tickle her arms. The night air was cool and pleasant, smelling like summer nights always do.

"You're probably not aware," Sealey began as he sat next to her, "that Luke is currently writing a missionary."

Alex sat up straight, feeling suddenly winded. No, she had not known that. She'd been encouraged by the fact that Lucas so rarely distinguished a particular girl above the rest, but now that she knew why, she felt the encouragement evaporate. "He is?" she almost wailed. "Who is she?"

"Her name is Olivia," Sealey responded. "They've been friends since they were kids."

"Is it serious?" Alex asked, really afraid to hear the answer.

"He's more serious about her than I've ever seen him about anyone else," Sealey replied. "But that's not to say his feelings can't change."

"So . . . why do you seem to want them to?" Alex pressed, noticing the furrow between Sealey's eyebrows.

"I don't . . . necessarily," Sealey hedged. He glanced at her face and sighed. "Look, Olivia is . . . well, she's beautiful. And I mean really beautiful. And she's smart and funny and . . . well . . ."

Alex squinted at Sealey, trying to figure out if he was purposely tor-turing her or something. But then suddenly everything slid into place in her head. "Oh my gosh!" she cried. "You want her! You're trying to distract Lucas from Olivia so that when she comes home, he'll no longer be interested and you can be there to pick up the pieces!"

Sealey winced. "Well, that makes it sound so much worse than it really is."

"No, I'm pretty sure it's every bit as bad as it sounds," Alex empha-sized. "You're seriously trying to steal your best friend's girl?"

Sealey looked at her. "Yes," he said straightforwardly.

"Wow . . . ," Alex muttered. "You know what I said earlier? I take it back. You are every bit as hardball as I've heard."

Sealey looked at her steadily, his face stony. "I'll see you later, Foamer." Without another word, he got to his feet and walked away.

{ Chapter FOUR }

ALEX SMILED AS she walked out of the hospital room of her last new mom for the day. While she considered herself more of a "grown-up person" than a "kid person," she loved being surrounded by the warm fluffiness that was the hospital maternity ward. You know, as long as all the new babies weren't screaming at once.

Alex, as one of the on-call dietitians for the maternity ward, was happy to consult with new moms on the best diet for themselves and for their babies once they left the hospital, but mostly, she acted as a certified lactation educator. She always found it somewhat ironic that she was expected to be an expert in something she had never actually experienced for herself, but the moms she consulted with didn't seem to mind. In fact, they were usually relieved and grateful every time she walked into their rooms, especially the first-time moms. Alex also kept office hours on Tuesdays and Thursdays so that these new moms could come in for help and advice once they'd returned home with their soft, cooing (or sometimes shrieking) new additions.

As Alex headed for her office to pick up her purse, she felt the pocket of her scrubs vibrate for what seemed like the twelfth time that day. She typically didn't carry her phone around with her on her rounds, but Sealey had forbidden her to so much as put it down. This afternoon was to be her first "drive by" with Lucas, and he wanted to be able to check in with her regularly as nuggets of wisdom and direction occurred to him. Sure enough, as Alex pulled the quivering device from her pocket, she saw that she'd received four text messages in the past twenty minutes. She was sure all of them were from Sealey.

"Man alive . . . ," she muttered as she swiped at the text message icon on the screen. Rolling her eyes, she began to read.

Change of plans. Luke just called, and the location is changing from Smith's Food and Drug to Lee's Marketplace. He's picky about his produce. For that reason, your rendezvous point is the strawberries—those are his favorite.

Alex shook her head in disbelief. What was she supposed to do, just stand there until he showed up? Or was she going to be bobbing in and out of aisles attempting to look busy until she caught sight of him, and then make a beeline for the fruit? She ground her teeth as she read the next message.

Don't doll yourself up too much. Remember you're supposed to be grocery shopping, not cat-walking down a runway.

Alex rolled her eyes again as she moved on to the next message. No worries there. She was planning on heading straight to the grocery store from the hospital. But a little mascara touch-up never went awry . . .

Don't hover. Just make sure you're within sight of the strawberries so you don't miss him when he gets there. Then drift over casually when you see him. Subtlety, Foamer. Subtlety.

Ah, well. That at least answered her first point of concern.

Don't talk to him unless he talks to you. I mean it.

Huffing as she pushed her phone back into her pocket, she pushed her office door open just long enough to grab her purse from the drawer and slip back out. Locking the door behind her, she headed for the exit. Now that she had an established plan, she felt a little better about this first encounter with Lucas. Squaring her shoulders, she felt a confident smile bloom across her face. She could do this.

* * * * *

Alex wondered how long she could conceivably be studying a cantaloupe for ripeness before she started to alarm the other customers. When she felt she had considered that fruit for too long, she moved on to the watermelon. Then the grapes. By the time she made it to the apples, she was getting desperate. She'd been haunting the produce section for a full twenty minutes and her basket was empty. The produce associate was eying her warily. Where was Lucas? Was she too late? Had she missed him?

Just as she was about to head for the nearest aisle, just to escape the awkwardness around her, she saw him. He had a grocery basket in his hand, containing only a bag of potato chips and a Gatorade. Alex froze next to the lemons and immediately began examining them, her eyes flicking back and forth between the bright yellow peels and the Adonis headed her way. Lucas shuffled past the grapefruits and headed straight for the strawberries, just as Sealey said he would. Alex began her slow, meandering journey, aiming to intersect her path with his.

The problem was, Lucas wasn't waiting for her. With no hesitation whatsoever, Lucas grabbed the nearest carton of strawberries, deposited it into his basket, and moved immediately toward the dairy section. *No!* Alex thought, panicked. *I thought Sealey said he was picky about his produce!* Determined to bag her prey, she began speed-walking after him. The next thing she knew, the world tilted and she found herself on her back in a sea of canned tuna. Cans were rolling in every direction as the display she had disrupted continued to collapse. The racket was spectacular. Cans of fish fell from several feet all around her, and Alex raised her arms defensively over her head. Sure she was about to meet her death by seafood, she marveled at the complete lack of poetic justice.

"Are you okay?"

The familiar voice was the very last thing she wanted to hear at this particular moment. She tried not to meet his vivid green gaze as she answered through clenched teeth, "I think so, but you may not want to get too close. I don't think the carnage is over yet."

She looked up at the teetering tower of tuna, imagining how fond Lucas would be of her after receiving a concussion by way of canned fish. *At least it's the good kind*, Alex thought weakly. *If he has to die with me, at least we'll be victims of name brand merchandise.*

Unexpectedly, she heard a chuckle. She glanced up at him, wondering how on earth he could laugh in the face of death. And then she stopped. Every mental faculty froze in the face of such magnificence.

She stared into his green eyes, entranced, as he attempted to pull her to her feet. Finally yanking her thoughts back to the present situation, she managed to get her legs under her, relieved to realize that the leaning tower of tuna appeared to finally be stationary.

"Oh no," she groaned, taking in the mess on the grocery store floor. "Do you think they'll make me pay for all of this?"

"I doubt it," Lucas said, smiling at her. "Nothing's broken. Most of the cans don't even look damaged. Come on, I'll help you put them back."

"Oh, you really don't have to do that," she protested. "It was my own fault. You shouldn't have to suffer."

"I don't mind at all," he said, smiling at her as he squatted to begin gathering cans. He glanced at her curiously a few times before opening his mouth again. "You look really familiar to me. Do we have a class together?"

"Oh," Alex murmured, half mortified and half relieved that he didn't remember her. "No, actually. We're in the same ward. My name is Alex Foamer."

"Alex!" Lucas exclaimed, dropping a can as he stretched out a hand to lay it softly on her arm. "Oh my gosh, I'm so embarrassed I didn't recognize my own date auction savior!" He squeezed her arm as he grinned openly at her.

"Oh, don't worry about it," Alex replied, trying desperately to sound offhand but unable to keep the breathlessness from her voice. Criminy, he was so beautiful. She wrenched her attention away from his face back to the mess of tuna cans, knowing her thinking would only remain coherent as long as she wasn't looking at him.

"I'm really looking forward to our date in a couple of weeks," he said as he too began picking up more cans of tuna and placing them back on the display. "I always enjoy getting to know someone new."

"Me too," Alex replied, still not looking at him.

She was pushing the tuna cans onto the display so fast that her vision was blurred as her eyes followed her hands. This encounter had been an unqualified disaster, and the only thing she could think of was to end it as quickly as possible and hope that the next one turned out better. She wondered how successful she would be at avoiding Sealey when he called to get a report. But that would be pointless. If Sealey couldn't get a satisfactory report from her, he'd simply use his wiles to get some semblance of a report from Lucas. She sighed as she thought of the scolding she was going to get from her mentor.

"Hey, don't worry about it," Lucas comforted, putting an arm around her shoulder as they both crouched next to the tuna. "No harm, no foul. I doubt anyone even noticed."

Alex smiled quickly at him, allowing him to think her sigh had been an indication of her embarrassment. She stacked the last can of tuna on the display as Lucas went to retrieve the ones that had rolled far and wide. She watched him, feeling her mouth pull into a smile. He caught her look and smiled back as he headed toward her, his arms full of the small cans.

"There we go!" he said, placing the cans on the display and wiping his hands on his cargo shorts. "Calamity officially nullified."

"Thanks, Lucas," Alex said sincerely to him. "I appreciate the help. I think we're probably even now. We've traded public humiliation for public humiliation."

"Not even close," Lucas insisted. "I'd have to save you from several hundred tuna collisions before we reached that point."

Alex winced. "Don't jinx me," she choked. Lucas laughed and picked up her grocery basket for her.

"Sorry," he said, smiling at her. He looked down into her empty basket. "Do you need to pick up a few things before you head out? I'm happy to walk with you."

Alex blushed, remembering why she was at the grocery store in the first place. "You know, I don't even remember what I was here for," she said, blushing deeper.

"Guess I don't blame you." Lucas laughed. "Come on, let me buy my stuff real quick and then I'll walk you out."

Alex stood awkwardly silent next to Lucas as he paid for his purchases. He smiled at her occasionally as he chatted in a friendly way with the cashier, who appeared to be someone he knew. Alex felt like an imposter, knowing she was there by design. For the hundredth time, she wondered what had possessed her to engage in this subterfuge. But as Lucas grabbed his grocery bag, reached back, and pulled her with him toward the door, she suddenly remembered.

I'd knock over a grocery display every day for a lifetime if I got to have him help me pick it up, Alex gushed in her head, following the adorable brown curls out into the summer heat.

* * * * *

Alex walked dreamily into her apartment, reliving the feeling of Lucas's hand on hers as he led her out into the sunshine of the grocery store parking lot. He'd smiled, his eyes crinkling at the corners, as he'd chatted merrily with her, although she honestly had no idea what he'd said. She was too focused on those green eyes. Sea foam. That's what they were. She sighed sappily.

"What's up with you?" Jaclyn asked from the couch as Alex sauntered by, her head cocked dreamily to one side.

"Oh." Alex straightened suddenly, realizing she was on public display. All of her roommates sat in the living room, watching a recorded episode of The Bachelorette. "Nothing. Just a good day."

"Uh-huh . . . ," Sage said, looking unconvinced. "A look like that can only mean one thing. Your meeting with Lucas went well."

"Well, actually, no, it didn't," Alex said, sinking down onto the floor and crossing her legs in front of her. "It was lousy and humiliating, but he was . . . just . . . ," she trailed off, and she could feel her eyes going all dreamy again.

"I hope you did something other than just stare at him with that look on your face," Kacey said straightforwardly. "If not, I doubt you made the impression you were hoping for."

"No, I was coherent," Alex defended. "Well, mostly."

"Hey, I don't blame you," Meredith said, coming to her rescue. "It's hard to keep your thoughts lucid with those eyes fixed on you. You could just drown in them." Her voice began to get a bit dreamy too.

Kacey rolled her eyes. Alex was starting to think that Kacey probably had the most success with men of all her roommates mostly because she seemed to be thoroughly unimpressed by them. Kacey was the kind of girl Sealey would need to find if he ever wanted to get married. She couldn't imagine a girl being brave enough to take *that* on.

Speaking of Sealey . . .

Alex groaned when she felt her phone vibrate in her scrubs pocket.

Again. She seriously considered ignoring it, but she knew that if she didn't pick up, he'd just show up on her doorstep in person. Scowling at her phone, she reluctantly hit the "Answer" button.

"You were supposed to call me," Sealey's flat voice echoed in Alex's ear.

"I just barely walked in the door," she replied. "Besides, I don't remember making that arrangement." She attempted to keep her voice light, hoping it would help keep the fear she felt from becoming too apparent. Had Sealey already talked to Lucas? Did he know about her failure?

"It was implied," Sealey informed her. "How am I supposed to help if you don't report back to me? So. Report."

Alex suppressed a groan with effort. "I'm pretty sure you really don't want me to," she said, wrinkling her nose.

"Oh, I definitely do," he answered smoothly. "Especially since I have the impression you made a complete fool out of yourself, therefore invalidating the purpose behind the entire exercise."

"Well, as you appear to already know the story, I don't see the good in rehashing it."

"Lucas is not known for his storytelling prowess," Sealey pressed. "All he told me was that he ran into Alex Foamer at the grocery store and had to save her from tuna fish. What did you do, fall into the fresh fish display case?"

"No," Alex said defensively. At least it hadn't been *that* bad. She'd escaped any kind of olfactory disaster. She doubted Lucas would have been as eager to walk her to her car if she'd smelled like raw fish. "It was canned."

"Oh . . . perfect." Sealey sounded like he was talking through clenched teeth.

"Hey, it wasn't entirely my fault," Alex protested. "I was insufficiently prepared . . . yet again. You told me that Lucas liked to take time over his produce purchases. He didn't give me enough time to approach him at the strawberries before taking off. I ended up having to chase him! So . . . get off me."

"Seriously, Foamer?" Sealey sounded incredulous. "You ran after him? It didn't occur to you to just casually follow and intercept him in the next aisle?"

"Well . . . I . . . you said . . . ," Alex trailed off. It did seem rather obvious now that he said it. "I was *nervous*, okay? I wasn't meant for this cloak-and-dagger stuff. I'm of the straightforward school of thought."

"Clearly," Sealey retorted. "Because what's more straightforward than crashing headfirst through a tuna fish display?"

"I didn't go headfirst," Alex said, sighing. "But point taken. It was a disaster. I know. Let's just move on and start planning for the next one so I don't have a repeat occurrence."

"I almost hesitate to encourage a 'next one,'" Sealey said scornfully. "If you can cause such havoc in a grocery store, I shudder to think what kind of damage you can instigate at a nice restaurant."

"As long as you just stick me in a place where he sees me and gets to decide whether or not to approach, all will be well," Alex insisted. "It's when you try to make me into a big game hunter that things go south in a hurry. You know I have no gift for subtlety."

"And how," Sealey muttered. "All right, fine. We'll make you the hunted instead of the hunter this time around."

"Many thanks," Alex said sarcastically. "So where am I going?"

"We made a schedule," Sealey reminded her. "Have you lost it already?"

"I don't think you gave me a copy," she responded, crossing her fingers. In truth, she knew he had given her a copy, but she had no idea where it had disappeared to. She had spent the better part of a half hour earlier that day looking through the thick folder Sealey had provided, containing Lucas's class schedule, campus walking routes, jogging routes, the USU football practice times and locations, as well has his favorite stopping places for fast food, groceries, and athletic wear.

"Oh," Sealey said, not bothering to question her. She sighed in relief. "Well, this next one is the day after tomorrow at the Elements restaurant. He's taking a client, so there's a chance he won't even notice you. Regardless, he won't approach you, because he'll have his attention focused on the client. Just be prepared to smile prettily at him. Maybe give him a careless sort of wave."

"Am I supposed to be alone or should I take someone with me?" Alex asked.

"Hmmm," Sealey considered. "Well, there are pros and cons to each one. You could take one of your roommates, but you run the risk of him liking what he sees a little too much and going for her instead of you."

Alex grimaced into the phone. The thought of watching Lucas date one of her roommates instead of her was torture. And some of them would gladly do it—roommate loyalties could only stretch so far.

"But if you take a guy, you also run the risk of him thinking you're already with someone and not bothering to pursue you," Sealey continued. "I say, let's just keep things simple and have you go alone."

"But me eating alone at a nice restaurant like that?" Alex wailed. "I'll look like a total loser! No self-respecting girl goes to a sit-down restaurant *by herself*!"

"Huh. Not a big fan of feminism, are you, Foamer?" Sealey murmured, and she could just picture him rolling his eyes. "All right, let's do it this way. Just go and sit in the front area of the restaurant like you're waiting for someone. When he walks in and sees you, smile and wave. He'll likely do the same. Once he's been seated with his party, act like you've gotten a text from your potential dining partner canceling the meeting, and then get up and walk out. Easy."

It certainly didn't sound too complicated. Compared to her last assignment, this was positively painless.

"Okay, I can do that," Alex claimed confidently.

"Good," he replied. "Feel free to dress up a little. Look like you're trying on this one."

"Got it."

"And Foamer?"

"Yes?" she said hesitantly.

"Let's avoid a fish collision this time."

"Right."

{ Chapter FIVE }

"ALEX? ALEX!" THE stressed accent on the other side of the door began at the same time as the frantic knocks. "Alex, are you in there?"

Alex sighed as she heard the familiar voice. Her most faithful patient was back. Again.

Eric Swithin was a British transplant who had lost his wife in childbirth two years before. He was helpless and hopeless to care for his young son without heaps of advice and support—which Alex felt duty-bound to provide.

She had been a brand-new dietitian at the hospital the first time she had met Eric. He was sitting with his head in his hands in the hospital waiting room, having just heard of his wife's death due to hemorrhaging after a difficult delivery. Alex had watched him, his eyes pressed into his clenched fists, his back convulsing with the force of his sobs. Her heart had positively ached for him. It was the memory of that scene that inspired her to keep seeing Eric and his son, Martin, despite the fact that he wasn't technically supposed to be on her radar anymore.

"Hi, Eric," Alex said as she swung open her office door. "How are you today?" She tried not to notice his panicked expression as she reached out a hand to stroke Martin's pudgy little cheek as he sat in his father's arms. Eric was a classic overreactor and Alex had learned long ago that the best method for dealing with his unjustified panic attacks was to

38

remain calm at all times. "Hi, Martin!" she said in a cheery voice. "Wow, what a great shirt! Red is really your color, you know that?"

Martin smiled cheerily up at her, raising his hands for her to hold him. She pulled him from his father's embrace and turned to face the look of terror on Eric's face.

"So what's up?" she asked, stubbornly retaining her cheerful tone.

"He won't eat! He just won't eat!" Eric wailed. "I don't know what to do! He's got to eat! He'll die if he doesn't."

Alex fought an eye roll with effort. "Eric, all toddlers resist eating sometimes. Trust me, when he gets hungry enough, he will eat."

"So I'm just supposed to let him *starve*?" Eric looked scandalized. This time Alex let the eye roll continue onto her face unobstructed.

"No, Eric. Didn't you hear what I just said?" Alex rubbed her forehead with her fingers, feeling a headache coming on. "He's a toddler. He's ruled by his needs. He won't let himself starve. Just keep offering him food at mealtimes. He'll resist only until it becomes uncomfortable for him, and then he'll eat again."

"But what if he gets hungry right after a mealtime?" Eric said, his face still showcasing his fear. "Then he'll have to wait for the next one? What if it's too much? What if it weakens him?"

Alex sighed. "If he gets hungry between meals, trust me, he'll let you know."

"I can't do this," Eric said, slumping against the wall. "I'm not cut out to be a single father. I should've put Martin up for adoption rather than kept him with me, motherless." For some reason, the British accent made his hopelessness all the more heartrending.

Alex felt a pang of guilt for her lack of patience with the young father. He was doing his best, and having lost the most important person in his world already, it only made sense that he would be constantly worried about it happening again.

"Oh, come on, Eric," she said bracingly. "You're doing great! You've learned so much in the past couple of years! You don't freak out nearly as much as you used to. I haven't seen you for at least two weeks. See, that's progress!"

And it was. For the first six months of Martin's life, Eric had contacted her several times a day. He seemed to forget that she was not a child development specialist, held no medical degree, and was thoroughly unqualified to assess his child's sleeping patterns. At that point, Alex had spent much of her time trying to ferry him to other specialists, knowing that she couldn't ethically advise him on anything other than Martin's nutrition. But for some reason, Eric always came to her first. She figured it was because she was, more than anything, a listening ear for the lonely father.

"It's just so hard when he doesn't clearly communicate," Eric despaired.

"You'll find that's common with two-year-olds." Alex smiled down at Martin as he reached up to pull her hair. "Look, you have my number," she said, glancing back up at Eric. "Martin appears to be in perfect health right now, but if you start to suspect that he's weakening from hunger, all you have to do is pick up the phone and I'll be there."

She'd made several house calls before, to assess everything from a strong-smelling white residue that Eric had found on Martin's lips (which turned out to be toothpaste) to the temperature of the baby's formula. She was well-acquainted with Eric's home.

"Couldn't you maybe stop by tonight? Just to check in? Make sure he's going on okay?" Eric pleaded.

"I can't, Eric," Alex said, handing Martin back to him. "I have an appointment at Elements tonight."

"What time? Maybe you could pop in after?" Eric seemed truly concerned as he stared down at his son, as if expecting to see him waste away before his very eyes.

"I'm supposed to be there about six," she answered. "Maybe if it goes more quickly than expected, I'll stop over on my way home. Around six-thirty. *Maybe*," she qualified. "But, Eric, I think I can safely promise you that Martin is in no danger of starving to death before bedtime."

Eric looked at her beseechingly, as if willing her words into fruition. "He's just so small. You'd think I'd be used to this by now, but I feel like every day brings me some new mystery or calamity."

"I suspect most first-time parents feel that way," Alex comforted him. "Hey, I have to go make my rounds. You going to be okay?"

"Yes," he said hesitantly, looking down at his son. "I think so. I'll talk to you later. Keep your phone on!" He added the last plea over his shoulder at her as he walked away down the hall.

She nodded seriously at him before watching him turn the corner, her mouth lifting slightly at the corners.

* * * * *

Alex stared at herself in the full-length mirror. She wore a knee-length green skirt, fitted at the hips but light and flirty at the bottom, with a white fitted blouse and chunky green necklace. Her long, dark red hair was full and slightly curled, and her face accented with her favorite makeup. Her legs—long, lean, and tan—were bare, a stipulation made by Sealey, who claimed that her legs were one of her best assets. She still had a hard time imagining him even noticing things like that. She wore a pair of nude pumps, which pushed her height to over six feet. It was a good thing Lucas was several inches taller than her. Flat-footed, Alex was taller than most of the guys she knew.

"Wow," Meredith whistled from her bed across the room, where she sat cross-legged. "You look fantastic. I don't know how you manage to get so much volume in your hair. It's like you're a life-size, red-haired Barbie doll. Life is so unfair."

"I may have volume, but my hair is really coarse. At least your hair is silky and shiny," Alex countered, turning to take a look at her rear end in the green skirt. She felt like this particular fabric tended to accentuate areas of her anatomy she'd rather hide.

"In signature Asian style," Meredith joked. She came from a family of Vietnamese immigrants, although she herself had been born in the United States. "So, are you ready? Have your script all prepared?" she asked with interest.

"No script this time," Alex answered, still studying her derriere. She shrugged and moved away from the mirror. "Sealey says there's no chance Lucas will speak to me, because he's taking a client to dinner and it's disrespectful to leave them standing there all alone to go and talk to someone else."

"Ah," Meredith replied, but she didn't look convinced. "Maybe you should be prepared with a topic of conversation, just in case. You never know what will happen."

"Sealey knows Lucas better than anyone," Alex said. "And Lucas

41

will be there on business for Sealey's company. I figure Sealey's probably right."

"I guess so," Meredith said, biting her lip. "It's so hard for me to think of Sealey as a big-time business owner. It's really impressive. He's super young to have his own company."

"'Big-time' might be a bit of an overstatement." Alex chuckled. "I don't get the sense that Trident Advertising is all that imposing. Like Sealey said, Logan is a small market."

"Still, to be a business owner at twenty-eight? That's pretty cool," Meredith insisted. "If Sealey weren't so rude and sarcastic and all-around terrifying, he'd be a pretty good catch. He's almost as good-looking as Lucas. He's tall, even taller than Lucas is. And he's smart and successful. I wonder if he'll ever get married."

"You interested?" Alex said. She tried to keep her voice teasing, but she couldn't keep out the note of incredulity. Meredith was sweet and good and funny, and she seemed exactly like the kind of girl that Sealey would eat alive.

"No, not me," Meredith said. "But if you found the right kind of girl . . . ," she trailed off.

"Kacey?" Alex asked, voicing her thoughts from a couple of days earlier.

Meredith's eyes lit up. "They would be perfect together! They even kind of look alike. Tall, blonde, athletic . . . they would have the cutest kids! You should suggest it to her. You know she gets any guy she wants."

"Maybe," Alex said noncommittally, searching through the piles of clothes on her bed for her purse. "Although Kacey doesn't usually take suggestions like that very well. She's too independent to go after a guy herself. She's used to them coming to her."

"Maybe I'll suggest it to Sealey then," Meredith considered.

"Be my guest," Alex said, pulling her purse from underneath a white corduroy blazer. "Better you than me."

As if on cue, Kacey's voice rang from the living room. "Alex! Sealey's here!"

Alex looked at Meredith, and Meredith stared back, wide-eyed. "Did you know he was coming?" Alex asked, her voice in a loud stage whisper.

"No, of course not," Meredith said, her face twisting into a look of confusion. "Why would I know a thing like that?"

Alex wasn't listening. "What is he doing here? You don't think he's *coming with me*, do you? How on earth am I going to play it cool with Sealey breathing down my neck?"

"He can't come," Meredith reminded Alex. "Lucas knows him, remember? It would ruin everything if he saw you sitting with Sealey."

"Oh, right." Alex breathed in relief. "He must just be here to check in before I go."

"Regardless, you'd better get out there," Meredith prodded. "Sealey Witchburn is not a patient man."

Alex groaned and opened the bedroom door. "See you later. My lord and master awaits."

* * * * *

"Lord and master . . . ," Sealey mused as he drove. "I like the sound of that."

Alex ground her teeth from the passenger seat. She had emerged from the hallway to see Sealey standing in the living room of the apartment, looking very fetching in a lightweight blue sweater that matched his eyes and dark, low-waisted jeans, his hands in his pockets. He had informed her that he was going to drive her to the restaurant so he could brief her on the way and see how things progressed.

"Don't worry, I'm not coming in with you," he said at her look of horror. "But judging from our last experience, you are unlikely to give me a timely and accurate report when this is all over, so I'm going to make sure I'm on-hand for a well-timed delivery."

"Lucky me," Alex had muttered as she'd followed him out to his black Lexus (if Sealey's car were any indication, his business was doing better than he'd suggested). Now, sitting on the plush leather seat, she was imagining all sorts of horrible happenings, ranging from Sealey pressing his nose to the window of the restaurant to keep an eye on her, to Lucas seeing her drive up with him and assuming they were dating. Nightmare.

"Okay, so recite the plan to me," Sealey prompted, poking her in the thigh.

"Smile and wave," she said dully, staring out the window with her arms folded.

"Short and sweet," Sealey replied, nodding. "The essence of a flawless plan."

"Mmm," Alex murmured. With Sealey here watching her every move, what had before seemed like an easy assignment was suddenly looking very daunting. She had no doubt that he would park in front of the restaurant in such a way that he would be able to see through the front windows. Swallowing her sigh and concentrating instead on getting her head in the game, Alex pulled down the visor to check her makeup in the mirror. She was determined to be a vision of feminine beauty when Lucas caught sight of her.

"You look fine," Sealey said, glancing at her. "Better than I expected, actually."

"Gee, thanks," she muttered as she attempted to separate her eyelashes with her fingernail.

"No, I really mean it," Sealey insisted, as though "better than I expected" was a legitimate compliment. "In line with your aforementioned lack of subtlety, I was expecting, when I told you to dress up a bit more for this one, that you would go to town on the makeup and wardrobe." He gestured to her green skirt appreciatively. "But this mermaid glamour look you have going . . . it's a good mix of eye-catching and classy. Nicely done."

Alex glanced at him in surprise. A real compliment? How unexpected.

They pulled into the restaurant parking lot a few minutes later in complete silence. Alex was starting to hyperventilate now that the moment of her performance was drawing near. The restaurant was very elegant looking, and she knew the food was good. She'd been there on a date before. In fact, she almost wished she was staying to eat. Almost.

As expected, Sealey parked directly in front of the windows of the rounded entrance, but a few rows back to make sure Lucas couldn't spot him. The waiting area was right inside the door, so he would have a nearly unobstructed view of whatever happened to occur.

"Perfect," he murmured as he shoved his car into park. "Now, Luke should be here around six fifteen. You'd better get inside."

Alex took a deep breath, glanced at Sealey, and nodded. She climbed from the car and began her walk toward the restaurant. It had been a long time since she had worn high heels, and she had forgotten the sense of confidence it gave her to be four inches taller. She felt very elegant and polished, walking toward the restaurant in her mermaid skirt and nude pumps. She straightened her shoulders, shook her hair out a little, and fearlessly entered the restaurant.

* * * * *

Alex sat calmly in the rounded entrance of the restaurant, feeling Sealey's ice blue eyes fixed on her back through the window behind her. She casually crossed her long legs and maintained the look of complete unconcern on her face. She pulled out her smartphone and began scrolling through her Twitter feed, looking as though she hadn't a care in the world. Inside, she was in turmoil. Lucas would be there with his client in tow at any moment. And then her show would begin.

Despite the fact that all she had to do was smile in a friendly way and wave vaguely in Lucas's direction, she felt like every detail, from the brilliance of the smile to the angle of the wave would be criticized in full by Sealey. And she couldn't help feeling that something was going to go wrong. In cases like this, where everything was supposed to be scripted and simple, unfortunate and unforeseen events had a way of cropping up.

She felt Lucas's presence before she saw him. It was as though her heart was aware that its perfect match was near and thumped away in furious joy. She forced herself to keep her head down and her eyes focused on her phone. After about thirty seconds of staring fixedly at the same word in her Twitter feed, she casually let her eyes drift up from the screen.

They immediately met Lucas's. He was talking to an older gentleman in a khaki-colored blazer, but his gaze kept drifting to her. When their eyes met, she smiled in cheery recognition, trying for all the world to look like seeing him was a complete surprise. She held up a hand in a discreet wave, and then pushed her eyes reluctantly back down to her phone. She felt her body relax. It was over. She had played her part, and now she just had to wait for his party to be seated, and she could leave.

Within five seconds, though, she knew something was wrong. A pair of black dress shoes approached from roughly ten feet away and stopped directly in front of her. She stared at them for a second before allowing her eyes to travel up the legs encased in dark gray slacks, the muscular torso sporting a dark plum-colored button-up, and finally to a pair of sea-green eyes. What was he doing here standing in front of her? Sealey had assured her he wouldn't approach her. She looked around frantically for his client, but the older gentleman had disappeared.

"Alex," Lucas's voice was warm and enthusiastic. "It's great to see you! You look fantastic."

"Ah, thanks, Lucas," she said, clearing her throat to try to clear away the dismay as she reluctantly stood up. "As do you. You always look fantastic."

Lucas smiled warmly at her. "So what brings you here?"

Crap. How had Sealey not instructed her to at least have a plausible backstory? It seemed very sloppy of him. "Um, I'm supposed to be meeting some family members here," she said quickly. It was the first thing she could think of, but it was just about the worst possible story she could have dreamed up. Alex had only one family member living in Logan. He was a second cousin from a small town in Iowa, and she barely knew him. They hadn't really said a word to each other since he'd moved out there a year earlier.

"Oh, really?" Lucas said, cheerfully. "A little family get-together, huh? Siblings, parents, cousins . . . ?" he prompted.

"Oh, um . . . ," she began, trying not to panic. "I'm from California, so I don't have any siblings or anything around here."

"Ooh, California," Lucas said, his smile widening. "Winters here in Logan must be difficult for you."

"That's an understatement," she said, managing to smile a little. She began twirling a chunk of dark red hair around her finger, a nervous habit she had never been able to break.

"So . . . cousin, then?" Lucas pressed again.

Alex suppressed a groan. It was as though he suspected her subterfuge and was determined to entrap her in her own lies. "Well . . . um . . . I—" she began, but she was cut off by the sound of her name spoken in a hysterical British accent.

"Alex!"

She spun around to face the door, already suspecting what she would see. Sure enough, Eric Swithin stood there, looking frazzled, with a bemused Martin in his arms, wrapped in a blanket, despite the warm August temperatures.

"Alex, I can't do it!" Eric moaned in distress. He approached Alex, holding his little son out toward her. "He needs his mother! I am not cut out for this fatherhood business! He keeps saying your name! I've never heard him say anything even close to 'daddy.' It's as though he knows that he needs a woman to care for him! I'm rubbish at this. Please, help me!"

Eric stood there, his small boy extended toward her as though he expected Alex to take him and raise him as her own. She stood bewildered, her eyes flicking between Lucas and Eric, taking in both expressions. Lucas looked stunned at the exchange but quickly hid his reaction.

"Hey, little guy!" he said cheerfully to Martin. He reached out a hand to the little boy as though to stroke his head, but Martin grabbed his arm and began attempting to climb it. Lucas laughed and pulled the toddler from his father's arms. He began talking quietly to Martin, as though trying to distract him from Alex and Eric, to allow them to talk.

"What's going on *now*?" Alex hissed at Eric. She couldn't believe he had actually shown up at the restaurant, especially when Martin didn't appear to be in any kind of distress or danger.

"He's not getting hungry!" Eric protested. "You said eventually he would get hungry!"

"Eric," Alex replied, rubbing a hand across her face. "You have to give it more than four hours. It might take *twenty*-four before he becomes hungry enough to give in. You need to exhibit a little *patience*."

She was about to scold further when she happened to catch what Lucas was softly saying to Martin, who appeared to have become mesmerized by one of Alex's earrings. He was reaching for it, and Lucas was trying to keep him out of range of her ears.

"Oh, you see your mama, don't you?" Lucas said in the little boy's ear. "She's pretty, isn't she? I know those things hanging from her ears are tempting, but I'm pretty sure she wouldn't like it if you got a hold of them. Why don't you just stay with me till she's done talking to your daddy?"

Lucas didn't appear to be paying any attention to Alex, so he didn't notice all the color leave her face. Lucas had somehow come to the conclusion that Martin was her son. That she and Eric had created the little body in his arms. Obviously, he knew her current marital status as she had saved his bacon at a singles date auction, but still, how on earth could he have gotten the idea that she had produced a child first? She was vaguely aware that Eric had started talking to her again, but she wasn't listening. She skimmed through the past five minutes in her head, trying to figure out what the trigger had been. When she realized that she herself had told Lucas she was meeting family, just in time for Eric to show up and make it sound like the whole reason for his presence at the restaurant was because Martin had needed his mother, everything clicked into place in her head.

"Oh, no . . . no, no, no, no, no," she began to say to Lucas, wasting no time disabusing him of the notion that she had mothered a child with a British psychopath before age twenty-four. "Martin isn't—" but it was already too late.

The client had returned. He approached them from the direction of the restroom, and Alex realized the eventuality that neither she nor Sealey had anticipated.

"Bill," Lucas greeted. "This is Alex and Eric, and their son, Martin." He introduced them as he handed Martin to Alex. She attempted to keep his little fingers from grasping her earring at the same time she opened her mouth to make sure he understood his mistake. But the fates seemed to be conspiring against her.

"Riley, party of two," came the voice of the hostess behind them.

"Right here," Lucas hailed her. He turned back to Alex. "It was so good to see you, Alex. Good luck with the little guy." He winked at Martin, who grinned at him. "I'll see you later, okay?"

He smiled brilliantly at Alex, nodded at Eric, and then turned to follow the hostess, his client at his side.

{ Chapter SIX }

ALEX COLLAPSED INTO the passenger seat of Sealey's car, her mind still reeling from the last ten minutes. Slamming the door, she scrunched down in her seat and refused to look in his direction.

"So, uh, what happened?" Sealey asked with a deadpan look on his face. "Who was the scrawny dude with the kid?"

"I really don't care to discuss it," Alex answered, a hand over her eyes. "Can you just take me home, please? I have a life to terminate. A couple, actually."

"I doubt Lucas would be interested in dating a murderer. You might want to rethink your diabolical plan," Sealey pointed out, and Alex could almost hear his eyes roll.

"I doubt he'd be interested in a deceased person too, which is why Lucas is no longer part of my diabolical plan," Alex muttered. "From now on, my sole aim is to put myself out of my own misery and to take Eric Swithin with me."

"Eric Swithin?" Sealey asked. "Was he the panicky-looking guy with the toddler?"

"Yes," Alex confirmed, glaring out the windshield. "And he *will* die."

"Where's the kid's mom?" Sealey asked, ignoring the drama in Alex's tone.

"She's dead . . . which is why I will never actually go through with my plan to annihilate Eric. Martin doesn't deserve to be an orphan so young." Alex sighed. "However, if you were to ask Lucas who Martin's

49

mother is, he would say 'Alex Foamer.'" She cringed, knowing she was seconds away from a hefty dose of Scorn a la Sealey.

He was silent for several seconds. Alex waited, dreading the barrage of insults she was sure was forming in Sealey's mind.

"I'm sorry, what?" Sealey said finally, his voice dangerously soft.

"Lucas thinks that Martin is my son," Alex almost wailed. "I tried to correct him, but everything just got away from me!"

"I . . . you . . ." Sealey seemed to be having a difficult time forming a coherent sentence. "How does a miscommunication that massive even *happen*?"

"I don't know," Alex said with a groan. "Seriously, the powers that be are combining against me. Everything is going wrong, and in the weirdest ways possible. First, I'm a tuna fish klutz, and now I'm an unwed mother."

"Well, luckily for you," Sealey said, his voice still tight but regaining some of its assurance, "you have me."

"Pardon?" Alex asked, sounding wilted.

"Well, if Lucas mentions to me that he ran into you tonight, I have no doubt that he'll mention your 'son.'" Sealey emphasized the word with his fingers. "I'll just make sure he knows that he's wrong about the kid. And if he doesn't bring it up, I'll find some way to introduce you into the conversation."

"Really?" Alex said in relief. "You would do that? Thank you! Thank you, thank you, thank you!"

"Stop groveling," Sealey grunted. "I'm not actually doing it for you . . . by all accounts, you haven't earned my help. But I have a stake in this thing too, so . . . ," he trailed off.

Ah, yes, Alex thought. *Olivia.*

Alex contemplated her conversation earlier that evening with Meredith about Sealey's romantic prospects. It would take a special kind of woman to steal Sealey's attention and keep it. She felt very curious about this Olivia. What kind of a girl could capture the heart of the kindest and most handsome man Alex knew and also nab the interest of the most frightening? Olivia must be a force of nature. The thought made Alex nervous. How could she ever be successful in distracting Lucas from such a woman?

* * * * *

In the following week and half, Alex made three more contact points with Lucas, the final two of which she hadn't even had to acknowledge him. Just make sure he saw her. And they went blissfully without incident. The first of the three had been much more stressful, but thankfully just consisted of Lucas approaching her at church to apologize for assuming that Martin was her son.

"I don't know why that was the first explanation to occur to me," Lucas said, his cheeks slightly pink. "I feel really stupid about it. Sealey told me that you were a pediatric dietitian or something like that, and suddenly everything just kind of made sense. I hope you're not upset with me."

Alex silently blessed Sealey's name as she smiled kindly up at Lucas. "Not at all," she replied. "It was definitely a bizarre situation, and it was easy to draw the wrong conclusion from it. But I have to admit, I'm glad it's all straightened out now. I wasn't really sure how to correct the misconception without making things awkward."

"'Cause I can make things awkward enough for both of us." Lucas laughed. "Thank heaven for informed roommates."

You can say that again, Alex thought as she laughed with him.

Now, displaying her wardrobe choice for her first official date with Lucas, she was once again grateful for Sealey's opinion.

"So? What do you think?" she asked as she turned in a circle for his inspection as he sat on the couch in the apartment living room. He studied her thoughtfully from head to toe, his eyes pausing on certain parts of her ensemble.

"Are you sure you want to wear those to go miniature golfing in?" he said, pointing at the strappy sandals on her feet. "They look horribly uncomfortable."

"Beauty equals pain." Alex shrugged. "Besides, these sandals look fabulous with my capris."

Sealey inclined his head with a "can't argue with that" kind of expression. "Just don't whine to him about the pain portion of that equation, okay?"

"No problem," Alex said, wiggling her toes and admiring her new pedicure. "Let me just grab my jacket and I'll be ready," Alex said, heading for the stairs.

"Don't take a jacket," Sealey said, stopping her. He rose to his feet, checking his watch. He had to be long gone by the time Lucas arrived to pick her up.

"No jacket? Why?" Alex asked. It was the second week of September, and already the temperatures in Logan were beginning to decline, particularly at night. "We'll be outside all night. I'm going to freeze."

"I know," Sealey said, yawning as he reached for his own jacket. "But Lucas will almost certainly have a jacket. When it starts to get cold, make sure you let it show. Don't complain about it, but don't try to stifle your shivers or teeth chattering or anything."

"We're being sneaky and manipulative again, aren't we?" Alex said, biting her lip.

"Yes," Sealey confirmed. "Lucas is a gentleman. When he sees how cold you are, he will offer you his jacket. Turn him down once or twice, express concern about him getting cold, talk about how silly it was to forget your own jacket, blah, blah, blah. He will insist you take it anyway. Feel free to do so at that point."

"Okay . . . ," Alex said, giving him a puzzled look. "And this helps the mission . . . how?"

"It's a couple of things, really," Sealey explained, sliding his hands into his pockets. "First of all, it wouldn't hurt for Lucas to see you showing a little weakness. You have an aura of confidence, and that tends to intimidate men sometimes. But allow him to see you in an uncomfortable situation and some of that intimidation will go away."

Alex nodded, seeing the logic behind Sealey's words.

"Second, guys tend to appreciate the things they sacrifice for. So let him sacrifice a little for you. It's not going to be erroneous enough that he'll resent you for it, but it will be uncomfortable for him, which means he'll have some invested effort in you."

"You have much wisdom," Alex said, eyebrows raised. "I'm lucky I have you on my side."

Sealey looked surprised at the comment as he reached for the door. "Thanks, Foamer," he replied. "I try to earn my keep."

Giving her a quick smile, he nodded and left.

* * * * *

"So . . . why don't you tell me about yourself?" Lucas said, smiling at her across the table. He picked up his cheeseburger and tried to keep all the fixings from falling out of it. "I feel like I've seen you all over the place these past few weeks, but I still don't know anything about you except that you're a Californian, a dietitian, and an enemy of canned seafood."

She laughed. "Well, I grew up in Malibu. My dad is a professor, my mom is a homemaker. They're both over six feet tall. It's a miracle I ended up an inch under."

Lucas laughed, and the sound sent a surge of warmth through Alex. This was the first time they'd actually had a full, non-scripted conversation. Alex was astounded at how easy it was. "I have three siblings. Two younger brothers, ages twenty-two and seventeen, and a younger sister, age nine. She was a surprise."

"Based on that age gap, I believe you," Lucas laughed. "Bet she's cute, though. Kind of like a miniature you."

Alex blushed. "She does look like me," she said with a self-conscious smile. "And, therefore, she's adorable."

Lucas laughed again. "So what are your brothers up to?"

"My brother Aaron served a mission to Puerto Rico. He got home in March of last year and married last September. His wife, Emily, is the cutest little blonde thing you'll ever see. Emphasis on little. She's nineteen."

"Wow . . . ," Lucas replied. "That's . . . young. But she must have been worth it to him."

"They're nuts about each other," Alex agreed. "And Emily's great. They live in Florida now, where Aaron's going to school."

"What about your other brother?"

"Austin," Alex replied. "He's a senior in high school and a basketball star. Naturally."

"I assume he's as vertically blessed as the rest of you," Lucas surmised.

"Yep, we're a family of freaks." Alex grinned. She dipped her fry in her chocolate shake and popped it in her mouth.

Lucas wrinkled his nose as he watched her. "You remind me of Sealey. He does that all the time."

"Does he?" Alex asked in surprise. "I didn't know he was a 'sweet and salty' kind of guy."

"How well do you know him?" Lucas asked innocently.

"Not well," Alex answered, much too quickly. "You know, as much as anyone really *knows* their ward executive secretary."

"He seems to know all about you. But I guess that doesn't surprise me," Lucas said, dipping a fry in ketchup. "He knows everything about everyone. No idea how he does it."

"He's a mystery, all right." Alex was itching to change the subject. The more they talked about Sealey, the more likely it was that she would blow everything. "So, now it's your turn. Tell me about your family."

"Well, my background isn't nearly as exciting as yours," Lucas claimed with a sigh. "I grew up here in Utah. My dad is an accountant, and my mom is an attorney. I have a little sister, Ashley, who's twenty-four, almost two years younger than me."

"Is she in school right now?" Alex asked, relaxed now that the subject of Sealey was off the table.

"She followed in my dad's footsteps. She just finished her graduate degree in accounting, and she's working for a big firm in Salt Lake. She's awesome but pretty intense."

"Really?" asked Alex. "How so?"

"She's kind of protective. She likes to 'save' me from people," Lucas said wryly, emphasizing the word with his fingers. "I have to tell her to cool it sometimes."

Alex could practically hear the words he wasn't actually saying. *Warning! My sister is a lunatic to girls who like me! Proceed with caution.*

"Interesting," Alex said, trying not to sound as intimidated as she felt. She cleared her throat. "So how do you think the football season is going? There's a game tomorrow, right?"

"Oh, it's going good," Lucas replied warmly. "I'm really proud of the team. They're really stepping it up this season. We play the University of Utah tomorrow. Should be a good game."

"Oh, sure, sure," Alex said, nodding like she knew what she was talking about. The subject of football carried Lucas all the way through the meal and onto the miniature golf course. Alex understood roughly an eighth of what he said, but she loved watching him get so excited about something.

"I'm sorry. I'm completely boring you, aren't I?" Lucas said as they walked onto the fourth hole. "I forget that not everybody loves football as much as I do."

"No, it's been interesting to hear you talk about it," Alex insisted. "I don't know much about football myself, but I've never been able to learn from an expert before."

Lucas rolled his eyes. "I don't know about the expert part of it, but I'm glad I could educate you on the greatest game ever played." He winked at her.

The sun had finally dipped below the mountains and Alex felt goose bumps start to rise on her arms. Dang it. The only scripted part of the evening was about to commence. She did her best to keep her face relaxed and unconcerned, even as she started to shiver slightly. Darn that Sealey. Was it really necessary that she suffer, just to make herself look vulnerable? She wasn't really that kind of girl. She was the kind of girl who was actually smart enough to remember a jacket so her date *wouldn't have* to save her. Well, according to Sealey, Lucas didn't need to know that about her.

Huffing quietly in frustration, she dropped her golf ball onto the fourth green and lined it up. In true Alex fashion, she smacked it much too hard, sending it ricocheting off the barrier at the other end of the green and flying back at her.

"Ahhhh!" she screamed, covering her head with her hands and dropping to her knees.

"Whoa!" Lucas yelled, ducking for cover as well. The ball landed in a thick bush behind them, and they both re-emerged, laughing.

"Um, would you like some pointers?" Lucas asked, breathless from laughing.

"Please," Alex said, clasping her hands in front of her. "Golf is not my sport of choice."

"All right, then," Lucas said, going to retrieve her ball for her. He dropped it onto the rubber pad and placed it just right. "Come here," he gestured to her. She approached him hesitantly. Taking her arms, he positioned her in front of him, her back to his chest. Sliding his hands down her arms, he corrected her grip on the putter and placed his hands over hers to take the shot.

Alex stopped breathing. The goose bumps on her arms became much more pronounced and she shivered even more violently at his closeness, every nerve tingling. Lucas was all but holding her in his arms. His head was right beside hers as he studied the green, their cheeks almost touching. He turned his face back to the ball but seemed to suddenly be distracted by something. She watched as he stilled, and his eyes narrowed. Unexpectedly, he began to run his hands softly up and down her arms again.

"Wow, you're freezing," he said in surprise. "Get a load of those goose bumps!"

"Ah, it's not too bad," Alex said, remembering Sealey's instruction to not complain. "It's my own fault for forgetting my jacket." She tried not to betray her reaction to his closeness. His hands were still sliding up and down her arms.

"Do you want mine?" Lucas said in concern. "Seriously, I can feel you shivering."

"I can't do that!" Alex exclaimed, relieved to realize that this actually took very little acting chops at all. Her natural inclinations were right in line with Sealey's instructions. "Then you'll be cold! I'm seriously okay." Then, without warning, a deep shudder ran through her body as a chilly wind rushed over the miniature golf course.

"Right," Lucas scoffed as he felt her shudder under his hands. "Nice try, Alex." He shrugged out of his tan jacket exposing his USU Football T-shirt and bare arms to the cold. He placed the jacket around her shoulders and once again placed his hands over hers on the putter.

Immediately, she felt warm and comfortable. With Lucas's jacket and his muscular arms around her, she thought she could stand like this forever.

"You ready?" Lucas asked, turning to look at her. Their faces were mere inches apart, and Alex once again stopped breathing as she stared into his sea-foam green eyes. They crinkled at the corners as he smiled.

"Ready," she said, a little breathless.

"All right," he replied, turning back to watch what he was doing. "It's all about the follow-through."

He guided her hands through the motions as he spoke. The putt was nearly perfect, landing her ball within inches of the hole.

"Nice!" Lucas exclaimed. "See, the secret is making sure the face of the putter is aimed where you want the ball to go, and make sure you follow your stroke all the way through. Don't just stop once it hits the ball."

"Oh, right, of course," Alex replied, as if this made perfect sense to her. All she really wanted was Lucas to stand here and hold her like this for several more hours. But Lucas let his arms drop and bent to put his ball on the rubber mat.

The date seemed to go very quickly after that. Though Alex had only partially understood Lucas's instructions, she managed to do much better on the rest of the holes. But Lucas still destroyed her with his effortless and infuriating lack of strokes. She was beginning to wonder if there was anything he wasn't good at.

"Thanks for coming with me tonight," Lucas said, walking her to the door at the end of the date. "I had a lot of fun."

"So did I," Alex replied, a little nervously. Doorstep scenes always made her antsy, even on nights like tonight when she was ninety-eight percent sure she wasn't kissing anyone. She trembled slightly due to the combination of nerves and chilly night air, and for a moment she wished she hadn't left Lucas's jacket in the car.

"We should do it again sometime," Lucas said.

Alex was immediately in turmoil. Did he mean it? She knew that phrase was generally thought by womankind to be a blow-off, but the very meaning of those words indicated that he was interested in seeing her again. Was Lucas the blow-off kind? He seemed too nice for that. He seemed like the kind of guy that would never have said those words if he didn't really mean them. She'd have to ask Sealey.

"I'd love that," Alex replied, trying to keep her voice and expression unassuming. "Good luck with the game tomorrow."

"Thanks," Lucas replied. They stopped at the door to the apartment, and Lucas turned to her. He pulled her smoothly into his arms and gave her a warm hug. "Have a good night, okay? I'll see you soon."

"Thanks again," she said, giving him a little extra squeeze. What if she never had the chance to do this again? Might as well take advantage. "Who would've thought five dollars at a date auction would buy me such a great date?" she teased.

Lucas chuckled. "Hopefully you got your money's worth." He pulled away and winked at her. "See you, Alex."

"Bye," Alex said, trying not to sound too swoony. She watched him walk back to his car before opening the door to the apartment, where she was sure to be immediately accosted.

* * * * *

"So? So?" Sage demanded. "How did it go? What happened? Did he hug you? Kiss you? Was he easy to talk to? Are you going out again?"

Alex froze in the doorway, taking in the sight of all five of her room-mates, squashed together on the couch in the living room, staring at her. The curtains at the window behind them were swaying in a suspect fashion, as though moments before, they'd had five curious faces peek-ing through them.

"Why bother even asking? You *saw* everything," she accused good-naturedly.

"No, we didn't!" Jaclyn protested. "The stupid window juts out too far. Hardly optimal for spying on doorstep scenes. It looked like he might've made a move, though. You guys certainly looked cozy . . . at least based on what we could see. Which was, you know, the tip of your elbow."

"He hugged me," Alex confirmed.

"And?" Meredith pressed. "How was it?"

Alex sighed in a dreamy sort of way. "Amazing. But it was noth-ing compared to what happened on the golf course. Listen to this . . ." She began her story, telling of how Lucas had taken her in his arms to improve her golf game.

"Wow," Sage said, sighing. "Who would've thought that just three weeks ago you were watching him from afar, coveting him, and now, he's voluntarily holding you in his arms." She sighed and sank back on the couch, accidentally elbowing Rachel in the ribs and bumping heads with Kacey.

"So did he say anything about going out again?" Kacey asked, giving Sage a dirty look. She slipped off the couch and onto the floor, bringing her knees to her chin. "'Cause, let's face it, if he doesn't want to see you again, Mission Score Lucas Riley has officially failed."

"I don't really know," Alex replied. "He said 'we should do this again,' but who knows if guys actually ever mean that when they say it."

Kacey groaned. "It's a cop-out, for sure."

"Oh, I don't know," Meredith defended. "If any guy could say those words and actually mean them, it would be Lucas."

Alex smiled at her. See? There was a reason Meredith was her best friend. "Well, I have a phone call to make," she said, heading for the stairs.

"Wait, you're calling him already?" Jaclyn cried after her. "Doesn't that look a little desperate?"

"I'm not calling Lucas," Alex responded incredulously. "I need to call and report to Sealey. He gets testy when I take too long."

She closed the door to her bedroom behind her, kicked off her sandals, winced at the blisters that had formed and uniformly popped during the course of the evening, and sank onto her bed. She pulled out her phone and dialed Sealey's number.

"Hey, Foamer," he said by way of greeting. "You're getting better. Luke just barely pulled in. Hang on a second while I duck into the other room so he can't hear me." After a few seconds, she heard the sound of a closing door on the other end of the line. "Okay," he said. "Report. How did it go?"

"Really good," she said honestly. "Really, really good. I was actually surprised at how much fun we had. Everything was so comfortable."

"Good to hear," Sealey responded. He sounded pleased. "How did the jacket thing work out?"

"Exactly how you said it would," Alex conceded. "Not only did he give me his jacket but it also gave us the opportunity to get a bit, um, physical." She felt herself blushing.

"Oh," Sealey said, sounding a little startled. "He . . . touched you, then?"

"Yeah, he was really just helping me with my golfing," Alex replied. "But he, you know, did it in the most physical way possible."

"Ah," Sealey replied. His voice sounded a little strange.

"Sorry, did I do something wrong?" Alex asked, worried. "Was there supposed to be a scheduled timeline for touching or something?"

Sealey cleared his throat. "No, nothing like that. Just . . . don't be too easy, Foamer, okay? I told you, he needs to chase you. Just make sure you don't allow him to catch you before he's done chasing."

"Uh-huh . . . ," Alex said, her tone skeptical. She knew all about the "playing hard-to-get" tactics that some girls employed, and while she knew a lot of girls who piqued boys' interest that way, she rarely heard of any who actually ended up with someone worthwhile in the long run. But she didn't feel like arguing with Sealey right now. No doubt he'd have plenty of time to further instruct her on how to keep Lucas at just the right distance. But for right now, she wanted to mentally relive her perfect date. "Sounds good," she said, just to get Sealey off the phone.

"Ready for the next steps?" Sealey asked. Without waiting for an answer, he continued. "Are you going to the game tomorrow?"

"The football game?" Alex asked. "I wasn't planning on it. Why?"

"You do recall something about Lucas being a football player, right?" Sealey prompted, his voice slightly sarcastic. "Don't you think it might be a good idea for you to actually watch him play? How much do you know about football, anyway?"

"Um, a little," Alex answered. "I know that a touchdown is supposed to be a good thing, right?"

Sealey snorted. "Yeah, you could say that. Okay, now that I've assessed your level of expertise, you're definitely going to the game tomorrow."

Alex groaned. "Do I have to?"

"Yes, you have to. I'll pick you up at eleven."

"Aye, aye, Captain." Alex sighed and hung up. She groaned and collapsed back onto her pillow. Apparently, tomorrow, she began her journey to football fandom. Yay.

{ Chapter SEVEN }

"**Y**OU OKAY?" ALEX pressed, eyeing Sealey with interest. They were on their way to Alex's first Utah State University football game, despite the fact that she had been a student there for four years. Sealey had been oddly quiet since he had picked her up five minutes earlier.

He had looked equal parts fashion model and sports fan in his usual low-waisted jeans and a dark blue T-shirt with a block USU on the front as he stood in her living room, waiting for her. She had silently watched him from the hall for a minute, smiling softly to herself. He carried a white hooded sweatshirt over his shoulder, and he stood with his hands in his pockets, looking uncomfortably around the room. Something seemed to be bothering him, but she wasn't quite sure what it could be. He was usually so unflappable . . . it must be something huge.

Now, driving toward the game, she was determined to pull it out of him. "Really, you don't look as put-together as usual. Is something wrong?"

"What makes you say that?" Sealey asked, glancing at her. "How can you possibly tell how 'put-together' I am? I promise you, I got dressed exactly the same way this morning as I always do."

"Okay," Alex said, but her voice rang with sarcasm. "So there's nothing wrong with the way you look, there's just something wrong with the way you sound."

"I don't sound like anything," Sealey said expressionlessly.

"Exactly," Alex said, pointing at him. "Usually you sound like a whole lotta cranky-pants, coming at me all at once. Why so silent?"

"Oh, come on," Sealey said, peering at her with a disgruntled look. "I'm not that bad."

"Oh no?" said Alex, raising an eyebrow. "Most of the time I can literally *feel* you chanting Olivia's name in your head, just to remind yourself that there's a reason you're subjecting yourself to my company."

Sealey looked startled. "Don't be ridiculous," he said. "I don't dislike your company. On the contrary, I find your company much easier to bear than most people I know."

Alex gave him a pointed look. "I assume that's supposed to be some kind of compliment?"

Sealey smiled slightly as he glanced at her again. "Let me put it this way. Do you ever see me spending time with anyone else other than Luke?"

Alex thought about that. "I guess not," she capitulated, eyebrows raised. "Well, then. Thanks, I guess."

"You're welcome," Sealey said, an amused smile playing on his face.

"So let me ask you something else," Alex said, changing the subject. "How well do you know Olivia? I mean, did you just meet her when Lucas started dating her or have you known her longer than that?"

Sealey flinched slightly, and Alex wondered if he disliked her talking about Olivia. She couldn't imagine why. After all, the only reason Sealey was doing any of this was for Olivia.

"We all grew up together, I guess you could say," Sealey said, somewhat hesitantly. "Our parents were friends, so even though we were all different years at school, we were thrown together all the time."

"How old is Olivia?" Alex asked curiously. "If she's on a mission, she's got to be several years younger than you and Lucas."

"She finished her bachelor's degree before she went," Sealey explained. "She's the same age as Lucas's sister, Ashley. Twenty-four. They're best friends."

Oh, great, Alex thought. *No wonder Ashley doesn't like any of the girls Lucas dates. She's trying to preserve him for Olivia.*

"So it was the four of you just hanging out all the time?" Alex asked. "Were you all best friends and everything? Did you go to the same schools and stuff?"

"No, not really," Sealey answered, shrugging. "Lucas, Ashley, and I all went to the same school, but I was two years ahead of Lucas, and Ashley was two years behind him. Olivia went to a private school."

"So . . . when did you fall in love with her, then?" Alex asked, wondering if she was about to get an earful for asking prying, personal questions. Instead, Sealey just smiled.

"I can't imagine anyone not falling in love with Olivia," he said. "She's the kindest, softest, most generous person I've ever met."

"But she dated Lucas instead of you?" Alex pressed.

Sealey's mouth tightened slightly, but a smile stayed firmly attached to his face. "Yes," he said simply.

"Did you ever try to date her?"

"No," he said and left it at that.

Alex was confused. Why had Sealey just let his best friend have Olivia up until this point? What had finally inspired him to fight for her? Despite all the time Alex had spent with Sealey thus far, it frustrated her how much she still didn't understand him.

* * * * *

Ten minutes later, they were walking through the stadium concourses toward their section. As the crowds grew denser, Sealey took Alex's arm, leading her toward the right stairway. It felt odd to have Sealey touch her. As she felt the warmth of his hand, she realized he'd never actually touched her before. She compared the way it felt to the way it felt when Lucas touched her. It was nice to have a reference point. While Sealey's touch felt warm and confident, Lucas's touch sent her stomach lurching and made her feel slightly feverish.

As Sealey led her up the stairs to their seats, she heard a female voice calling.

"Sealey! Sealey! Up here!" Alex and Sealey both raised their eyes to the voice. It was issuing from a petite, tanned little thing with copious amounts of curly, light-brown hair. Her eyes were a curious shade of green. It looked familiar.

"Ashley," Sealey greeted pleasantly.

Oh no.

Alex's middle immediately erupted in nauseous nerves. She was completely unprepared to meet Lucas's overprotective little sister. Why hadn't Sealey warned her that Ashley was going to be here?

63

"I saved your seats," Ashley said, pointing to a jacket spread over a couple of chairs. "We've had people try to take our reserved seats before, so I figured I would be proactive this time. I don't like to get nasty if I can avoid it." She smiled, her pouty lips parting to reveal a row of perfect white teeth.

"So who's this?" she asked, gesturing to Alex. Was it Alex's imagination, or did Ashley already have a steely, disapproving look in her eye? How could she *already* suspect that Alex was crazy about her brother?

"This is Alex Foamer," Sealey introduced. "She's a friend of mine and Luke's."

This introduction surprised Alex. She never expected to hear Sealey concede that she was a friend of *his*. But the thought pleased her, somehow.

"Hi, Ashley," she said cheerfully. "It's nice to meet you."

Ashley just smiled at her, her sea-foam eyes looking rather frosty as she studied Alex. "So you're Alex," she said, her tone cool. "Lucas was telling me about you just this morning."

"Really?" Alex said, trying to suppress her smile. *Lucas had told his family about her!*

"Yes, he mentioned he had a date last night," Ashley said, her mouth twisting in a smirk as she combed her fingers through her hair. "The word *pity* may or may not have been thrown in there somewhere as well. I can't really remember."

"Well, naturally, it would have been," Sealey said, giving Ashley a significant look. "That date was the result of Alex taking pity on Lucas. After all, she had to pay five dollars so he wouldn't be humiliated at a date auction." He narrowed his eyes at her.

"Right, that's what I meant. Obviously," Ashley said with a look that was entirely too innocent.

As Ashley turned away, Alex raised her eyebrows at Sealey, surprised that he would stand up for her like that. He just smiled gently at her and quickly reached out to squeeze her hand in a comforting way. She turned back to look at the field, still puzzled. Why was he so different today? He'd never championed her like that before. She felt a sense of deep gratitude. And confusion.

But with regard to Ashley, Alex was torn. All right, so she wanted to make a good impression on Lucas's family. Of course she did. But she was not the kind of girl to sit and take insults from an uppity, pint-sized accountant, either. She longed to put Ashley in her place, but she held her tongue.

Ashley did not follow suit. "So, Alex, what do you do?" she asked with false sweetness, swinging her miles of thick, curly hair forward as she leaned over to get a good look at Alex. "Lucas didn't mention anything about you beyond your height. But don't worry about that. I'm sure there are plenty of guys who don't mind being shorter than their wives."

Alex ground her teeth. She wouldn't let Ashley goad her. She would be the bigger person. "I'm a dietitian," she replied, her voice determinedly polite. "I work primarily with new mothers over at the hospital."

"I see," Ashley said, her look slightly superior. "Well, that can't be terribly complicated, can it? I mean, new babies really only eat one thing, don't they?" She laughed airily. "But don't feel bad. Some people can't handle high stress careers, so it's good that jobs like yours exist."

Alex clamped her lips together, determinedly keeping her smile fixed on her face, although it felt strained. "While I definitely do work with new moms to make sure their babies get the best nutrition, I also work with them on their own nutrition," she said. She was seriously wrestling with the urge to grab the pretty little thing by her curly-haired head and fling her down the stairs. "A mom's level of nutrition translates directly into her baby's nutrition, especially if she's breast-feeding. So I help moms know the best kinds of foods to eat to make sure their babies benefit as well. I also do some consulting to help women who are concerned about losing their baby weight."

"Sounds like a pretty important job to me," Sealey said, although he didn't seem to be paying much attention to the conversation. He was studying the football field closely, apparently looking for Lucas.

"Maybe," Ashley said, giving him a dirty look. Apparently, she was hoping he would back her up.

"So, Sealey," Ashley said, threading her hand through his arm. "I just got an email yesterday from Olivia. She's so close to coming home! Can you believe it's only a couple of months away? I know Lucas is just counting the hours. The four of us should double that first weekend she's back."

Suddenly, the clouds parted in Alex's mind. She could see exactly what was going on. Ashley had a crush on Sealey. She wanted her brother to end up with Olivia, and she wanted Sealey for herself. But judging from Sealey's reaction to Ashley, he wasn't biting. Which, given Sealey's proclaimed preference for Olivia, made perfect sense to Alex. But, of course, Ashley had no idea that Sealey was interested in Olivia. Man alive, what a soap opera.

"We'll see," Sealey replied, patting Ashley's hand and pulling away.

The rest of the game proceeded in this way. Ashley completely ignored Alex, cozying up to Sealey instead, and made marked comments about either Olivia and Lucas or herself and Sealey. Sealey would answer in short, noncommittal sentences and then turn to Alex, explaining to her the rules and points of the game.

By the end of the first half, Alex was actually starting to enjoy what she was watching. It was pleasant to be sitting there in the sun with Sealey, his arm across the back of her seat as he pointed out Lucas's form running back and forth on the field. Her enjoyment of the afternoon might also have had something to do Sealey markedly ignoring Ashley, but it made her feel petty to think such things, so she pretended like that had no bearing on her mood.

As the marching band began playing their halftime show, Sealey turned once again to Alex. "You hungry?" he asked. "Want to come grab something to eat with me?"

"Sure," she answered, rising to her feet. Ashley watched them go, her arms folded sourly across her chest and her eyebrows scrunched. The sight made Alex want to laugh.

"How about pizza?" Sealey asked as they walked past the various food vendors. "I'm craving bread and cheese right now."

"Sounds good to me," Alex said, reaching in her purse for her wallet. She was always up for a good pepperoni pizza.

"I got it," Sealey said, gesturing to the wallet in her hand.

"Huh?" she asked vaguely.

"I'll pay," Sealey clarified. "I pretty much forced you here. Lunch is on me."

"Oh . . . well, thanks," Alex said, disconcerted. The Sealey she was seeing today seemed like a completely different person than she was used to. She wondered if all the talking about Olivia had improved his mood.

"By the way, I'm sorry about Ashley," Sealey said, not looking at her. "I wasn't sure if she would be here. She doesn't come to all the games. But if Lucas really told her about your date last night, then I'm not surprised she's here."

"Yeah, she's . . . you know, charming," Alex replied, biting her lip.

Sealey chuckled. "Yeah, she's a piece of work."

"She seems to like *you*, though," Alex said, elbowing him in the ribs. "Have you ever been out with her?"

"Not really . . . not in the way you mean," Sealey replied, shrugging. "We've been out before, I guess, in the sense that she's invited me as her 'plus one.' But there's nothing going on between us."

"No thanks to you," Alex said, laughing. "I'm sure she'd like nothing better than to rectify that situation."

Sealey smiled wryly and shrugged again. "She's not my type," he said simply. "She's beautiful and really smart, but she's also incredibly manipulative. Her dad spoils her rotten, so she's gotten used to getting her way. She gets downright irritating when she wants something."

"Sounds about right," Alex surmised.

Once they had their personal-size pizzas in hand, they headed back for the stairs to their section.

"Hey, let's stay down here and eat, if you don't mind," Sealey suggested. "Ashley's driving me nuts, and I'd rather postpone going back up there until Luke's on the field again."

"Sure," Alex agreed, rather relieved that he suggested it. They sat on a bench side-by-side and opened their pizza boxes. "So, how long ago did you start your company?" Alex asked, taking her first careful bite of the steaming pizza. "Have you been doing this long?"

"Well, technically, I started my company while I was still in grad school," Sealey responded, trying to detach a string of cheese from his slice with his fingers. "I knew I didn't want to work for anyone else, so I decided to do my own thing and focus on advertising for smaller businesses here in the valley." He took a big bite of pizza and immediately coughed, his eyes watering. "Holy moly, that's hot!" he exclaimed.

Alex started laughing. "I've never heard you use an expletive before.

It's nice to know that you do that kind of thing, even if you used the goofiest one you could've chosen."

Sealey looked at her through his tearing eyes and shook his head. "I don't know where you come up with these ideas about me," he sputtered, trying to keep his mouth open to let the heat from his pizza escape. "Why wouldn't I use expletives? *Everyone* uses expletives. Even goofy ones."

"Yeah, well, you're not everyone," Alex claimed, taking another tiny bite. "You're the untouchable, imperturbable Sealey Witchburn. Nothing and no one surprises you. Well, except for thoroughly heated pizza, apparently."

Sealey rolled his eyes. "Well, *anyway*, I picked up a few clients while I was finishing up my MBA. But once I graduated and was able to focus solely on my company, the business really took off. Turns out the small mom-and-pops in the valley really like a locally owned firm promoting them. Plus, due to my 'single and fancy-free' status, I'm able to travel wherever and whenever I need to for work, so I can do some advertising for them in other areas of the state if needed. Sometimes in other areas of the country."

"Wow, that sounds exciting," Alex replied. "I have to admit, I'm really jealous."

"Jealous?" Sealey asked, his eyebrow raised. "Have ambitions in advertising yourself, Foamer?"

"No, not about that," Alex said, smiling. "I just . . . I've always wanted to make a difference, you know? Not just here in Logan, but out there." She gestured widely with her arms. "In the wide world. I feel so strongly about the importance of nutrition, especially for children. I just wish I could do more to educate people."

"It sounds like you make a big impact where you are right now," Sealey reminded her. "Don't sell yourself short."

"Oh, I know I make a difference with the individual people I work with," Alex assured him. "I just wish that I could reach more. That I could, I don't know, change the world." She laughed self-consciously. "Wow, that sounds really corny."

"Sure does," Sealey said and winked at her. "No, it's not corny. I think it sounds kind of noble, actually. It's not like you're aspiring to become famous or wealthy. You're aspiring to change people for the better. It's a very unselfish goal."

"Yeah, well, it's unlikely I'll get anywhere with it."

"Probably not, with that attitude," Sealey said, with a smirk. "Come on! Where's that confidence you're so famous for?"

Alex chuckled. "I'll find it someday." She watched him as he enthusiastically downed the rest of his pizza. "Sealey?" she finally said, capturing his attention.

"Yeah?" he asked, looking at her with his mouth full. It was adorable.

"I just wanted to let you know"—she looked down at her half empty pizza box so she wouldn't have to meet his eyes—"I'm grateful for all you're doing for me." She looked back up at him, her expression sincere. "And I'm really impressed with you. You've done really well for yourself. I hope I can someday accomplish all that you have."

Sealey was quiet for a moment as he studied her expression. "Thanks, Foamer," he finally replied, nudging her with his shoulder and grinning. He had pizza sauce stuck in his teeth. She laughed.

* * * * *

The last half of the game passed quickly, now that Alex understood the rules. She cheered at all the right moments and kept her eyes focused on Lucas's form. When he caught a pass and ran it in for a touchdown, she thought she might have screamed louder than anyone in the stadium. By the end of the game she was slightly hoarse.

"Well, let's head down," Sealey said, as the navy-clad USU fans began to stream gloomily toward the exits. Utah State had fought bravely, but unfortunately, the University of Utah had managed to emerge victorious. "Lucas will likely need some cheering up after that whooping."

"Are we meeting up with him?" Alex asked, the fluttering of butterflies beginning in her middle.

"Yep, we're going to take him to dinner," Sealey replied. Alex heard Ashley huff behind them.

"Honestly, I don't know why we have to change plans last minute," Ashley protested. "We told him that you and I were going to meet him. He's not expecting Alex. Don't you think he'll be a little irritated?"

"I doubt it, Ash," Sealey said over his shoulder as he once again took Alex's arm above the elbow and led her toward the exit. "Lucas really likes Alex."

Ashley muttered something under her breath, but Alex didn't catch it. She gritted her teeth for what felt like the fiftieth time that day and clenched her fists, trying to stifle her irritation.

Twenty minutes later, the three of them stood outside the stadium in an uncomfortable silence.

Alex didn't want to say anything to Sealey, knowing that Ashley would hear every word, and she assumed Sealey felt the same way. She rocked back and forth on her heels, willing Lucas to hurry up.

"There he is," Ashley said suddenly, pointing to the form of her brother emerging from a metal door to their left. She raised her arms and waved, even though he was only twenty feet away and couldn't possibly have missed the tall, white-blond figure of Sealey Witchburn.

"Oh, hey, guys," Lucas said in a slightly morose voice. "I almost wish you hadn't—" Suddenly he froze, his eyes falling on Alex. "Alex!" he exclaimed. "What are you doing here?"

It was at that point that Alex realized she didn't have a story. She couldn't tell him that Sealey had insisted she come because she didn't know football. She glanced, panicked, up at Sealey's face, but he looked utterly unconcerned.

"Oh, I invited her," Sealey said easily. "I ran into her this morning and mentioned I was going to the game. She told me she didn't know much about football, and since I had an extra ticket and knew you two went out last night, I figured it would be a good thing to educate her. After all, how can you ever expect to get a repeat date with her if she doesn't fully appreciate your football brilliance? I mean, really, what motivation does she have to say yes?" Sealey smiled teasingly at his friend.

Alex glanced at Lucas, noticing how red he appeared. Wait a minute, was he blushing? Could it be possible that Lucas had mentioned something about wanting a repeat date with her to Sealey? She suddenly felt like singing.

"Well, if I was hoping to impress her, I've done a poor job," Lucas said ruefully to Sealey, rubbing the back of his neck with his hand. He glanced self-consciously again at Alex and shifted his gym bag uncomfortably on his shoulder.

"Well, we're giving you the opportunity to redeem yourself," Sealey announced. "We're going to take you out to dinner."

"Not sure I'll be the best company tonight," Lucas said, wincing. "This was a painful one."

"Oh, come on," Ashley said, running to him and giving him a hug. "Even if your team lost, at least you did well personally."

"Wish I could see it that way," Lucas said glumly.

"Well, not that what I think means anything, but you certainly seemed faster than anyone else on the field," Alex spoke up, feeling stupid for her contribution to the conversation. "I imagine that makes a big difference."

"Speed is very important for a wide receiver," Sealey agreed, nodding. "And nobody is faster than Luke."

Lucas grinned. "Well, if you're trying to cheer me up, you guys are definitely off to a good start." They started toward the parking lot.

"Hey, Alex, why don't you drive with me?" Lucas said, brushing his fingers down her arm to get her attention. "I'd love to hear your impressions of your first real college football game."

Alex opened her mouth to enthusiastically agree, but Ashley interrupted her.

"Oh, don't be silly, Luke," she said with a saccharine smile. "Alex doesn't want to talk football with you. Alex, why don't you come with me? I'd love to get to know you better." Alex could see the cunning behind Ashley's offer, but Lucas looked at her with an expression of shocked approval on his face.

"That's a great idea!" he exclaimed. "We'll meet you guys at Angie's."

Alex had to stifle a groan at the choice of restaurant. Angie's was always packed to bursting after sporting events, which was why she always made a point to avoid it. But at least she was going with Lucas. She would put up with anything to be with Lucas. Even his snotty sister.

"So, Alex," Ashley said as they climbed into her sleek, black Infiniti. "I'm just going to be straight with you, okay?"

"Please do," Alex said, again through gritted teeth. She felt a headache coming on.

"Lucas is taken," the curly-headed witch said bluntly. "Okay? He's off the market. You really shouldn't waste your time. Sorry to disappoint you."

"I appreciate you letting me know," Alex said, melting her voice into sugary tones. "But if Lucas really was taken, I doubt he'd be interested in dating me, would he? He doesn't seem like that kind of guy, and I assure you, I have no intention of forcing myself on him."

Ashley looked at her disbelievingly. "Then what are you doing here? If you have no interest in snatching my brother away from his steady girlfriend, then why did you show up today?"

"Sealey invited me," Alex returned simply. "Like he said, I'd never been to a football game before, and I'm all about new experiences. So I said yes. And if Lucas really does have a steady girlfriend, then there is no reason to expect that he'll ask me out again. So you needn't worry your pretty head about it, Ashley." She turned her head to stare out the window, willing the scenery to go by faster, desperate to escape the bratty brunette's company.

"Look, I'll be blunt," Ashley said, and Alex rolled her eyes, wondering how on earth the girl could have been classifying her communications up to this point if not as "blunt." "Lucas is too nice for his own good. Seriously, he will ask you out just because he feels sorry for you. But he is in love with someone else. A girl who is a much better match for him than you are. So I'm telling you now, really, for your own sake, back off."

Alex turned to face Ashley, full-on, eyes narrowed and snapping with furious energy. She'd promised Sealey she would keep tight rein on her tongue when speaking to Lucas, but he'd said nothing about Ashley. She decided to take that oversight as his permission to completely unload on Lucas's nasty sister.

"I appreciate your concern, Ashley, and I understand that maybe what I've said thus far could be construed as vague, or maybe even a little timid, so let me just take this opportunity to clear things up for you. I currently do not have any kind of diabolical plan to force Lucas to date me. However, if he happens to ask me out or express interest in me, I will respond as I see fit. With no reference to you or anyone else. Quite frankly, my dating habits are none of your concern. I am a big girl, and your brother is a big boy, and I'm fairly certain we can handle ourselves without your input or guidance. Because you are Lucas's sister, I'm sure he is ready and willing to hear your concerns about his relationship status. However, you are not my sister or my mother or my maiden aunt, so I have no such obligation. So let's just consider this topic closed, shall we?" She turned back to the window, her fists clenched in her lap.

Alex could practically feel the waves of hot fury emanating from Ashley. But neither said another word.

* * * * *

"So, ladies, how was the drive?" Lucas asked as they converged on the entrance to Angie's Restaurant. Although the restaurant was less than two miles from the stadium, due to game day traffic, it had taken nearly ten minutes to get there. Ten very uncomfortable minutes.

"Oh, it was fantastic!" Ashley said with expertly faked enthusiasm. "Alex and I really used the time to get to know each other. I think we're off to a good start. I feel like I know exactly what kind of person she is already."

"Glad to hear that," Lucas said, smiling warmly at Alex, and suddenly she felt all of her former irritation evaporate. "Sealey went in to put his name down. It's a thirty-minute wait."

The wait passed quickly, mostly with banter between Lucas and Sealey. Alex was thoroughly entertained, but Ashley was oddly quiet. It made Alex nervous. What was she planning in that demonic head of hers?

Once seated at their table, orders taken, Lucas turned to Alex. "So how are Eric and Martin doing? I hope you haven't had Eric showing up in a panic to any of your other family dinner dates."

"Oh, uh, no," Alex said, trying to smile. Why did she have to get so shifty whenever he brought up one of their staged meetings? She couldn't afford to arouse suspicion from Ashley's direction. "Thankfully, Martin responded to my advised tactic and all seems to be well for now. At least until the next crisis." She looked quickly down at her hands, pretending to be pushing back a stubborn cuticle.

"Who's Eric?" Sealey asked politely, even though he knew perfectly well.

"He's that guy I told you about," Lucas reminded him. "The one that showed up at Elements that time Alex and I ran into each other. The one with the cute little kid I assumed was hers." He reddened slightly, but smiled broadly at Alex.

"Ah, right," Sealey said, nodding and stirring his ice water with his straw. "Isn't that the guy who's become pretty much a perpetual patient for you?" he asked Alex, seemingly as an afterthought. The question sounded offhand, but Alex could feel him attempting to steer the conversation in a certain direction. She wondered what he was up to.

"Yes, he's the most nervous parent I've ever encountered. That's pretty uncommon for a father, but it makes a bit more sense once you understand Eric's history."

"What is his history?" Lucas asked. "Or can you not tell me? I don't know, do you have something like doctor/patient confidentiality?"

"Well, as long as I'm not revealing their medical history, I should be okay," Alex replied. She explained Eric's history, starting with their first meeting on the day Martin was born and Eric's wife had passed and ending with the day Eric had accosted her at the Elements restaurant with a perfectly content Martin in his arms.

"Wow," Lucas said, his eyebrows raised. "That's really good of you to spend so much time consulting with him when technically Martin shouldn't be your patient anymore."

"Couldn't you get in trouble for that?" Ashley asked. Alex thought Ashley sounded almost hopeful.

"No, because I generally refer him to other specialists whenever Martin has any kind of real medical problem. It's only in regard to Martin's diet that I consult with Eric," Alex informed her. "And even in that case, I'm consulting as more of a friend than anything. I mean, say you had some kind of digestive issue that caused you to have per-petual diarrhea," Alex said, smiling inside when she saw Ashley flush and look around to make sure no one was listening to their conversa-tion. "I could consult with you as a friend who happens to be a dietetics professional, couldn't I? It's the same kind of thing."

"Sounds like the kind of skill we should keep around," Lucas agreed. "It's valuable information to have at your fingertips."

"Alex was telling me earlier today that she has global aspirations," Sealey said, taking a sip of his water.

"Really?" Lucas looked back at her. "Global, huh?"

"That's kind of overstating it," Alex said, reddening. "I just wish I could do more to encourage people to live healthy lifestyles, particu-larly with regard to raising kids. I feel very limited where I am now."

"So you're interested in furthering this agenda outside of Logan, I take it?" Lucas clarified.

"Outside Utah, if I can. While every state has its health struggles, Utah regularly tops 'Most Healthy' lists, so I feel I could do more good elsewhere."

"Interesting," Lucas said, considering her words. "That's great you have such ambitious goals. Kind of intimidating, really."

Ashley snorted softly and rolled her eyes, but Lucas was watching Alex and didn't notice. Alex tried not to, but it was difficult.

"You remind me of Sealey," Lucas continued, grinning at his best friend. "Sealey has all kinds of expansive goals for the business. Nothing seems to hold him back."

"Really?" Alex said, raising her eyebrows at Sealey. When he had told her of his business, he hadn't mentioned plans to expand.

"Not really," Sealey said, waving them off. "We're rooted locally. My dreams of expansion are pretty limited."

"But you could if you wanted to," Ashley crooned, leaning forward to take his arm over the table. "You could take that company public if you wanted to!" She turned to Alex and explained with a condescending look on her face, "That means the company would be traded on a public stock exchange."

"Thanks, I got it," Alex replied with a seriously fake smile. She wondered if she could get away with "accidentally" kicking Ashley in the shins as she unfolded and refolded her legs.

"I have no desire to take my company public anytime soon." Sealey smiled at Ashley and moved his arm away. "I'm having way too much fun right now being in charge. If I were public, I'd have shareholders to answer to."

Their food came then, and the conversation moved to other topics. Alex couldn't help but consider pinching herself as she looked over at Lucas and saw him smiling at her. The feeling intensified when he reached out for no apparent reason and squeezed her hand. She smiled radiantly back at him and glanced at Sealey. His eyes were fixed on their clasped hands and when his eyes met hers, the corner of his mouth twitched. Things appeared to be progressing right on schedule.

{ Chapter EIGHT }

"**G**UESS WHAT TODAY is?" Alex cried with unrestrained delight. Her swimmers looked just short of rolling their eyes at her. "It's *hypoxic* day! Yay!"

The team groaned in unison.

"Trust me, when the region and state meets come around, you'll thank me," she said, the unmerited glee gone from her tone. She turned to write the hypoxic set up on the whiteboard, inwardly thanking her stars, yet again, that she was no longer on the swimmer end of this deal. Hypoxic day was Hades. But it bred results, as she well knew.

"Whaaaat?" Jason Green cried as he read the whiteboard. "Eight fifties freestyle, no breathing, on a minute? When the heck are we supposed to breathe then?"

"So swim the fifty in less than a minute. You'll have until the top to breathe. Simple math, Green," Alex said, supremely unconcerned. She heard Jason continue to mutter behind her back and she grinned to herself.

She eyed the pace clock on the wall as she snapped the lid back on the marker. "Okay, set starts on the top!" she called down the pool. As the second hand hit the sixty, splashes erupted in six lanes as her swimmers pushed off the wall. She strode along the side of the pool, watching for stroke improvements and cheating on the breathing restrictions. As Jason Green finished his first fifty, she called to him, "I saw that breath, Green! Remember, you owe me ten push-ups every time you cheat!"

"Yeah, yeah," he gasped as he slid his goggles back over his eyes in preparation for his second fifty.

Alex laughed as she kept walking down the deck. As her eyes continued their scan of the pool, a figure standing near the lifeguard station caught her eye. Her heartbeat faltered as she realized it was Lucas. He stood in his basketball shorts and cutoff T-shirt, gym bag on his shoulder, smiling at her. When her eyes finally met his, he waved. She smiled back and immediately started toward him.

She tried to look pleased and unconcerned at his presence, but inside she was all of a flutter. It was the first time he had approached her without her somehow devising a way to catch his attention. She was thrilled he decided to stop by all on his own.

"Hey!" she said cheerfully as she approached him. "What are you doing here?" She was proud of herself for thinking of the line. No one would ever suspect that she watched for him to walk by the pool area every day.

"I work out here with some buddies pretty much every day," Lucas said, and she was elated when he stepped forward and pulled her into a quick hug. "How long have you been coaching the swim team?"

"This is my third year," she said, trying to sound like being hugged by Lucas Riley was no big deal to her. She would've done all right if her breath hadn't been coming so fast. "I started in my last year of college. It was actually supposed to be a temporary thing, but I loved it so much I decided to stay on."

"Coach!" Mark Peters's voice rang through the pool area, deeply out of breath. Both Alex and Lucas turned to look at him. His chest was heaving, as he swiped the fog from his goggles. "I'd just like to take this opportunity to say . . . I hate you." He grinned playfully at her and pushed off the wall.

She turned back to Lucas and bit her lip, trying not to smile.

"Well, they obviously think the world of you." Lucas laughed, and she joined in.

"Today is hypoxic day," she explained. "They don't like it very much when I mandate how often they are allowed breathe." She winked at him. She felt light and happy inside. Lucas's voluntary presence had that effect on her.

"Why do you do that to them?" Lucas asked, raising an eyebrow. "Seems a little cruel to me."

"Trust me, it's not to make them miserable," Alex explained. "It trains their muscles to use oxygen more efficiently. The less air their muscles require, the less often they have to take a breath, and the faster they move."

"Ah . . . ," Lucas said, turning to watch the swimmers. "I guess that makes sense. We don't worry about such things on the football field."

"Yeah, it's kind of a 'water sports only' concern."

"So how long do their workouts usually last?" Lucas asked, turning back to her.

"They go till six," she replied, slipping her hands into the pockets of her workout pants. "Four to six every day. Why?"

"Well," Lucas said, looking slightly uncomfortable and running a hand over the back of his head. "I was just wondering if maybe you'd like to go get a smoothie or something with me afterward. I'm usually wrapping up around six thirty. I could cut out a little early and come down and get you."

"Oh, uh . . . ," Alex said, taken very much off guard. Stupidly, the first thing that popped into her head was, *What would Sealey say about this?* He seemed to have a very carefully thought-out strategy. Would going out with Lucas now spoil everything?

"You totally don't have to," Lucas said, holding up his hands. "You've kind of seen a lot of me lately. If you're all 'Luked' out, I completely understand." He emphasized his name with his fingers.

"Oh no!" Alex said quickly, reaching out to touch his arm. Forget Sealey. Having Lucas ask her out all on his own was a pure miracle. If anything, Sealey should be happy about this development. "I'd love to. I was just, uh, you know, not wanting to be the cause of a short workout for you. I know how much you football players love your workouts." She smiled brightly, feeling ridiculous for hesitating at all to accept his invitation.

"Ah, it's no big deal," Lucas replied. "I probably spend far too much time in the gym as it is. It'll be good for me." He pulled his bag further up on his muscular shoulder and grinned at her. "Well, all right, then. I'll see you at six."

"See you then." She beamed at him, her middle erupting with hyperactive butterflies. She watched him walk away, feeling like the luckiest girl in the world.

* * * *

"Seriously, Foamer, I can't hear a word you're saying." Sealey's voice was distracted and slightly distant, as though his mouth wasn't actually aimed at the receiver. He was probably still working.

"I'm at the pool. It's echoey," Alex explained. "But Lucas just—"

"Uh, nope. Still can't make out a single syllable."

Alex sighed, glanced back at the pool to make sure the team was still occupied by the set on the board, and then ducked into the locker room.

"I *said*," she began again, "Lucas just asked me out for tonight."

The line was silent for a moment.

"As in, by himself?" Sealey finally asked, his voice louder now. The conversation appeared to have captured his interest. "He walked up to you and asked you out? How? When? Where are you?"

"I'm at the gym. He just showed up in the pool area five minutes ago and asked me out! Did you know anything about this?"

"No . . . he didn't mention anything about it to me," Sealey replied. Alex couldn't place his tone. He didn't sound angry, exactly . . . but he didn't sound particularly happy either.

"Are you going to yell at me for accepting?" she asked. "It kind of came at me out of left field and I wasn't sure how you would want me to respond, so I decided to respond how I wanted to. Which was to say yes." Her tone clearly stated how much trouble he would be in if he told her to back out of her commitment now.

"No, I'm not going to yell at you," Sealey said, and she could hear a slight smile in his voice now. "I'm just a little surprised. This turned out to be much, ah, easier than I was expecting. I may have to revamp my plan a little."

"Maybe I'm just that much more lovable than you thought," Alex teased him. It was a testament to how far they had come in the past few weeks that she could manage to tease Sealey Witchburn.

"Maybe," Sealey said, surrendering unexpectedly. "Well, let me know how it goes. What are you guys doing?"

"Oh, just going to grab a smoothie. No biggie," Alex replied nonchalantly as though this weren't the biggest and most important event in her life up to this point.

"Sounds harmless enough," Sealey observed. "Well, have a good time."

"Um, thanks," Alex replied, surprised that he wasn't offering her any kind of advice or direction. "Are you sure you don't have any instructions for me?"

"Not this time," Sealey responded. "You earned this date all on your own. You got this."

* * * * *

"Medium strawberry banana, please," Alex said to the girl behind the counter. The blonde nodded and turned to begin working on the smoothie.

"Large peanut butter protein blast," Lucas said to the guy behind the blonde waiting to take his order.

After Lucas had paid, the two of them sat down at a nearby table, waiting for their treats.

"So," Alex began, feeling a little awkward at the silence. "You work for Sealey's company, right?"

"Yep." Lucas nodded. "Kind of pathetic, isn't it? Working as a staffer for my best friend. I try not to let it bother me, but I manage to feel inferior to him pretty regularly anyway. He's certainly done more with his life than I have."

Alex looked at him incredulously. "What are you talking about?" she said. "Sure, he may own his own company, but you are probably the most well-rounded person I know. Given your calling and your talents, it's obvious that you've put in a lot of effort in just about every area of your life."

"Being elders quorum president doesn't necessarily mean I'm super spiritual, you know," Lucas said, waving away her comment. "It just means I'm the poor schmuck who said yes."

Alex smiled. "But you obviously have your spiritual ducks in a row," she pointed out. "And Sealey told me you do really well in school. And, on top of that, you're a starter on the football team and you have a job. Only a certain kind of person can manage that many responsibilities at once."

"The job is only part-time," Lucas said, running a hand over the back of his head in a way that Alex was beginning to recognize. It was his nervous habit. "You're giving me a lot more credit than I deserve." He looked at her ruefully.

Alex just smiled at him. The more she talked to him, the more she found to admire. "So what are your long-term goals, then? Do you want to stay with Sealey's company?"

"I don't think so," Lucas replied. "It's a good gig for right now because Sealey is really good about working with my schedule, plus he's giving me lots of exposure to potential business contacts, but I think eventually I'd like to move into a more finance-centered role."

"You're an MBA student, aren't you?" Alex asked, smiling at the girl who had just set her smoothie on the table in front of her. "Do you have an emphasis?"

"Um, finance," Lucas answered, grinning at her.

"Duh." She laughed at herself and coughed, nearly choking on her smoothie.

"My dad actually pushed accounting really hard," Lucas said, smacking her on the back to clear her windpipe. "'It's the language of business, Lucas,' he said to me, but he's already got his CPA clone in the family. And Ashley actually *likes* accounting, the weirdo." He grinned. "I like looking at investments and market trends. But actually, more than anything, I enjoy the private equity or venture capital side of things."

"Come again?" Alex said, blinking cluelessly at him. "I'm pretty sure I've heard those words before, but I won't bother pretending I know what they mean."

"Well, in layman's terms, I like the idea of investing in new businesses. The ones with really brilliant and promising concepts, and then supporting them until they're profitable. If you go about it the right way, you can really make something of yourself."

"So you fund the businesses and Sealey promotes them?" Alex smiled. "You two should set up shop together."

"Nah, Sealey is much more ambitious than I am," Lucas said as he took the peanut butter smoothie from the neon green–shirted employee who was holding it out to him. He nodded his thanks. "For all Sealey's claims that he's rooted locally, he really does have big dreams for his company. There's no way he'll be content staying here in Logan."

"But you don't want to leave?" Alex asked. "You have no ambitions outside Logan?"

"Well, I wouldn't limit myself to Logan," Lucas claimed, taking a sip of his smoothie. "I'm originally from Salt Lake, so I think after graduation, that's probably where I'll head. But I don't really have any ambitions outside of Utah right now. There's a lot of opportunity in state. It's a good place to get started."

"So when do you graduate?" Alex asked.

"Not for a while," Lucas said with a grimace. "I've had to keep my credit hours relatively low while I've been playing football, but this is my last season, so I'll be able to up my credit hours considerably next year. I'll have about a year and a half left. They're going to let me integrate into a normal MBA schedule at that point. The business school has been really great about working with me and my football schedule."

"Well, chances are, they want you to excel at football as much as you do," Alex said, winking. "We all have a stake in your success."

"Oh, don't say that," Lucas said, rubbing a hand fretfully over his flat stomach. Alex saw the defined outline of his muscles as his cutoff T-shirt momentarily tightened over his chest. She felt heat creep up her neck and onto her face, and she determinedly looked away to keep her expression under control. "I can't handle the idea that so many people are watching me and relying on me to uphold their school pride. It makes me seriously nervous." He winced and played with the straw in his smoothie.

"Well, with great talent comes great responsibility," Alex replied loftily and then laughed at his panicky expression. "Honestly, you're just really fun to watch. Even I enjoy it, and I'm nowhere near a football aficionado."

"Now that, I can handle," Lucas said, pointing at her. They sat grinning at each other in silence for a few seconds. "So, would you be interested in maybe seeing a movie with me sometime or something?" Lucas suddenly asked. "Whenever you're free. I'm pretty open most of the time. I mean, as long as I don't have practice. Or church responsibilities. Oh, or a huge school project. Or, you know, client meetings for work."

Alex looked at him incredulously and laughed. "I'd love to, but why don't you let me know when you're free? I think you and I have two very different definitions of the word."

Lucas smiled at her and reached across the table to place his hand softly over hers. "Deal," he said. "But let's plan on sooner rather than later, okay? I'm not sure why, but I have a feeling you are going to be a very important part of my life, Alex Foamer."

Staring at him, Alex couldn't trust herself to speak.

* * * * *

The next few weeks passed in a haze of tingly butterflies for Alex. Lucas took her out twice, once to dinner and a movie and once to a concert. Each time she felt herself falling faster and further for him. He was considerate and chivalrous, affectionate and complimentary. Alex thought she must have found the one perfect man on earth.

She continued to call Sealey after every date, reporting on the general happenings, but leaving the truly personal stuff out wherever she could. Sealey seemed to be growing less and less demanding, and Alex took that to mean he had grown more confident in her ability to handle herself. He hadn't mentioned Olivia again since the day of the football game, but Alex was sure that the beautiful missionary was often on Sealey's mind. Alex felt strangely satisfied that Sealey trusted her to attract Lucas's attention on her own, and therefore he didn't need to worry about his chances with Olivia. As for the ethical ramifications of helping Sealey to steal his best friend's girl, Alex tried not to think too deeply about that.

Lucas had yet to specifically mention Olivia to Alex, and she had no plans to ask. As far as she was concerned, the further they stayed away from that subject, the better.

"But don't you think you should at least test the waters?" Meredith had asked her after she had returned from her last date with Lucas. "Just to see how attached he really is to her?"

Alex shook her head. "To be perfectly honest, I don't really want to know. He's a good, honest guy. If he were truly devoted to Olivia, he wouldn't be wasting his time with me. The fact that he keeps asking me out makes me even more confident that he never made her any promises before she left."

"I don't know, Al," Meredith said, biting her lip. "He hasn't made *you* any promises either. Just because he likes you doesn't necessarily mean he's stopped liking her, does it? She's coming home in a month . . . are you sure you're prepared for that?"

"I really haven't thought much about it," Alex lied. "And, anyway, it's not like my worrying about it will keep her from coming home. I just need to make the most of the time I have left. Maybe if I can make Lucas fall hard for me in this last month before Olivia comes home, I won't have anything to worry about when she finally arrives."

"Okay," Meredith capitulated, but she didn't look convinced.

Neither was Alex, really. But she didn't know what else to do, except to keep accepting Lucas's invitations to go out. Their next date was to Lagoon, the only real amusement park of which Utah could boast. And to tell the truth, there wasn't much to boast about. But since they were now in the first week of October, Lagoon was hosting their annual "Frightmares," for which the amusement park became a Halloweentown of sorts. Nothing overwhelming, but it afforded a bit more interest than usual. And, of course, Alex was looking forward to simply spending time with Lucas, regardless of where he wanted to go.

It was a crisp and cool October afternoon when they walked through Lagoon's parking lot toward the park entrance. Alex couldn't help but think of one of her favorite quotes from L. M. Montgomery's *Anne of Green Gables* as she walked. "I'm so glad I live in a world where there are Octobers." With her hand warm inside Lucas's and her lungs full of the smell of October, she didn't think life could be more perfect.

The park entrance was haunted by various ghouls and zombies, mulling through the crowd with shuffling steps. The gruesome specters stopped for pictures with people, grimacing as their photo compatriots grinned with excitement. Alex dodged a particularly miserable-looking zombie as she and Lucas made for the ticket counter. Within five minutes, hands stamped, they were in the park.

"So, where to?" Lucas asked, rubbing his hands together with relish. "I haven't been here in forever. I want to ride *everything*."

Alex laughed. "Hey, I'm up for anything. I haven't been here for years myself."

"Okay, let's go . . . this way," Lucas said, leading them off to the right. "Let's start with something fast."

They were off. They focused on the most intense attractions in the park, Lucas's hair getting more and more disheveled as they exited each ride. They wandered through the Halloween attractions and got their pictures taken with various bloodied and battered characters. Alex was having the time of her life. They took a break from rides around dinnertime and stopped at a sandwich place inside the park for a bite to eat. They talked and laughed animatedly through the entire meal, anxious to get out on the midway again.

"So . . . you up for something *really* scary?" Alex asked, poking Lucas in the arm.

"Scarier than we've already done?" Lucas asked, eyebrows raised. "We've ridden all the fastest rides in the park, haven't we?"

"Not yet, we haven't."

Lucas looked slightly apprehensive at the adventurous look in Alex's eye. "Which one did we miss?"

"The Sky Coaster," Alex said with increased drama. "You know, it's that one that's like a giant swing, where they stick you in a harness, strap you to a cable, take you up a hundred and fifty feet, and then . . . they just drop you and you swing back and forth. It's spectacular."

Lucas looked faintly ill.

"It costs some extra money to ride, but it's my treat," Alex claimed. She nudged him again. "Come on, Riley. You can't possibly be scared. A big, tough football player like you."

"I'm . . . not scared," he protested weakly. "I just . . . don't love heights."

"You've been riding roller coasters all day!" Alex laughed. "That's kind of a key component of a roller coaster, you know."

"Right, but I've had a track and a seat beneath me for all of that," Lucas reminded her. "On the Sky Coaster, you're just kind of, you know, *hanging* there, face down."

"I swear to you, you won't regret it," Alex promised.

Finally, Lucas nodded weakly. "Okay," he said. "But if I scream like a little girl or throw up or something like that, you're sworn to secrecy."

Alex crossed her heart.

"Oh, and if I die, I'm not leaving you anything in my will," he tacked on for good measure.

"Well, if you die, chances are I'll be in the same situation, so I agree to that condition as well," Alex said, rolling her eyes and pushing him out the door of the little deli toward the attraction.

Given the intensity of the ride, there were very few people in line. After paying the extra charge and getting their tickets, they waited for ten minutes or so in the shelter of the ride shack. In which time Lucas had the chance to turn slightly green. When it was finally their turn, he was oddly silent as the park employee strapped him into his flight suit and led them to the launchpad.

"You okay, there?" Alex asked, trying not to laugh.

"No comment," Lucas muttered, barely opening his mouth.

Once they were attached to the cables, the bottom dropped suddenly out of the launchpad booth and Lucas gasped as they flew forward, suddenly parallel with the ground. They hung, suspended six feet in the air, Alex laughing as Lucas attempted to catch his breath. And then, they began to rise. Alex thought Lucas might begin whimpering as the ground sank further and further away. Once they reached the top, the tiny park employee below instructed them through the speaker to "Fly!" Alex paused, her hand on the ripcord, to look at Lucas. His eyes were tightly closed.

"Lucas Riley, I am not pulling this cord until you open your eyes," she said sternly. "You won't get the full effect otherwise."

"I don't want the full effect," he gasped, squeezing his eyes even more tightly shut. "I'm really okay missing that part of this experience."

"Luke," she said, making her voice soft and soothing. It was the first time she had ever used his nickname and her honeyed tone of voice made him look at her. "Trust me," she said softly as his eyes stared into hers. And she pulled the cord.

They immediately went into a free fall, the ground racing toward them at eighty miles per hour. To his credit, Lucas did not scream, but it might have been because he looked too horrified to manage it. By the time the cable caught them, six feet from the ground, and they began to soar back and forth, Lucas's face had broken into an exhilarated smile. He whooped and spread out his arms, enjoying the sensation of flying. Alex laughed, watching his face.

Once back on the ground and free of their flight suits, Lucas watched the pair after them plummet toward the ground, howling and laughing.

"Wow, is that what we looked like?" he cried, his voice full of excitement. "Man, oh man, what a *rush*!" Alex laughed again, and he looked down at her, his eyes bright with energy. "Thanks for making me do that," he said, his voice softening a little. "I never would have dared do something like that on my own."

"No problem," she said, staring up into his sea-foamy eyes. "I told you you wouldn't regret it."

She leaned into him, meaning to nudge him playfully, but he used her momentum against her, grasping her arms and pulling her tight against him. He studied her face, his expression mesmerized as they slipped over her features. He slid an arm around her, holding her firmly against his solid frame, and pushed her long, dark-red hair away from her face with his other hand.

And then he kissed her. Her breath stopped as his lips pressed warm and confident on hers. Her legs immediately went weak. She was grateful he was holding her up, because she was certain she would be shaking and tottering like an idiot otherwise. He slid his hand underneath her hair, pulling her closer and deepening the kiss. Alex could have sworn her feet had left the ground.

When he finally pulled away, she was sure she would have to reteach herself to breathe. The air felt lodged in her chest and her head was light and fuzzy from either lack of oxygen or an excess of Lucas.

"I've wanted to do that all day," Lucas said, his breathing slightly quickened. "Thanks for giving me the perfect opportunity."

"Oh . . . well . . . sure," she said stupidly, her head still buzzing.

* * * * *

The rest of the evening passed quickly and dreamily. Lucas stopped suddenly in his path on two separate occasions as they walked through the park, just to kiss Alex quickly. And he kept his arms looped comfortably around her as they waited in various lines throughout the night. As they drove back to Logan, their hands clasped between the seats of his car, Alex wondered if she would be able to find words to describe to Meredith how happy she was when she got home. It seemed unlikely.

"Given the, uh, events of tonight, I think I should probably tell you something," Lucas said suddenly. He turned off I-15, heading toward Brigham City.

"Okay . . . what's up?" said Alex, suddenly nervous but not sure why.

"I am . . . sort of . . . I'm kind of . . . well, I'm kind of attached to someone," he said, his voice hesitant.

Uh-oh. Here it was. Olivia.

"I'm sorry, what?" Alex said, straining to keep her voice light and unassuming.

"Well, I've been writing this missionary. Her name is Olivia. I've known her pretty much my whole life, and we dated, you know, kind of seriously before she left."

Despite the fact that Alex already knew all this, she was curious to hear Lucas's side of the story. She played along.

"So, are you supposed to be waiting for her or something?"

"No, nothing like that," Lucas answered, shaking his head. "I never promised her anything, but given that I've written her regularly for nearly her entire mission, and that she's coming home in a month, I think she's probably expecting something to happen."

"I see," Alex said, and she could feel the shiny happiness inside her fading a little. Was she about to hear that this was her last night with Lucas? Was he feeling guilty about kissing her? Maybe so much so that he wouldn't want to see her again?

"Don't get me wrong, I'm not implying anything by telling you this, I just . . . I don't know, I . . . I just felt like you should know," he finished somewhat lamely. In his discomfort, he began to rub his thumb over her palm absentmindedly. Shivers of pleasure reverberated through her. She quickly pulled her hand away, not wanting to be distracted. Lucas mistook her sudden movement as a sign that she was angry with him.

"I'm so sorry, Alex," he apologized immediately. "I should have told you sooner. I promise I wasn't trying to use you or mislead you or anything. And I don't want to stop seeing you."

"I appreciate the fact that you want to be honest with me," she began, her tone uncertain. She needed to tread carefully here. "But I guess I'm not sure why you felt the need to tell me this. Are you regretting what happened tonight? Are you trying to tell me that we need to back off?"

"No," he said, firmly and immediately. "I don't want to back off. I'm not regretting anything that happened. Tonight was . . . incredible." He reached over and squeezed her hand again. "I guess I just needed to tell you about Olivia because it's likely that when she gets home there will be some potentially awkward moments. And I think it's likely that they will involve both of us." He gave Alex a meaningful look. The shivers returned, and she squeezed his hand back.

"Well, then," she cleared her throat. "In that case, thanks for letting me know."

{ Chapter NINE }

"SERIOUSLY, FOAMER. I never thought it would have taken me this long to say this, but I'm right on the brink of really regretting that I ever agreed to this," Sealey complained to Alex as they sat on the grass at the park, enjoying the October sunshine.

"Oh, stop your whining," Alex said, lying back on the grass and tucking her hands beneath her head. She closed her eyes, feeling the soft heat on her face. "Just keep focusing on the fact that in less than a month, Olivia will be attractively crying on your shoulder." The words sounded more callous than Alex had meant them. But Sealey didn't seem to notice.

"But until that happens, I get to hear over and over how amazing and perfect and beautiful you are," Sealey griped. "It's not that I don't concur with those sentiments, but it's getting to the point that the more he says it, the less I agree with him."

Alex laughed, squinting up at his face. She was getting better at recognizing when he was teasing and when he was serious. "Well, we can't have that," she said. "I'll buy you some earplugs. I'd rather you didn't turn against me at this critical juncture."

"I'm not going anywhere," Sealey assured her, watching the kids play on the playground several feet away. He burrowed his fingers in the grass, tearing up the delicate blades and piling them on Alex's stomach. "When's your next date? Homecoming?"

"Yep," Alex replied. "We're going to the dance next Friday, and then I'll be at the game on Saturday."

"Cool. I'll be there too," Sealey replied.

"The game or the dance?" Alex clarified.

"Both."

Alex scrambled upright, the little pile of grass scattering everywhere as she gaped at him. "You're going to the dance? The USU homecoming dance? Why? And with whom, may I ask?"

"Ashley," Sealey said simply, shrugging. "She's coming up on Friday anyway and she's staying with us, so we decided to make a night of it."

The thought of Sealey and Ashley in the vicinity while Alex and Lucas were attempting to have a romantic evening together made Alex very nervous. She could only imagine the earful she would get from Ashley if Lucas kissed her or something while Ashley was watching.

"I thought you didn't like Ashley," Alex said, sounding much whinier than she meant to. "Why on earth would you volunteer to go to a dance with her?"

"Of course I like Ashley," Sealey claimed, giving her an incredulous look. "She's one of my oldest friends."

"But I thought you said she wasn't your type. Don't you think this will just encourage her to keep pursuing you?"

"Probably," Sealey said unconcernedly. "But, quite honestly, Foamer, she's been pursuing me since she was three. I'm pretty sure she's used to the lack of reciprocation by now. In fact, I'm convinced that nowadays, she flirts just to annoy me. She doesn't actually want it to go anywhere. Not anymore."

Alex studied him out of the corner of her eye. Despite the fact that she felt he was slowly revealing his true nature and personality to her, sometimes he really did surprise her. She would have never in a million years supposed that Sealey Witchburn would attend a college dance (at a college he didn't even attend anymore, no less) with a girl he had no real interest in.

As Alex studied him, the question flew from her lips unrestrained. "So, is Olivia going to be completely blindsided when you admit you're in love with her?"

Sealey turned to look at her, fatigue evident on his face. "Oh, we're back to this topic now, are we?"

"Well, I'm just curious how that's all going to work out," Alex said, shrugging. "I mean, have you even had any contact with her since she left?"

"Of course," he replied, looking away from her. "I write her all the time."

"You do?" Alex said, surprised. "Does Lucas know?"

"I really don't have any idea," Sealey said, unconcerned. "But if he did, I doubt he'd suspect anything. We've all been friends so long it would be perfectly natural for me to write her."

"I'm really interested to see how this all plays out," Alex said again, chewing on the inside of her lip.

"You and me both," Sealey muttered.

Alex began to reply but was halted by the sound of a shockingly familiar voice calling her name from behind them—a voice that had no place being in Logan, Utah. She whirled around to see an extremely tall, thickly built man jogging toward them.

"Al!" called the man again, his thinning blond hair blowing in the slight breeze.

"Dad!" Alex exclaimed, jumping to her feet. "What on earth are you doing here?" She threw her arms around her father, still reeling at the unexpected fact of his presence.

"Just flew in," Alexander Foamer replied, hugging his oldest daughter and kissing her soundly on the forehead. "I have a conference at the University of Utah this weekend, and I thought I'd take the afternoon to stop by and surprise my favorite namesake. I stopped by your apartment first, but, obviously, you weren't there. Your roommates told me where to find you."

"I'm so glad you came!"

"Yes, well, your mother wouldn't have forgiven me if I'd been this close and not stopped by to check up on you. Consequently, is there a *reason* you haven't called her in nearly a month?" Alexander's voice took on a note of sternness as he gave her a meaningful look.

Alex winced, but smiled up at him quickly to hide it.

At six feet eight inches tall, her father was one of the few men alive who had the ability to make her feel small. His height was probably his most defining characteristic and had been a significant advantage to him in his life. He had played basketball in college, and thanks to his success, now was the head basketball coach at Pepperdine University in Malibu, where he also worked as a professor of finance.

"So, who's this?" Alexander motioned toward Sealey, who had risen to his feet at the sight of the newcomer.

"Dad, this is Sealey Witchburn," Alex introduced. "He's a friend from my ward." She didn't think it wise to elaborate further on that, and she was sure Sealey would agree with her. "Sealey, this is my dad, Alexander Foamer."

"Alexander?" Sealey questioned, holding his hand out to shake that of the larger man. "Does that get confusing around your house?" He gestured between the two of them. "Do you both go by Alex?"

"Nah," Alexander responded, waving a hand. "At home, I'm Dad, and she's Al."

"Very feminine," Sealey said, winking at Alex.

"So, do I have you to thank for my wife's current lack of information with regard to her firstborn daughter?" Alexander asked Sealey.

"I'm sorry?" Sealey replied, baffled.

"Grace, my wife, hasn't heard from Alex for quite some time. Is it you I have to blame for that?"

Sealey glanced at Alex, his look subtly pleading for her to intervene. "No, sir," he finally said when she just watched him, blinking innocently. "I would never do such a thing. In fact, if I had known that Alex was neglecting her mother, I would have frog-marched her right back to her apartment and refused to talk to her until she immediately rectified the situation." He attempted to keep his tone light, but Alex could still detect some uneasiness in his demeanor. It was hilarious.

"Good man," Alexander said, laughing. "Al isn't much for keeping us up-to-date on her love life, so when I catch sight of her talking to a boy, I have to assume that he's the 'one,' you know? The one fated to keep me up at night until I commission a thorough background check?"

"Stop while you're ahead, Dad," Alex finally spoke up. "Trust me, you're way off base with that one. Sealey and I are just buds."

"Huh," Alexander responded, looking Sealey up and down, unconvinced. "Well, that's too bad. He reminds me of myself at that age, if a little runtier than I was."

Alex snorted with laughter, while Sealey nodded with an expression of affected misery on his face. "Yes, I actually get that quite often. Six foot six . . . it's a curse."

Alexander laughed and pounded Sealey good-naturedly on the back. "I like this one, Al. Hang on to him."

"Dad, I told you we're *not together*," Alex emphasized. "In fact, if you must know, I—"

"Hey, Alex, why don't we take your dad over to Aggie Ice Cream? Nobody should visit Logan without getting a taste of our primary accomplishment here at USU," Sealey interrupted. His voice was light-hearted, but he shook his head slightly at her as she looked at him questioningly. Why didn't Sealey want her dad to know about Lucas?

By the time Alexander Foamer drove out of her apartment parking lot nearly two hours later, Alex was bursting with questions for Sealey. The three of them had gone together to the USU Creamery, where Sealey had expertly maneuvered the conversation to various topics engineered to keep Alex from being tempted to mention her recent romance.

It all seemed to be going swimmingly until Lucas's name cropped up unexpectedly. Alexander had mentioned how USU's football team had had an unusual amount of success in the current season, seemingly due to some very able players, namely that wide receiver, Lucas Riley. Sealey agreed wholeheartedly and then immediately steered the conversation to USU's much more decorated basketball team. That was all that was necessary to keep Alexander occupied for the rest of his visit. As he drove away, headed for a dinner appointment in Salt Lake with a colleague, Alex whirled angrily to face Sealey. They stood in front her apartment building, and her fierce look caused him to take a defensive step backward toward the curb.

"What was that all about?" she demanded. "Why are you making me withhold information from my parents?"

Sealey raised his eyebrows at her. "Hey, I'm trying to *help* you," he claimed innocently. "Don't you think your parents would be a little curious as to why you're spending time with me if you're dating another guy? Besides, your dad didn't seem to take much to the idea that you and I weren't actually a couple."

"He just likes to tease me," Alex defended. "I'm sure he wouldn't think anything of it if I told him I was dating someone else."

"Well, feel free to call him and tell him all about Lucas," Sealey said, shrugging. "I just thought maybe you'd want to hold off on making any big reveals about your relationship with him until everything is on, you know, sure footing."

"What is *that* supposed to mean?" Alex demanded, folding her arms tightly in front of her. "You were just telling me earlier today about how Lucas won't stop talking about me!"

"Yes, but until Olivia comes home and everything is settled between the four of us, your relationship with Lucas is very much hypothetical," Sealey reminded her. "Is that really something you want to be updating your mother on regularly?"

Alex considered, biting her lip. She hadn't thought about it from that perspective. "You're right," she finally said. "I'll wait until Olivia is home, but as soon as the dust has settled and we all are organized into our established romantic arrangements, I'm calling my mom and telling her everything."

"Deal," Sealey agreed. "Although I recommend you don't tell her *everything*. And by that I mean, feel free to leave my role in the entire project completely out of it." He took a step toward the street, heading for his own apartment building. "Oh, and by the way, I feel duty-bound to remind you that you have not spoken to your mother for almost a month. I recommend you take care of that," he said, pointing toward her apartment. "Especially since I have a feeling that if you don't, it will make it back to her that I'm the reason you didn't. I'd rather not have her hate me before she has the pleasure of meeting me." Sealey winked at her and walked away into the deepening darkness.

* * * * *

"Alex?"

Alex heard the soft voice of her boss outside her office door, just as the timid knock sounded. She smiled to herself before she called, "Come on in, Karen."

Karen Waters, Director of Dietetics at the hospital, was a thin brunette with skin so pale it was almost translucent. She had long, delicate limbs and an awkward, insubstantial air. Her physical appearance matched her personality exactly. She was quiet and timid and preferred to fade into the background. Unfortunately, necessity had pushed her into her current position of authority and it did not suit her. Still, she was kind and sweet, and Alex adored her.

"What's up, sister?" Alex asked, signing a chart with a flourish before putting down her pen and gazing up at Karen. "How was your trip?"

"Oh, it was very nice," Karen said with a soft smile. That was about as much enthusiasm as she was capable of. "The weather was beautiful and Thomas took me to see six different lighthouses."

Karen's husband, Thomas, was a lighthouse enthusiast. From how much Alex heard about it, she would swear that he had visited every single one in the United States at least four times.

"New ones this time?" Alex asked hopefully.

"Two of them," Karen agreed. "But I have to admit, my favorite part of the trip was the color. Everything is so green in Oregon. The drives were just beautiful."

"I love that area," Alex agreed, nodding. "Well, I'm glad you had fun. We missed you."

Karen waved the comment away. "I had something I wanted to talk to you about."

"Okay, sure," Alex agreed, motioning to the seat across from her. "What's up?"

"While I was in Oregon, I attended a symposium on the research supporting the DASH diet," Karen said as she sat down. "I went up after the presentation to tell the presenter how much I enjoyed it. Her name is Dr. Fiona Welch. Have you heard of her?"

"Sure," Alex shrugged. "She's one of the foremost researchers on childhood obesity."

"Yes, she is," Karen agreed. "Anyway, she asked about my background and when I told her that one of our main goals here at the hospital is to educate mothers early about appropriate childhood nutrition, she asked if I might be interested in joining her in a speaker series." Karen looked positively horrified at the very thought.

"I imagine you said no," Alex said, smiling at her. "I know how much you loathe public speaking."

"I did," Karen admitted. "But I also told her about you."

"Me?" Alex squeaked. "What about me?"

"I told her we had a dietitian on staff who was very passionate about fighting childhood obesity and was interested in doing more," Karen said, her voice gaining a little bit of strength. "She said she'd like to meet with you."

Alex stared at her. "What does that mean?"

"Well, she's going to be in Salt Lake City on October 21 doing another symposium. I told her you could probably meet her then."

"Karen!" Alex squealed. "Oh my gosh! Are you serious?"

Karen nodded, her face breaking into another one of her signature soft smiles. "I thought you'd be excited."

"What kind of speaker series is she doing?" Alex asked eagerly.

"It's a traveling series," Karen explained. "I don't know the details or locations they have planned, but her group is holding conferences in various cities to speak about different aspects of childhood health. If Dr. Welch feels you're appropriate, she'll have you join the group. There are about ten of them, I believe. She said they originally had fourteen, but four of them were given the opportunity to go on a humanitarian trip to Africa, so they dropped out. She's kind of desperate for people to make up the difference."

"That's my kind of job opportunity!" Alex exclaimed, rubbing her hands together with relish. "October 21. I'm so there."

"I think that's wise," Karen said, smiling at her and getting to her feet. "I gave her your information, so she should be in contact shortly. In the meantime, you might want to take some time to put together a new resume highlighting the relevant work you've done. That community center class you taught last winter on healthy school lunches would be something valuable to highlight."

"I'll do that, thanks," Alex said, and Karen left the room. Alex watched her go, her mind racing with new and exciting possibilities.

* * * * *

Alex studied herself in the mirror, liking how the sleek green dress emphasized her figure just the right amount. It was a kind of a modified mermaid-style gown, fitted from the shoulders to the upper thighs, finally flaring out slightly from there to the floor. As she turned in front of the mirror, the light caught the shimmery fabric, giving her a luminescent glow. She wore her hair down past her shoulder blades. It was long, full, and shiny—like burnished copper. She felt stunning. It was a nice feeling.

Meredith sighed. "You look incredible," she said in a dreamy voice. Meredith herself wore a fitted red sheath, her hair piled high on her head and tumbling down in curls. She had been asked to the dance by a boy in one of her classes. A boy that she had been shamelessly flirting with since the beginning of the semester.

"Thanks." Alex smiled at her. "I still feel kind of stupid going to this dance . . . it's a little like reverting back to high school, don't you think?"

"Bite your tongue," Meredith said, shunting Alex out of the way as she moved in front of the mirror to apply some mascara. "I don't care if we're reverting to a middle school stomp if it means I get to spend an evening with Collin." She stuck her tongue out as she attempted to perfectly apply the product to her lashes.

"Man, you must really like this one," Alex said, raising her eyebrows. "You're usually the first one to pass on the organized social events in favor of homework."

"Yeah, well . . . he kind of . . . he's really . . . ," Meredith sighed, giving up on her attempt to find substance. "He looks like a Ken doll, okay?" she said, giving Alex a pointed look. "I'm sorry, but no one can expect me to pass up the opportunity to date a Ken doll."

"Point taken. I'm pleased to see your priorities are so aligned," Alex said, rolling her eyes. She turned in a circle, trying to locate her shoes in the bedroom that looked like a clothing-centric tornado had struck it. Finally finding them in a corner beneath a pile of half-folded T-shirts, she sank onto her bed to put them on.

"So . . . are you ready for this?" Meredith asked as she applied some bright red lipstick. The effect next to her creamy skin, black hair and eyes, and red dress was spectacular.

"Ready for what?" Alex huffed. She was attempting to locate her feet beneath the yards of shimmery green fabric. It wasn't going well, thanks to the fitted bodice of the dress that refused to let her bend more than two inches toward the floor.

"For an evening of attempting to pretend like you know Sealey half as well as you actually do, charming Lucas, and refraining from murdering Ashley." Meredith smacked her lips together and examined her expertly made-up face. "It sounds like a big job to me."

"Well, I don't expect to see Sealey and Ashley much," Alex said, finally managing to hook one of her delicately silver shoes over her right foot and fasten it. "After all, he has just as much investment in making sure Lucas doesn't find out about our past dealings as I do."

"Geez, the whole thing sounds so scandalous when you say it like that." Meredith giggled. "Your *past dealings* . . ." She stepped easily into her matching red shoes and picked up a shimmery black shawl to drape over her shoulders. "Well, I'm ready." She headed toward the bedroom door. "You'd better hurry. The guys will be here in less than five minutes."

"Right behind you," Alex said, gasping as she leaned forward with all her might to fasten her left shoe. Once the exhausting task was done, Alex stood and straightened her dress around her frame. The fabric skimmed the floor as she turned to the left and right to examine herself in the mirror.

The doorbell rang just as she emerged into the living room of the apartment where Meredith was arguing with Kacey. The rest of the girls sat around the room, watching the confrontation.

"I don't care if it's idiotic and juvenile," Meredith insisted, her hands on her hips. "Besides, I wouldn't be talking if I were you. Of the two of us, one of us has a date tonight and it isn't you." She gave Kacey a superior glance.

Kacey smirked at her and rolled her eyes. Nobody needed to ask why. Of all the girls in the apartment, Kacey was the one who never failed to have a date whenever she wanted one. Meredith's argument was a weak one indeed.

"Guys, let's not scare the visitors," Alex cautioned as she headed for the door. "Some of us have a vested interest in their sense of well-being, okay?"

Kacey rolled her eyes a second time and snuggled back into the couch to recommence reading her book. Jaclyn and Rachel turned back to the television, but Sage, who sat right next to Kacey on the couch, was on the edge of her seat. Her eyes were fixed on the door as though a movie star was about to walk through it.

She wasn't far off. Alex couldn't seem to locate her lungs when Lucas sauntered into the apartment, wearing a black suit and a silver tie. His light-green eyes seemed strangely illuminated.

"Evening, ladies," he said cheerfully. Kacey grunted, but Jaclyn, Rachel, Sage, and Meredith all smiled admiringly at him.

"Well, hello," Jaclyn said, winking at him playfully. Rachel elbowed her. Alex was about to suggest they leave to escape her roommates prying eyes, but she suddenly realized that the room seemed awfully crowded. Turning to look at who had entered the apartment behind Lucas, she saw a tall, tanned, muscular young man with light-brown hair smiling at Meredith; a gorgeous, short, skinny girl in dark blue with curls piled on top of her head; and . . . Sealey.

Alex felt the dismay invade her face before she could stop it. What was Sealey doing here? He was supposed to be avoiding her! She was on the point of opening her mouth to say something remarkably stupid, but thankfully, Sealey anticipated her.

"Hi, Alex," he said loudly, talking over the beginning of her sentence. "Lucas suggested the four of us drive together instead of separately tonight. Good idea, don't you think?"

"The four of us?" Alex repeated, still trying to get her expression under control. She had just realized that the beautiful girl in blue was Ashley. She hadn't recognized her with her hair done up and the copious amounts of makeup on her face. Ashley gave her a smile that was an impressive mix of scorn and superiority and moved close to Sealey, taking his arm.

"Hi, Alex," she said in a falsely sweet voice. "Nice to see you again."

"Ashley," Alex replied, dully. She felt suddenly and completely unprepared for this experience. She turned to look at Meredith but found her best friend's eyes focused on the life-size Ken doll standing a few feet away. No help there.

"Well, shall we go?" Lucas asked, rubbing his hands together. "Nice to see you guys," he said to her roommates. "Have a good night, okay?"

Her roommates called well wishes after them as they left the apartment, but Alex barely heard them.

* * * * *

"You look fantastic," Lucas said to her, his eyes taking her in appreciatively. Alex saw Ashley roll her eyes at Sealey behind Lucas's back. Great. So *this* was how the evening was going to go.

"Thanks, Lucas," she replied, taking his arm. "You look pretty amazing yourself."

Lucas smiled in response.

"So we thought we'd hit Elements for dinner, since that seems to be a favorite haunt of yours"—he winked at her—"and then we'll head to the dance afterward. How does that sound?"

"Sounds perfect," Alex replied, her voice still strangely choked. She had not anticipated spending a romantic evening with Lucas constantly observed by his bratty sister and watchful best friend. Her expectations of enjoying the date evaporated.

Thankfully, within an hour her initial outlook appeared to have been overly pessimistic. Dinner was surprisingly agreeable, thanks to Lucas and Sealey's constant banter back and forth. It kept her laughing and negated the need to make conversation with Ashley, which was always a plus.

By the time they made it to the dance, Alex was much more relaxed. Especially with the sea of couples on the dance floor that seemed to be inviting Alex and Lucas to get lost in their midst. She resisted the urge to immediately pull him to the middle of the floor and leave Ashley and Sealey behind. After all, she was attempting to be a more malleable version of her usual pushy self, consistent with her efforts since the beginning of the "Woo Lucas Riley" project. Yanking him away from his sister and best friend probably wasn't the best way to show her flexibility.

"I feel like I'm back in high school," Ashley moaned, looking around the decorated lounge in the student center.

At last, something Ashley and I can agree on, Alex thought. Still, a chance to be in Lucas's arms for a solid two hours was not something she was eager to complain about.

"Come on," Lucas said to her enthusiastically, grabbing her hand and pulling her onto the dance floor. A slow song was starting right as they entered the fray and Lucas's strong arms immediately encircled her. She felt heat climbing up her cheeks as his warmth invaded her space. She resisted the urge to lay her head on his shoulder, feeling like she might want to warm up to such a forward gesture. Still, he held her extremely close. Close enough that instead of just letting her hand rest on his shoulder, she could nearly rest her chin there instead. In that position, she had the chance to observe the couples dancing around them. They were all staring at her.

"Why is everybody looking at us?" she whispered in Lucas's ear. "Did I rip my dress or something?"

"Your dress is fine. More than fine," Lucas replied softly in her ear. "As for the staring, I hadn't really noticed. But I can't say I blame them. I would be staring at you too."

Alex felt tingles invade her extremities but pulled back to give Lucas a doubtful look. "Somehow I don't think I'm the one they're staring at. I'm not the hero of the USU football team."

Lucas smiled self-consciously. "I manage to ignore the staring most of the time," he finally conceded. "I actually don't love the sensation of having all eyes on me, so I've learned to blur out everything around me except the focus of my attention. And for right now, that's you." He softly brushed his lips against the side of her face, and Alex closed her eyes, her fingers clenching on his suit coat. The song merged into another slow melody, and Alex and Lucas swayed silently, lost in the moment.

"Hey, can I cut in?"

And the moment came to a screeching halt. The voice came from behind her and was infuriatingly familiar. She wanted to turn and give Sealey the dirtiest look he'd ever gotten in his life.

"Well . . . ," Lucas said unwillingly.

"I really am sorry to interrupt," Sealey said, and he truly sounded sorry. "But Ashley actually sent me over. I think she wants a dance with her brother."

Alex refrained from rolling her eyes with extreme difficulty. She suspected that what Ashley actually wanted was a chance to separate her brother from Alex. The little monster. Alex managed to keep her face expressionless for Lucas's benefit, but it took a lot of effort.

"Oh," Lucas said to Sealey, sounding a little mollified. "I guess I should make an exception for the little sis." He winked at Alex and gave her hand to Sealey, who enveloped it within his long fingers. "Now don't let her run off to anyone else," Lucas said to Sealey with a significant look at Alex. "I'm entrusting you to keep her safe for me." He smiled at Alex teasingly.

"I'll do that," Sealey said, not quite meeting Lucas's eyes. Alex wondered if he was thinking about the betrayal in the background. Olivia.

She watched Sealey's face closely as he pulled her against him, sliding his arm around her waist. His hand felt surprisingly rough in hers.

"So how's it going so far?" he asked her, glancing down at her face. He was taller than Lucas by nearly three inches, and at this angle, it was noticeable. It was rare for Alex to feel so short.

"Well, we've only had one song to enjoy, so I'll probably have to get back to you on that," Alex said, not attempting to keep some of her frustration out of her voice.

"Sorry about that," Sealey said with a grimace. "But I do as I'm told."

"Since when?" Alex scoffed, and he laughed. "Actually, I'm more interested in how things are going with you," she said with a significant look. "Is Ashley still hanging all over you like she was at dinner?"

"Well, if she is, can you blame her?" Sealey asked with teasing arrogance. "I'm considering sending a picture of myself in this getup to GQ. I'm fairly certain I'll get some favorable results."

Alex laughed and looked him up and down conspicuously. "You do look pretty good tonight, Witchburn," she said, really meaning it. Although she didn't expend much energy checking Sealey out regularly, there was no doubt that he cut an impressive figure.

"And you're completely heart-stopping," Sealey responded in her ear. His voice sounded so deadly serious that she was sure if she looked up, she'd see another affected look on his face.

But when her eyes did meet his, she was astonished to see that he was sincere. His blue eyes were calm and genuine as he smiled at her.

"Now, now, don't go getting all awkward on me," he said, noting the look of discomfort on her face. "But given the occasion, and the unexpected success of the project thus far, I feel justified in finally admitting to you that you are one of the most beautiful women I have ever seen. I've tried to not stroke your ego too much, but I think you've earned this one."

Alex smiled sardonically at him. "Oh, really? Well, thank you, kind sir."

"You're welcome," Sealey said, apparently deciding to mistranslate her sarcasm into sincerity. His fingers brushed across the back of her hand, and his arm felt too warm around her waist. Her stomach clenched with unease. All of the sensations at once were so uncomfortable—being this close to Sealey, his arms around her, her hand in his. He was too tall, too intense, and he smelled really good. Too good. She longed to be back in Lucas's arms, where her thoughts and feelings generally seemed to make sense. It was an interesting reversal, now that she thought about it. A month ago, her internal reactions to each man would have been the opposite.

Finally, *finally*, the song ended. Lucas appeared almost instantly at her side, pulling her from Sealey's arms. In fact, he appeared so quickly that neither she nor Sealey were expecting him, and for a brief period of time, she had both men's arms around her. Sealey quickly released her, however, and after giving her a somewhat unreadable look, he disappeared into the crowd to find Ashley.

* * * * *

Alex closed her eyes, her head having finally made it to Lucas's shoulder, breathing in his scent, relishing the feeling of his hands on her back.

"Hey, I have something to ask you," Lucas said, startling her into looking up.

"Okay," Alex said, smiling encouragement at him.

"Next Saturday is my dad's birthday," he began. "Ash is throwing a big party for him. It's kind of an all-day thing. I was wondering if maybe you might want to come with me. Possibly meet my parents?"

Alex's heart leapt with joy at the same time her stomach erupted in a combination of knots and butterflies. The idea that Lucas wanted to introduce her to his family was possibly the best thing she'd heard, maybe ever. But this was the same family that was fully expecting him to marry Olivia when she came home. What if they all held Ashley's view on the matter? What would Lucas do if his family disapproved of her? Would he break things off? But what else could she say but yes? If things were to ever progress between them, meeting his family was something that would eventually have to happen. Better it happened now, before Olivia returned home and reminded everyone how incredible she was.

"I'd love to," Alex said, hugging him gently. "That sounds perfect."

Lucas kissed her cheek again. Then, his face breaking into a mischievous grin, he suddenly spun her out, her dress flaring out around her. She laughed as he pulled her back in tight against him, but the sound died in her throat at what she saw over his shoulder.

Sealey and Ashley were dancing only a few feet away. Given that they had come to the dance together, this was not all that unusual, but the way they were dancing caught Alex's eye. They swayed gently like every other couple, but to Alex's astonishment, they were staring intently into each other's eyes. Sealey's hand was resting on Ashley's face, and the expression on his was fiercely focused. Suddenly, Sealey's head bent purposely toward Ashley's and their lips met.

{ Chapter TEN }

ALEX WATCHED IN shock. In turmoil. There were so many feelings, ranging from confusion to amusement to indignation to pity to fury. So many feelings. What was Sealey *doing*? After all he'd said about not caring for Ashley in that way! Had he lied to Alex about that? Had the feelings developed within the past hour? And if so, what about Olivia? Or was he just playing with Ashley? At that thought, furious bursts of resentment erupted inside her. She may not like Ashley, but she could never condone any woman being led on like that, no matter how generally annoying she was. And from the look of Ashley's arms clasped around Sealey's neck, she at least seemed to think the kiss was genuine.

Alex's gasp caught Lucas's attention. He turned to see what had her transfixed and froze.

"What the?" she heard him breathe as he watched Sealey and Ashley pull apart.

"Did you know anything about this?" Alex asked him.

"No," Lucas said, his surprise evident on his face. "I know Ashley's had a crush on Sealey forever, but I never thought Sealey was interested. I never really asked him, but it always seemed like he saw her more as a little sister than anything else. Maybe he's finally changed his mind."

Alex couldn't tell whether Lucas considered this possible change in his best friend as good news or bad news. She wasn't sure how she herself felt about it. She knew she was angry. That was obvious. But she wasn't sure if the anger resonated on Ashley's behalf or on her own. How could Sealey not tell her about something like this?

But . . . then again, when did Sealey tell her anything, really? At least without her pressing him about it? He wasn't one to volunteer information. It was perfectly consistent with his personality for him to have told her nothing. So why did that irritate her so much? Was it because she had laid her entire life bare for him? He knew everything about her deepest wishes and feelings, with regard to her career, with regard to Lucas . . . and she knew nothing. Nothing except that he was supposedly in love with a missionary he'd known all his life. But was that even true anymore? And if it wasn't, what did that mean for Alex and Lucas?

* * * * *

"So, are you ever going to voluntarily speak to me again?" Sealey's voice came from her left as she sat in the bleachers the next day. The football game had not yet begun, and excited shouts, cheers, and conversation surrounded them on every side. Thankfully Ashley had not yet made an appearance, so they had the chance to talk unobserved and unheard.

The night before had ended on a somewhat awkward note. Lucas had wasted no time in razzing his best friend and sister about what he and Alex had seen, and Alex's lack of lighthearted conversation had made it clear that she didn't agree with Lucas's favorable opinion of the development. She wasn't sure why she cared, especially when she saw that Ashley was much more smug than excited at the new turn of events, which made Alex like her even less.

If things truly were turning romantic between Ashley and Sealey, then Ashley didn't even seem to realize how lucky she was. Sealey, although intimidating to those who didn't really know him, was truly a catch. But Ashley just seemed to care that she had finally emerged victorious. And for some reason, she kept giving Alex self-satisfied grins, as though she knew something Alex didn't. It was infuriating.

And through all this, Sealey continued to act as if nothing of real importance had happened. That was *worse* than infuriating.

"Why do you care?" Alex replied to Sealey's question. "It's not like you fill me in on the details of your life when we *are* talking."

"Oh, come on. Don't be like that." Sealey nudged her. "I tell you stuff. Actually, I probably tell you more than I tell anyone else."

Alex gave him an incredulous look. "If that's the case, then why didn't you tell me that your feelings for Ashley were changing? It would've been nice to be forewarned, given that"—she lowered her voice to a stage whisper—"this entire project was based on the idea that you wanted Lucas's old girlfriend for yourself." She gave him a significant look. "I assume that's no longer the case?"

"Alex, what does it even matter anymore?" Sealey said, and his voice sounded tired. She almost couldn't even hear it over the noise of the crowd. "You got what you wanted. Luke is head over heels for you."

"Maybe, but without you there to distract Olivia when she gets home, who's to say that he'll *stay* head over heels for me?" Alex asked pointedly.

"A little lacking in confidence, aren't we?" Sealey said, his eyes on the football field, which was emptying as the beginning of the game drew near. "Look, why don't you just abandon this whole scheme and let the chips fall where they may?"

"What do you mean *abandon this whole scheme*?" Alex nearly screeched. "Olivia gets home in three weeks and you want to just forget the whole thing *now*? Have you really fallen so fast and so hard for Ashley?"

"Ashley has nothing to do with this," Sealey retorted. He still wouldn't look at her.

Alex, confused, studied the practiced lack of expression on his face. "Ahhh," she sighed as realization began to dawn. He was right. Ashley really did have nothing to do with it. "It's finally happened. You've actually sprouted a conscience, haven't you?"

"I'm sorry, what?" Sealey said, turning to look at her. His face was finally displaying an emotion, and it looked a whole lot like anger.

"You're starting to feel guilty about going after your best friend's girl," Alex stated bluntly, nodding at him with narrowed eyes. "I wasn't sure it would happen, but your guilt finally overcame your self-serving nature. I guess I should be proud of you for that, but I have to admit, your timing could be better." She gave him a scornful look.

"It's not about feeling guilty," Sealey defended vehemently. "I don't feel guilty. Not yet. I'm just trying to stop before I get to that point.

We've gone far enough, don't you think?" Sealey gestured widely around them. "Luke's crazy about you. He now, officially, considers you an option. You are on equal footing with Olivia. Now, let's leave it that way. Let him make a fair, informed decision between the two of you."

"Since when was the point of this a *fair, informed decision*?" Alex spat. Her white-hot panic was forcing the words to exit her lips before she actually had the opportunity to consider them. "The point was to make Lucas want me more than he wanted Olivia so I could have him and you could have Olivia! That was the entire goal! So now that you've decided that maybe you don't want Olivia as much as you thought, you're just going to leave me hanging? Well, I guess I shouldn't be surprised, Sealey. After all, when do you ever do anything for *somebody other than yourself*?"

The noise of the crowd pushed in on them as Sealey shook his head disbelievingly, his eyes narrowed. "You are a piece of work, Alex Foamer. Do you hear yourself? You are trying to make me feel guilty for wanting to spare my friends potential heartache, while you sit there scheming a way to cause it. You lecture me about being self-serving, while you happily doom everyone around you to impending misery, just so you can have what you want." He made a disgusted sound in the back of his throat.

"Oh, don't act all innocent. It doesn't suit you," Alex said with a matching look of contempt. "Let's not forget that you were the one who dreamed up this whole *scheme* in the first place." She emphasized the word with her fingertips.

"I know," Sealey said forcefully, and he even looked as regretful as he sounded. "I know I did. And I thought it would be worth it. But now . . ." He trailed off, looking away from her.

Alex watched him silently for a minute. "Really?" she asked, her voice clearly indicating her mystification. "Have you really lost all interest in Olivia? Just like that?"

Sealey glanced at her as the tone of her voice changed from anger to bewilderment. "I just want to be fair," he replied quietly. "I want her to have a choice. I want him to have a choice. A real one."

"What changed your mind?" Alex asked, and she tried to keep the distress of what she was hearing out of her voice and off of her face. She didn't want to admit to Sealey that without his help, she felt she was at a significant disadvantage. "You were all gung-ho to control the situation a couple of months ago. Why are you suddenly so willing to give it up?"

"I never had control," Sealey said with a humorless laugh. He looked at her earnestly, his expression a startlingly unhappy one. "Not for one second."

He looked away, and Alex knew the conversation was closed.

* * * * *

Alex drummed her fingers nervously on the steering wheel as she headed south on I-15 toward Salt Lake City. In less than thirty minutes, she would be trying to convince one of the foremost researchers on childhood obesity that she was worth hiring. But Alex had done her research too. She had practiced in the mirror. She knew her stuff. Now if she could only get her hands to stop shaking and her salivary glands to start working again so she could actually speak, she'd be in business.

She was set to meet with Dr. Welch in the downtown Salt Lake City Marriott, where the researcher was holding her latest symposium. Alex had hoped to arrive early so she could sit in on a bit of the lecture, but she had spent too much time in front of the mirror trying to make herself look like an experienced nutritional lecturer. Now she was almost running late.

Breathing a sigh of relief as she pulled into the Marriott parking garage with five minutes to spare, she quickly parked and headed for the elevator to the lobby. Within minutes, she was seated outside the ballroom where the lecture was just finishing up. Her knees bounced nervously as she watched the room slowly empty. Finally, she caught sight of Dr. Fiona Welch talking earnestly to a young blonde woman holding a clipboard and pen.

The master dietitian looked just like her picture. Medium height, very fit (a characteristic which Alex considered job security for someone in her line of business), with short, dark brown hair and black-framed glasses. As the blonde girl Alex imagined to be Dr. Welch's assistant walked away, Alex took a deep breath. Rising unsteadily to her feet, she silently mouthed what she planned to say to the intimidating woman.

"Dr. Welch?"

The woman looked up from a pile of papers she was shuffling

through and smiled in a friendly way at Alex. "Are you Alex Foamer?" she guessed.

"I am," Alex replied, gratefully acknowledging the woman's smile. "Do you still have time to meet with me?"

"Of course!" Dr. Welch exclaimed. She gathered the papers and deposited them in a black leather bag on a nearby chair. "Let's head out into the foyer. I saw a sitting area out there where we can chat."

Alex followed her toward a cluster of chairs near the stairs to the lobby, mentally running through all the points she wanted to make about her experience, her goals, and her enthusiasm for raising awareness about childhood nutrition. She felt like all her hopes were riding on this one conversation and she was terrified she would forget the one key point that would make her dreams a reality.

"So, Alex, tell me about yourself," Dr. Welch asked once they'd gotten settled. "Karen mentioned that you currently work for her at the hospital?"

"Yes," Alex confirmed. "I'm the primary dietitian in the maternity ward. I spend most of my time working with new mothers on their own nutrition and how it translates into their baby's nutrition. I also work as a certified lactation specialist."

"So what interests you about our childhood nutrition symposium coming up?"

"Oh, everything!" Alex cried. "Really, absolutely everything. It's exactly what I've always wanted to do with my life, but I've had no idea how to get started. I feel very strongly about starting nutrition education early in a child's life, especially in areas where childhood obesity is rampant. I feel like most parents don't fully realize how unhealthy and processed most foods available today are. They *intend* to feed their children healthy foods, but instead provide a diet that is low in nutrients and high in sugar, all because they are uneducated on how to recognize and locate healthy options."

"And that is exactly what this symposium is meant to accomplish," Dr. Welch commented with a nod. "We want to bring nutritional education to those who don't have access to it. The classes and lectures we're offering are mostly free to anyone who wishes to hear them, thanks to some government funding we have received. We will be providing these classes in twenty cities across the United States. We're doing most of our advertising for the event in low income areas, as those tend to be where obesity is at its highest."

"How many classes are you planning on providing?" Alex asked excitedly.

"Twenty to thirty per city," Dr. Welch replied. "We are planning to spend three to four days in each city with, hopefully, about fifteen lecturers. Which means that each lecturer will likely be presenting their topic—or topics—multiple times, so as to provide people multiple opportunities to attend each lecture. Ideally, we'd like each attendee to be able to make it to each lecture they're interested in."

"Say I was lucky enough to get the job," Alex asked with a sheepish grin. "How many lectures or classes would I personally be responsible for?"

"Three, most likely. Possibly more if we can't fill our open lecturer positions."

"And would I come up with them myself, or would I choose from a list of acceptable topics?"

"I have a list of topics I'd like to cover," Dr. Welch answered. "But once you have your topics, your class is completely yours to create. I only ask that you provide me with a transcript beforehand so I can be prepared to answer any questions that may come my way, whether it be from media outlets, interested parties, potential sponsors, or what have you."

"This sounds amazing!" Alex said, clasping her hands together. "I'd really love to be a part of it."

"Let's talk about your prior experience," Dr. Welch suggested. For the next twenty minutes, Alex walked her through the internships she'd done while working on her degree, her experience at the hospital, and the volunteer work she did in the community, which mostly involved classes taught at the community center. She even included some examples of when she had consulted with personal acquaintances, eager to overwhelm Dr. Welch with examples of how qualified she was to participate in the symposium. Dr. Welch responded enthusiastically to many of Alex's points of experience, even going so far as to share similar experiences that she had had in the early days of her career.

"Well, this is all very impressive," Dr. Welch replied after Alex had finished. "I admire all that you've tried to do in your own community to encourage nutritional education." She smiled warmly at Alex. "Now, I have a few more people I need to meet with for the childhood nutrition symposium before I can make any kind of offer. But I should have an answer for you within the next couple of weeks. Does that work for you?"

"Yes, absolutely," Alex replied immediately, nodding. "I'll be waiting to hear from you. It was so good to finally meet you, Dr. Welch. I've read so much of what you've written and I've always wanted to work with you." Alex stopped, knowing she was on the verge of gushing. She didn't want to be remembered as a groupie, she wanted to be remembered as a competent candidate and possible colleague.

"I enjoyed meeting you as well," Dr. Welch said, smiling as she rose to her feet. "I will let you know one way or the other as soon as I can. But I hope you'll keep in touch, regardless of whether or not I'm able to include you in the symposium. I'd love to hear about your work in your own community."

Alex enthusiastically agreed and bade farewell to her role model. Nearly skipping down to her car, she allowed her mind to go over and over the conversation. She felt that the interview couldn't possibly have gone better. She didn't want to be overconfident, but if she were being completely honest with herself, she suspected that she had totally nailed it.

Great big world, here I come, she thought with a sigh.

* * * * *

Alex twisted her fingers anxiously in her lap as Lucas turned the Toyota a sharp right and they began driving up the abrupt incline. As they ascended the curved driveway, Alex could see the huge house towering over them from above, surrounded by trees and a stone wall. It clung to the side of the mountain, stone and brick, looking impenetrable. The structure reminded her of a version of *Beauty and the Beast* she had seen a long time ago, and as she looked up at the rounded third-floor balcony, she almost expected to see the hulking figure of a hairy beast glaring down at her.

Lucas stopped the car in front of a stone fountain merrily trickling away, and Alex noticed all the other cars lining the driveway in front of them. Her nerves kicked up a notch. So many people. How many of them would see her as the imposter she was, attempting to displace Olivia? In the months she had been engineering this relationship, she had never felt like more of a fraud than she did at that moment. Perhaps Sealey's accusations from the weekend before were still stuck in her mind.

"You ready?" Lucas asked, trailing his fingers down her arms and entwining his fingers through hers.

"Sure!" she said. She had been going for bright and cheery, but instead her tone registered as an anxious squeak. Lucas laughed.

"Little nervous?" he squeezed her hands. "Don't worry. I won't let anyone eat you."

"Literally or figuratively?" Alex asked, attempting a brave smile.

"Either one," he answered. "As long as you promise to return the favor when the time comes for me to meet your family."

At his confident smile, her nerves quieted. She followed him up to the heavy oak front door, taking a deep breath as he pushed it open.

The house was deathly quiet. It occurred to Alex to wonder if the party was actually a surprise party and they had been mistaken for the guest of honor, but as Lucas guided her quickly through the professionally decorated house, she realized that the party was actually taking place in the backyard. As they emerged on the massive back patio, Alex saw the fire pit blazing to combat the early November chill, as well as the strategically placed outdoor heaters. People were spread everywhere, talking and eating, lounging in a hot tub, playing horseshoes, badminton, and even dancing in a grassy area where a DJ had been advantageously positioned.

"Wow," Alex breathed. "Ashley certainly does know how to throw a party."

"Yeah, she missed her calling. She should've been an event planner." Lucas chuckled. "She's wasted on accounting."

"A DJ? Really?" Alex whispered.

"Ah, don't be too impressed," Lucas replied. "He's a cousin and practically begged Ashley for the opportunity to show off his mad skills."

Alex laughed and looked around, her eyes caught by an imposing figure with white blond hair, pulling himself out of the hot tub. Sealey.

"Oh, I didn't realize Sealey was going to be here," Alex said, trying to hide her discomfort. They hadn't talked at all for the rest of the football game the weekend before. Sealey had spoken intermittently to Ashley, but not to her. After the game, she had considered going to dinner with them all again (Lucas had texted her directly after the game to invite her), but she had begged off with a phony excuse. She couldn't handle another double date. Not with the fake lovebirds—who were faking their relationship for some strange, unknown, and undisclosed (naturally) reason.

Likewise, Sealey hadn't spoken to her all week, and she had been surprised at how much she had missed his needling texts. With his avowal that, as far as he was concerned, the project was over, she wasn't surprised that he hadn't contacted her to discuss Lucas. But for some reason she thought that, at some point, he might have wanted to talk to her anyway—just to clear the air or something. But her phone had remained ominously silent.

"Luke!" Sealey said cheerfully, rubbing a towel roughly through his hair and across his chest as he approached. "I think your mom's about ready to kill you. Not awesome, when all the party guests manage to arrive before the guest of honor's firstborn son. I think she was expecting you a couple of hours ago."

"I know," Lucas replied sheepishly. "But I had a few places I wanted to show Alex. You know, the high school, the golf course. All the old haunts. Mom'll forgive me."

"You'd better hope so," Sealey teased. He turned to Alex and gave her a kind smile. "Hey, Foamer," he said.

"Hey," she almost whispered. It was a distinctly awkward situation. She didn't want to meet his eyes, because she was still feeling slightly ashamed from their last encounter. But she couldn't keep her eyes focused on his shirt or anything either, because he wasn't actually wearing one. And his lack of shirt revealed a frankly surprising physique. In fact, if everything had been normal between them, she would've given him a teasing compliment about it. But with the way things were since their argument, all she could manage to do was turn her blushing

114

cheeks away from his swimsuit-clad frame and focus her eyes on the empty flower pots to her left.

"You okay, there?" he asked, reaching out to nudge her shoulder with his fingers.

"She's a little nervous," Lucas replied, putting his arm around her and pulling her into his side.

Nervous. Right. She could run with that.

"You know, meeting the family," she said, allowing her eyes to flit up to Sealey's momentarily. "It's a big step."

"Yes, it is," Sealey agreed, and he ducked his head slightly as he attempted to keep eye contact with her. "But I think it'll all turn out okay."

Something in his tone caught her notice, but she wasn't sure why. It almost sounded like a warning.

"Well, better go appease the matriarch," Lucas said, pulling her toward the tables loaded with food. "Good to see you, man. Let's play some ball later."

"Sure thing," Sealey agreed, heading toward the house. "See you later, Alex." He smiled at her quickly before disappearing inside.

Lucas grabbed her hand and led her to the side of a petite woman with short, caramel-colored hair. She was talking animatedly to a couple who could have been either thirty-five or sixty. Alex studied them, wondering if what she was seeing was the result of plastic surgery or just unfortunate coordinated pre-mature aging.

"Mom," Lucas said, clasping the petite caramel-haired woman around the shoulders when she noticed him standing beside her. "Sealey told me you're mad at me, but I figure he was exaggerating. After all, who can stay mad at a face like this one?" He pulled an angelic face as he drew her into his chest, where the top of her head barely reached his shoulder.

"I should be mad," she said, laughing. "You were supposed to come early to help us set up the heaters. Your dad and Sealey had to do every-thing themselves."

"I know," Lucas said, having the grace to look ashamed. "But I got distracted showing Alex around my old stomping grounds."

"Yes, I assumed as much," said the woman, turning to look at Alex. "And this must be the woman herself."

"Yep," Lucas said, smiling broadly at Alex. "Mom, this is Alex Foamer, my current fixation." He winked at her. "Alex, this is my mom, Candace Riley. Everyone just calls her Candie, though."

"Hello, dear," said Candie, her face breaking into a smile. Alex thought she might be paranoid, but it looked like the smile was a little stiff at the corners.

"It's very nice to meet you," Alex replied. "Your home is breathtaking. And this area is absolutely beautiful. I've never seen anything like it."

"Thank you," Candie said politely. "We certainly like it. Are you familiar with North Salt Lake?" she asked.

"No, actually," Alex replied. "I passed by this past week on my way to a job interview downtown, but I didn't get the chance to look around much. Most of my travel is a straight shot between Logan and California."

"Oh, are you from California?" Candie asked, raising an eyebrow in expertly feigned interest. But Alex could tell the difference. It was a very Ashley-esque expression and it was now clear to Alex that she had learned it from her mother.

"I told you that, Mom," Lucas broke in, and he looked a little embarrassed. "Remember? Alex is from Malibu."

"Oh, that's right. I'd forgotten," Candie said, airily waving a hand.

"Hey, did you say that you had a job interview in Salt Lake this past week?" Lucas asked, frowning slightly at Alex. "I don't remember you mentioning that before. What job were you interviewing for?"

"Oh, it's for a traveling speaker series," Alex said, her voice gaining enthusiasm. "It's a bunch of different classes on childhood obesity and nutrition, and I interviewed for a spot as a lecturer. My boss recommended me for it."

"Traveling?" Lucas asked, his eyebrow raised.

"Yeah, just for a few months," Alex replied. "We'd be doing symposiums in at least twenty different cities. It's a really great opportunity for me."

Lucas cleared his throat. "It sounds like it," he said. But he didn't sound very enthusiastic about the idea. "I guess I just don't understand why you didn't tell me about it."

"Excuse me," Candie said, in a tactful attempt to give them some space. "That water looks like it needs some refilling." She walked away, leaving them alone.

"I'm sorry I didn't tell you about it," Alex said. "I've been really distracted this week and it honestly didn't occur to me to tell you. I kind of just thought I'd tell you about it if I got the job."

"So you'd tell me about it once you had already decided to leave me for three months?" Lucas said, and his voice sounded almost angry now. She'd never heard him like that. "Gee, that's thoughtful of you."

"Luke, I'm sorry," she said, reaching out to lay her hand on his arm. "I promise, I wasn't trying to keep anything from you. I just didn't think you'd be interested."

This didn't seem to appease him at all. "We're dating, aren't we? Alex? This is a relationship, isn't it?"

"Um, is it?" Alex asked, biting her lip, afraid the question would make him even angrier. "We've never really established that formally," she went on quickly. "I wasn't sure that was what you wanted."

Lucas appeared to be calming down. He stepped forward, sliding his hand across her cheek. "Trust me, it's what I want."

"But what about . . ." She glanced around furtively and lowered her voice. ". . . Olivia?"

"Let me worry about Olivia," Lucas said, pulling her against him. "From now on, I just want you to worry about us."

Alex sighed. For some reason, the thought of not worrying about Olivia seemed to lift a ton of bricks off of her shoulders. "I would love to just worry about us." She smiled up at him.

"Well, just as long as *I* don't have to worry about the two of you," said a strong voice from a few feet away.

They jumped apart, startled. Alex looked behind her to see a large, muscular man with curly hair and sea foam eyes.

"Dad!" Lucas greeted, throwing his arms around his father. "Happy birthday!"

"Thanks, son," the large man replied with a wide grin. "And who's this young lady?"

"Dad, this is Alex, the girl I told you about. Alex, this is my dad, Marcus Riley."

"Alex, it's nice to finally meet you," Marcus said, his grin widening as he took her hand in his huge one. "Luke has told me a lot about you. Dietitian, right?"

"That's me," Alex replied, smiling. It was nice to meet someone so overtly friendly, especially after the coolness of Candie's greeting.

"Great profession," Marcus said, nodding. "Very important. And you're from California, right? Malibu? Is your family all out there?"

"Yes. I am." She nodded. "My parents and two of my younger siblings are. My dad teaches at Pepperdine, so they're kind of rooted there for now. And I believe you're in accounting, right?"

"Deep in it," Marcus said, chuckling. "I'm a partner at one of the big firms downtown. It's a difficult job but a lucrative one."

Alex smiled and nodded, not sure exactly what to say to that. *Oh really, sir, how lucrative?*

"Well, anyway, it was nice to meet you, Alex." He smiled at her one last time, clapped his son on the back, and then moved away.

"Well, he's a cheerful guy," Alex said to Lucas.

"Yeah, he's super friendly," Lucas agreed, but he was watching his dad with a slightly troubled look on his face.

"Hey, you okay?" she asked, putting a hand on his shoulder. He absentmindedly reached out and slid his arm around her waist, pulling her tight into his side.

"Yeah, fine. It's just . . ." He turned to look at her. He studied her face for a second and then smiled. "You know what? Never mind."

* * * * *

After meeting Lucas's parents, Alex felt like she could relax a little. Lucas introduced her to several more people, most of them family friends. None of them accused her of stealing Lucas away from his perfect match, and most of them seemed genuinely happy to meet her. She was relieved at the lack of enmity.

About an hour after their arrival, Sealey turned up again to formally challenge them to a two-on-two basketball game against him and Ashley.

"Absolutely," said Lucas, as Alex nodded enthusiastically. She loved basketball, and her height made her pretty good at it. "I have a brand-new ball in my room upstairs. Hang on a sec and I'll grab it."

Lucas jogged toward the house, leaving Sealey and Alex alone to stare awkwardly anywhere but at each other.

"So . . . ," Sealey began, shoving his hands in the pockets of the jeans he'd thankfully changed into. "How have you been?" His white Abercrombie T-shirt emphasized his tan and his clear blue eyes. Blue eyes that flitted in discomfort to Alex's face and away again. Alex allowed herself to look at him, feeling a little bit better about the awkwardness she felt, knowing he felt it too.

"Pretty good." Alex shrugged noncommittally.

"I haven't talked to you in awhile. Anything new with you?" he questioned, quirking an eyebrow.

"It's only been a week."

"Seems longer." Sealey shrugged.

Alex looked down, trying to come up with something to fill the silence.

"Oh, I wanted to tell you!" she exclaimed, suddenly excited about what had occurred to her. "I had a job interview in Salt Lake this last week. It's for a lecturer position in a traveling speaker series on childhood obesity. It's just like what I told you I wanted to do! A chance to make a difference!" She grinned happily.

"Really?" Sealey said, smiling broadly at her. "That's fantastic, Alex! So how do you think the interview went?"

"Good, I think," Alex replied enthusiastically. "I met with Dr. Welch—she's done all kinds of research in the childhood obesity field—and we really hit it off. We just talked like old friends. If she can get past the idea that I haven't been to grad school and I'm probably horribly inexperienced compared to all the other candidates, I think I'm in."

"I'm so proud of you," Sealey said, putting his arm around her shoulders and squeezing her against him. "You really did it. You went out and found what you were looking for."

"Well, I was mostly just lucky," Alex admitted. "My boss put me up for it. But still, I can't believe it's all happening!"

"So, what does Luke think about it?"

The smile slid off of Alex's face. "Well . . . ," she began. She imparted her conversation with Lucas, highlighting the fact that he didn't seem all that pleased about her plans.

"Well, at least you know he likes you enough to want to keep you around," Sealey pointed out, with a slight grimace. "Sorry he wasn't more excited for you, though."

"Well, it's more my fault than anything. I should have told him sooner. I can't believe I didn't. I'm not sure what I was thinking."

Sealey looked as though he wanted to say something, but he didn't. Talking about Lucas reminded Alex that it had been awhile since they'd seen him.

"Hey, where do you think Lucas went, anyway?" Alex said, looking around to see if he'd been waylaid by old acquaintances. "His bedroom can't be *that* far away."

"Not sure. He might be in the house somewhere," Sealey replied, also craning his neck for his friend. "Why don't you go check the kitchen and I'll check over by the ball court. Maybe he headed over already and we missed him."

"Okay," Alex agreed, and she moved toward the house. She stepped through the patio doors into the kitchen and found that it was deserted. She could hear voices coming from down the hall, however, so she went in search of them. The voices were emanating from the den right off the front entryway. The door was partially closed, which indicated that the inhabitants were looking for privacy, so Alex turned to continue her search for Lucas somewhere else. But the sound of her name made her pause.

"I'm sure Alex is a very nice girl," said the deep, calm voice. Marcus. "And I'm sure she would do everything she could to make you happy. But I need you to think about just one thing."

"Olivia," broke in a higher, sterner voice. Candie. "You've known her your entire life, Lucas. You've loved her your entire life. Why would you throw all of that away now? She'll be home in two weeks!"

"Why do you think she'll even want me?" Lucas's voice came fast and hard. "People change on missions, Mom! She's been gone for a year and a half, she'll want completely different things when she gets home. She'll be a completely different person. And Alex is . . . well, she's amazing. I love being with her."

"I'm not saying Alex isn't a delightful girl, Lucas, but why? *Why* would you give up a girl you've known and loved your entire life for a girl you've only known for a couple of months?" Candie's voice pressed hard against Alex's eardrums. She could almost feel the pressure of the words as they weighed down on her shoulders. "All I'm asking is that you hold off on making any promises or doing something you may regret later until Olivia gets home and you have the chance to see where things stand with her. For all you know, she expects you to be waiting for her."

"She doesn't," Lucas's voice returned immediately. "She made it very clear when she left that she didn't want me to wait. What does that tell you, Mom? I don't think she expects us to end up together."

"Or maybe she was just being the sweet, angelic girl that she is," Marcus replied. "You know her, Luke. She would never expect you to put yourself on ice for her. One of Olivia's defining characteristics is her tendency to put everyone else before herself. She'd sacrifice almost anything if she thought it would help someone else."

"I know," Lucas said, and his voice was gentle, as though he was thinking of past experiences with Olivia. "I'm not saying I don't want her anymore. I'm just saying that I don't know. Alex is—"

"Practically a stranger," Marcus cut in. "That's the long and the short of it. I mean, what do I know? Maybe she'll end up being the one for you. But we don't want you to be too hasty about this decision. At least give Olivia a chance to let you know what she wants before you decide for her."

"Why are you guys acting like I've already proposed to Alex?" Lucas demanded, and Alex couldn't help nodding her head in agreement. As much as she wanted things to work out between her and Lucas, this conversation seemed rather premature. "I just brought her to a birthday party!"

"No, you brought her to a *family* birthday party," Marcus emphasized. "The only girl you've ever brought to a family function before is Olivia. And you give us too little credit for being able to read you, Lucas. You forget, we *created* you. We know when you're getting excited and ready to leap into something."

Lucas made a huffy noise, but he didn't argue.

"I'm sorry, I just need to say this," said Candie suddenly. "I can't help but think that this Alex is just a mistake all around. Again, she's a nice girl, but she doesn't feel like a good fit. I mean, didn't she say she was leaving to take a traveling job for a few months? And she didn't even tell you about it? Is that really the kind of life you want?"

Alex bit her lip, hard. She'd known right from the moment of meeting her that Candie hadn't particularly liked her. This was what she'd been afraid of all along. Suddenly, a large hand grabbed her shoulder. Alex jumped a mile and narrowly escaped issuing a terrified squeak that surely would have alerted everyone to her presence. She turned to see Sealey standing behind her. He opened his mouth to say something, but Candie's voice rang again from the den, stopping him.

"Alex is certainly attractive, and I know you have a bit of a weakness for the tall, leggy types, Lucas, but don't you think your wife should have more substance? She'll be the most important part of your life. I can't help thinking that you'll regret it for as long as you live if you give up a girl like Olivia for a girl like Alex."

Sealey's eyes narrowed as he stared at the partially open door. He reached out and grasped Alex's arm, pulling her down the hall and away from the room.

{ Chapter **ELEVEN** }

"**S**EALEY, I—" **ALEX** began, but he rode right over her.

"Trust me, you don't need to listen to any more of that," Sealey muttered as he led her through the Rileys' kitchen.

Instead of guiding her out the back door onto the patio as she expected, he led her to a side door that emerged into a side yard, densely populated with trees and wild-looking shrubbery. They walked in silence until they arrived at a decorative wooden arbor with a bench underneath. Sealey sat and pulled her down next to him.

"Look," he began. "Despite what that sounded like, Marcus and Candie are really great people. They're like second parents to me. I wouldn't want you to judge them too harshly based on what you just heard."

"I'm sure they're wonderful people," Alex said quietly. She kept her eyes focused on her hands, playing with the ends of her tan sweater. "Look, I don't blame them," she said honestly, looking up at Sealey. "I mean, it's not a picnic to hear yourself spoken about like that, but I'm not stupid. I know they don't know me at all. And I know they've hoped for Lucas and Olivia to end up together for probably most of Lucas's life. I get that. I must be a major disappointment after so many years of hoping for something different."

"You are taking this surprisingly well," Sealey said, looking at her skeptically. "After our conversation last weekend, I would've thought something like this would devastate you."

"Well, luckily, I've had a week to reflect on what you said," Alex replied. "Don't get me wrong—I'm not going to just roll over and give up on me and Lucas, but I think you're right that the time for scheming is over. Now that Lucas actually knows me and has chosen to keep me around anyway, I think Olivia and I are as close to equal footing as we're going to get." She bit her lip and then glanced up at Sealey. "And I should probably take this opportunity to apologize for the things I said to you. I was just scared about having to take responsibility for my chances with Lucas, and I took it out on you."

Sealey shrugged. "I get that. And I wasn't exactly a charmer either, so, you know . . . I'm sorry too."

Alex waved his apology away, not feeling like she deserved it. She had definitely been the antagonist in that particular conversation. "You know, the fact that Lucas was actually defending me to his parents in there makes me feel a bit better about my chances. Is that stupid?"

Sealey smiled softly. "There's nothing wrong with that." He reached out and laid a tentative hand on top of Alex's.

"But doesn't it make you nervous at all?" Alex asked. She turned to face him more fully, wanting to be able to read his expression. "What if Olivia comes home, and Lucas decides he wants her instead of me? What if we lose?"

"Well," Sealey replied, pulling his hand back and folding his arms across his chest. "In that case, I guess I just have to trust in your ability to keep Lucas's attention."

Alex stared at him. "What?" she gasped. "You're really going to pin all of your hopes for a happily ever after with Olivia on me? You can't do that!" She wanted to reach out, grab his T-shirt with both of her hands, and shake some sense into him. "Sealey, I can't take that much pressure! It's hard enough having my own happiness resting on my ability to keep Lucas's interest, but I can't be responsible for yours too!"

"Well, unfortunately, you are," Sealey said, shrugging. A small smile tugged at the corners of his mouth. *Why wasn't he more anxious?* Alex wondered. It was infuriating!

"I really don't know what else to tell you," Sealey continued when he saw her disgruntled expression. "Nobody has more power over my fate right now than you do. But don't let it worry you. Like you said, Lucas was defending you in there. I think he's probably more attached to you than you think."

This really didn't make her feel any better. Sure, she liked to think that her chances with Lucas were relatively good overall, but she'd assumed that she'd at least have Sealey's advice per usual to help her through the rough patches. Particularly when Olivia returned home and everything got even more complicated. Now he was effectively saying that even from a consultation perspective, he was out.

Alex studied him as he smiled serenely at her. She sighed as she felt herself accept his words. He was right. It was her turn. It was thanks to him that she'd even made it this far, but her relationship with Lucas was now beyond his help. Could she do it? Was she confident enough in her knowledge of Lucas and of herself to defeat a relationship that had infinitely more history?

Looking over at Sealey and knowing that she shared some responsibility for what happened to him, she really hoped so.

* * * * *

Lucas was very quiet on the drive home that night. The rest of the day had been relatively uneventful and his parents had been kind and generous to Alex. They, of course, had no reason to suspect that she had overheard their conversation with their son. And she didn't give anything away either. She meant what she'd said about not resenting them.

"You okay?" Alex finally asked, squeezing Lucas's hand. He'd been silent for nearly half an hour, and she was a little concerned that he might be taking what his parents had said a little bit too much to heart. If that were the case, she really wanted to know about it sooner rather than later.

"Fine," Lucas said, forcing his voice to be cheery. But Alex could hear the difference. "I'm sorry about my parents."

"Um, what do you mean?" Alex asked. For a second she panicked, thinking that maybe he had known all along that she had overheard his conversation with Marcus and Candie. "They were perfectly friendly to me."

"Yes, they were friendly," Lucas agreed. "But they weren't warm. I don't know, maybe you didn't notice the difference. You don't really know them. I shouldn't have brought it up."

"Well, you can't expect them to adore me right away," Alex replied, trying to be as diplomatic as possible. "They don't really know me yet."

"And they didn't even try to get to know you," Lucas said, and his voice had an edge to it. "They could have at least tried."

"Come on, Luke," she said, reaching over and massaging between his shoulders. "There's no need to get all worked up about it. We'll have plenty of time to get to know each other, I'm sure." *Did that last sentence ring false?* she wondered, as Lucas glanced at her quickly. Sighing, she finally decided to drop the façade for once. "This has something to do with Olivia, doesn't it?"

Lucas flinched a little. His hand tightened almost painfully on hers. "Why do you say that?" he asked.

"Well, I know you guys have known each other forever, and I know your parents know and love her. Sealey said as much," Alex said quickly to explain her knowledge of Olivia's connection with Marcus and Candie.

"You talked to Sealey about Olivia?" Lucas asked, eyeing her warily. "Why?"

"I was just . . . ," Alex said, thinking fast. "Curious. You know. I wanted to know more about her, but I thought it might be awkward to ask you. You mentioned that you'd dated her for a while, so I figured Sealey must know her, since you guys are such good friends."

"What did he tell you?"

"Well . . . you know. Not much."

Lucas waited, indicating that her answer was not good enough. She attempted to come up with a better one.

"You know . . . just . . . everything." She finally gave up, letting her breath out in a whoosh. "I know you all grew up together, and that she is Ashley's age and that they're best friends. I know that you and Sealey and Ashley all went to the same schools, but that Olivia attended private school. And I know that pretty much everyone you know wants you to end up with her."

Lucas made a funny face at her last sentence. "Well, I wouldn't say *everyone*," he defended. "Sealey doesn't seem to care one way or the other. Actually, he's been really supportive in my relationship with you. I've never known him to ask so many questions about my love life."

"He's a good friend," Alex said quickly. "Maybe he wanted to encourage you in something that seemed to be making you happy. Just a guess, though." Blushing, she looked away. She was not off to a good start, here.

"You do make me happy," Lucas assured her, squeezing her hand.

"I'm glad," Alex replied. "You make me happy too."

After that, Lucas seemed to relax. His outlook was sunnier and he spoke merrily of his memories of many of the party's guests, entertaining her with funny stories about them. By the time they got back to Logan, it was as though the conversation with his parents had never happened.

* * * * *

"Hello?" Alex gasped as she struggled to grab her purse, keys, sweater, and hold her phone to her ear all at once. She was already ten minutes late for her shift at the hospital and while she knew Karen would never confront her about it, Alex hated to agitate her.

"Alex?" said a female voice on the other end. "Alex Foamer?"

"You got her," she replied breathlessly as she attempted to shove her feet into her tennis shoes.

"Alex, this is Fiona Welch," said the voice on the other end. Alex froze, one finger stuck behind her heel as she attempted to force her foot into the stubborn sneaker. Attention now totally focused on the other end of the line, Alex fell backward onto the couch, her finger still wedged in her shoe.

"Dr. Welch!" she exclaimed. "It's great to hear from you!"

"I'm sorry it's taken me so long to get back to you."

Alex made a nonchalant, snorting sort of noise that sounded more disturbing than she had meant it to. "It's only been a week and a half," Alex said quickly to cover the noise. "It's no problem. I know how busy you are."

"I appreciate your patience," Dr. Welch said. It sounded like she might be smiling. "But between our current symposium series and all the interviewing I've been doing to fill these positions for our next one, I really have had very little time. But at least I'm calling with good news. I am pleased to offer you a position in our next conference series if you'd like one."

"Seriously?" Alex gasped. She had hoped and wished and pleaded with the heavens that this phone call would come, but the longer silence reigned, the more she had suspected that it never would. "You really want me?"

"Absolutely," Dr. Welch responded, and now there was no doubt that she was smiling. "What you lack in professional experience, you make up for in energy. And what we really need is someone to excite the audience about our goal, and quite frankly, to speak to them on a less technical level. What do you say?"

Alex nearly opened her mouth to shriek in the affirmative, but suddenly Lucas's face was swimming in her head. Three months without him? For some reason it had never actually occurred to her that she would have to be separated from him until that moment. She suspected that she had been suppressing the thought.

"I know this is going to sound ridiculous after that display of enthusiasm, but can I have a bit to think about it?" Alex asked. "I actually just recently had a big change take place in my personal life and I need to make sure I have all my ducks in a row before I commit to a three-month absence. When do you need my answer by?"

"Hmmm," Dr. Welch replied uncertainly. "That might be tough. The symposium begins in mid-December and while I do have enough solid applicants that I think I can give you a little wiggle room, I can't offer much. How does Thanksgiving weekend sound? That should give you another week and a half to decide. Do you think you'll have an answer for me by then?"

"That I can do," Alex said quickly. A week and a half was much more than she'd hoped for. That would give her plenty of time to talk this over with Lucas. "Thank you so much, Dr. Welch! I can't tell you how excited I am by this opportunity."

"Well then, I hope you decide to join us," Dr. Welch answered. "We'll talk in a week and a half, Alex."

Alex hung up and collapsed against the back of the couch, her tardiness completely forgotten. She had just been offered her dream job—something she had never really believed she'd get the opportunity to do. It had just fallen into her lap . . . and at the very moment she would have the hardest time accepting it. Why did life always have to throw you curve balls like that? Sighing, Alex closed her eyes and tried to figure out how to broach the subject with Lucas. Would he be excited for her, or would it just be a continuation of the last time they'd discussed the opportunity the week before? She didn't want to argue with him.

That wasn't exactly all of it, she knew. Olivia would be coming home in just a few days. Did Alex really want to leave Lucas at home with his former love for three months, especially when their relationship was so new? Was that the wisest strategy?

And just as though her thoughts had called Lucas forth, her phone rang and his name appeared on the screen. She smiled brightly as she lifted the phone to her ear.

"Hey, handsome," she greeted, her voice sultry and inviting, mostly in jest. Sort of.

"Well, hello," came the voice on the other end that was not Lucas's.

"Sealey!" Alex exclaimed, feeling her cheeks go pink. She checked her phone again. Yes, it was indeed Lucas's number. "What are you doing with Lucas's phone?" she demanded.

"Beats me," Sealey replied. "He dialed your number and then threw the phone into my lap. I think he finally heard the timer in the kitchen that's been going off for the past ten minutes. His macaroni and cheese is done."

Men. "Nice to know I rank second to Kraft Specialty," Alex muttered.

"Hey, at least he dialed first," Sealey consoled. "Oh wait, he's back. Here."

"Alex!" Lucas's voice burst onto the line, the word sounded garbled through the mouthful of his precious mac and cheese.

"Hey," Alex replied, not able to work up the energy to re-create her "come hither" tones from before. "What's up?"

"I was just wondering if you were free tomorrow," Lucas replied. "I'd like to head up Smithfield Canyon before all the fall colors fade and I wondered if you wanted to go with me."

"Love to," Alex replied enthusiastically. A romantic stroll along the rosy canyon's famous "river walk" would be the perfect time and place to broach the looming subject of her job offer. How could he refuse to lovingly support her dream and faithfully wait for her return while she stood in front of him, surrounded by vibrant hues?

"Great, I'll pick you up at eleven, if that's okay," Lucas said, his words still mixed with macaroni.

"I'll be ready," Alex responded. "See you then."

"Bye, babe," Lucas said and disconnected.

Babe. He'd called her babe. It was her first official pet name! Alex felt the sudden and driving need to document. Knowing it would take far too long to hunt down the journal she hadn't written in since she was fifteen, she grabbed her phone and opened up her note-taking app. That would have to do. Tapping the conversation out furiously with the tips of her fingers, Alex felt the almost painfully wide perma-smile hanging goofily on her face. She didn't care. Despite the fact that Alex knew she still had a difficult conversation ahead with Lucas, at that moment, she felt ready to take on anything.

* * * * *

"So, just curious, are we ever going to be allowed to go on a date *without* you?" Alex teased Sealey from the front seat of Lucas's car. Sealey rolled his eyes at her from the backseat where he sat passing his iPod back and forth between his hands.

"Trust me, the only reason I'm here is because my car is in the shop and I still haven't had the chance to run the canyon this fall. As soon as this vehicle stops, I'm outta here and you two can have your private romantic interlude."

"I'm just too nice of a guy," Lucas sighed from Alex's left. "I would have just made him walk, but I figured by the time he made it to the canyon on foot, he wouldn't have the energy to run anywhere, let alone walk home again. So I'd end up having to pick him up anyway."

"Sound reasoning," Alex agreed, nodding. Sealey muttered something indiscernible from the backseat.

"So what do you lovebirds have planned, anyway?" Sealey asked a few minutes later. "Romantic stroll through the exotically colored flora and fauna?"

"Your vocabulary is too big and too fruity for your own good," Lucas replied with a smirk. "But, yes, that is the general idea."

"Original." Sealey snorted, kicking the back of Lucas's seat. "And let me guess, you have an adorable and oh-so-cheesy picnic set up in a little grove of trees, just off the path." His tone was teasing, but Lucas was uncomfortably quiet. "Oh, um . . . do you?" Sealey asked suddenly, registering the awkwardness in his best friend's silence.

"Well, I hope you don't like surprises, Alex, because you've just had one completely ruined for you," Lucas replied, ignoring Sealey.

Alex melted, and she reached over to take Lucas's hand. "You came up here and set up a picnic for us?" she asked, her voice sounding a bit more sickly-sweet than she really liked. But she couldn't help it. What a guy.

"I know it's corny, but I wanted to do something special for you and I lack creativity," Lucas replied, shrugging. "I would've asked Sealey, who, believe it or not, is a wizard at putting together schemes of that sort, but I didn't want to go on a date with you that someone else had planned. Not this time."

"It's perfect," Alex said, squeezing his hand. She glanced behind her into the backseat, expecting to see Sealey pretending to vomit or something, but he sat quietly, expressionless, looking out the window.

The moment the car was parked, Sealey was out the door and running down the riverside path away from them.

"Um, see ya!" Alex called after him, surprised at the suddenness of his departure. He waved vaguely over his shoulder and kept going, shoving his earphones in his ears. He disappeared quickly around a bend.

"Well, shall we go?" Lucas asked, holding out his hand to her. She smiled at him and took it.

They walked in silence for several minutes, enjoying the pleasantly cool temperatures and the fiery colors surrounding them, although to Alex they looked a little tired. Pretty soon, the multi-colored leaves would abandon the trees and the snow would arrive in their wake— and boy, was Logan, Utah, enthusiastic about snow. Alex sighed, thinking of the miserably frigid temperatures that were only a few weeks away. Winter was her least favorite part of the year in Logan. In fact, she flat-out dreaded it. But this year, she had the opportunity to miss it altogether . . . if she took the symposium position.

"What's wrong?" Lucas asked, studying her face. "What's with the heaving sigh?"

"Oh, I'm just regretting the future," Alex replied, smiling wanly at him.

"Come again?" he asked, running his thumb over the back of her hand. "How can one regret the future? You have some kind of psychic powers you haven't told me about yet?"

Alex laughed. "No, no psychic powers. It usually doesn't require much foresight to anticipate that with winter will come snow. And cold."

"Ahhh," Lucas realized, nodding. "Mourning the absence of California winters, are we?"

"Always." Alex sighed again. "It's Logan's one major defect."

"Well, I hope we can eventually convert you to the awesomeness that is winter in Utah," Lucas replied. "We need to get you on a snowboard, stat."

"Trust me, if the sport in question requires the presence of frozen water, it is not for me," Alex claimed loftily. "I only appreciate water in its liquid state."

"You poor, unfortunate soul," Lucas mourned. "You have no idea what you're missing."

"And let's keep it that way." Alex laughed. "But speaking of the possibility of missing out on an encounter with a Logan winter . . ." Alex took a deep breath, feeling rather proud of herself for this smooth segue. "I've been given an opportunity to do so."

Lucas looked at her, his expression a mixture of confusion and apprehension. "What exactly do you mean by that?" he asked carefully.

"You know that job I mentioned at your dad's birthday party?" Alex asked, trying to keep her tone light and fluffy. The last thing she wanted was for him to get upset again. "Well, I found out yesterday that I got it!" She injected her voice with a healthy dose of enthusiasm. She prayed he would focus on that and realize how much this opportunity meant to her.

"The traveling speaker series job?" Lucas clarified. "The one that will take you away for three months?"

"Yes!" Alex said, attempting to hold on to her excitement but sounding almost manic instead.

Lucas watched her closely, saying nothing. Each passing second stretched her nerves closer and closer to their breaking point. She wasn't even sure what she wanted him to say. A huge part of her wanted to take this opportunity, but there was still that small piece that hoped he'd insist that she refuse. Their relationship was so new, could it survive something like a three-month absence? Especially a three-month absence with Olivia in the picture? She certainly hoped so, but at the same time, she somehow doubted it. But she also doubted that a career opportunity like this would come around again.

And what if Lucas decided he couldn't support her? From the look on his face, that was looking more and more likely. Would she really turn the opportunity down? She tried to imagine herself doing that. Had she ever really considered the possibility that Lucas would make her choose between the job and him? And if he did, how could she choose anything but him? Oh! She didn't even know what *she* wanted anymore!

"Well, uh . . ." Lucas rubbed a hand over the back of his head, his expression uncertain. "Congratulations, I guess."

"Thanks," Alex replied, her tone just as uncomfortable as his. "It's a really great opportunity for me."

"So you're going then?" Lucas asked, his eyes boring holes into hers.

"Well, that's actually why I'm bringing it up," Alex replied, shrugging. "I'd like to get your thoughts. I told Dr. Welch that I needed time to consider the position, and I wanted to talk to you about it before I decided."

Lucas's shoulders relaxed and his face softened into a relieved smile. "So there's a chance I can convince you not to go?"

As soon as the words hit her eardrums, Alex realized that that was not the response she had been hoping for. She hadn't even known what she really wanted until that very moment. She had subconsciously been envisioning Lucas exclaiming his happiness for her, immediately insisting that she go, and ensuring her that he would be waiting faithfully for her return. In hindsight, this dream was probably slightly unrealistic, but still, to have both of these amazing options pitted against each other felt like a cruelly unfair twist of fate.

"You can try," Alex replied, deflated. "But this has been a dream of mine for a really long time, Lucas. I kind of hoped you'd support me in it."

"But it's three months," Lucas pointed out. "Don't you think it's a little soon in our relationship to spend so much time apart?"

"Maybe," Alex conceded. "But do you really think we can't work

133

through it? And I wouldn't even be gone for the full three months. I get some time off for Christmas, so I could spend a week or so back here in Logan." The argument sounded feeble.

"You know," Lucas began, his tone hesitant. His hand clenched uncomfortably around Alex's and his steps shuffled along as unwillingly as his words. "Olivia comes home the day after tomorrow."

Alex stiffened as her insecurity about Olivia reared its ugly head. She pulled her hand away from Lucas and glared up at him. "What's that supposed to mean? Because it sounded an awful lot like a threat."

"It wasn't a threat!" Lucas defended, raising his hands as though to ward off her sudden anger. "Just an observation. You probably don't know this, but my parents are very set on the idea of me marrying Olivia and if you leave for three months, they will use that time as an opportunity to throw us together as much as possible. I'm just saying it like it is."

"You realize you're all grown up now, right?" Alex snapped, her nerves finally cracking under the strain. This conversation was hard enough without Lucas throwing Olivia in her face. "You realize that Mommy and Daddy can't make you do anything you don't actually want to do?"

Lucas narrowed his eyes at her. "Don't talk to me like I'm four years old, Alex. I'm just saying that being apart for three months so early in our relationship will be hard enough without an old girlfriend thrown into the mix. Please understand, I have no intention of getting back together with Olivia, but it would be a lot easier to make that case to my parents if I had you beside me while I did it."

Alex took a deep breath, attempting to calm herself and feeling stupid about her outburst. "You're right," she admitted. "I'm sorry. It's just hard for me to see an opportunity like this slip away. I'd like to make sure that it's unavoidable before I give up my dream like that."

"I can understand that," Lucas replied, reaching out to pull her to him. His arms slid around her, holding her firmly against him, her head on his shoulder. "And I don't want you to have to give up on a dream either. Really, I—" His voice cut out and Alex felt his chest expand as though he were taking a deep, unsteady breath.

"Alex," he tried again, taking her by the shoulders and pushing her back so he could look into her eyes. He looked suddenly very nervous. "I want you to have everything you want. Everything. But the more I get to know you, the more I think that whatever it is that you want, you should have it with me. I—I love you." He looked at her, his eyes wide with terror at what he had just revealed.

Alex stared back at him. "You do?" she gasped. "Al-already?" Sealey was better than she thought. There's no way she'd have been able to accomplish such a feat on her own in barely three months.

"I was going to tell you once we'd gotten to the picnic area, but I felt like the revelation was needed, given our current topic of conversation." Lucas eyed her pointedly. "Now do you maybe understand why I'm so hesitant to see you leave? I really don't want to be separated from you for so long."

Alex was in absolute turmoil inside. Lucas was in love with her! The thought made her feel like she could never possibly be depressed again. But a part of her, the part with the lofty career aspirations, didn't seem to be listening to that logic. She was furious with herself. Why couldn't she just be happy? This was a miracle! She'd wanted this man for so long and now he was standing here, telling her that he was hers, and she was going to mope about missing out on a job opportunity?

No. Lucas deserved better than that. She could mope later.

She pulled Lucas's head down to hers softly. "I love you too," she said, feeling warmth permeate her as she spoke the words. She pressed her lips to his and felt him respond enthusiastically. He pulled her tightly against him, his hands pressing into her back. As his warmth combined with hers, Alex felt all the regret vanish.

{ Chapter TWELVE }

"**W**HY ARE YOU two so . . . giddy?" Sealey asked as they drove back to Logan from the canyon. "Foamer, I don't think I've ever heard you giggle before."

"I am *not* giggling," Alex defended, affronted. She'd never been a giggler, thank heavens.

"You are," Sealey emphasized, a deadly serious look on his face. "What happened?"

"Seriously, man?" Lucas asked, eyeing him in the rearview mirror. "You're really going to ask what happened on our ridiculously romantic picnic? That you have already openly mocked?"

"Point taken," Sealey muttered, looking out the window. "Just wanted to share in the merriment, but I guess I'll just, you know, pass."

"Wise move," Lucas replied, smiling.

Alex glanced back at Sealey, noticing the glum look on his face. She wondered if maybe he just seemed down in comparison to her incandescent happiness. But no, he'd been moody on the way to the canyon.

"What's your deal?" she asked him. She reached back to nudge his knee with her fingertips. "You've been awfully grumpy lately."

Sealey glanced at her but said nothing. His eyes stared somewhat vacantly out the window, his hands limp in his lap. She studied his expressionless face for a second longer and then turned back to the front, eyebrows furrowed.

"Don't mind him," Lucas replied, still smiling. "He's just in a crappy mood today."

Alex wasn't sure about that, though. What reason did Sealey have to be in a bad mood? With Olivia due home in a couple of days and with Lucas and Alex so happily connected, what did he have to complain about? And for crying out loud, he'd just been running down a colored canyon in cool, sunny weather! What more could you do to improve your general outlook on life? No, something was bothering him. Something big. The thought made Alex nervous.

* * * * *

"I'm freaking out. I'm really freaking out," Alex muttered as she paced back and forth across the apartment living room. Jaclyn watched her with a raised eyebrow.

"Didn't Lucas *just* tell you that he loved you?" she prodded. "Like, two days ago?"

"Yeah, so?" Alex replied, now wringing her hands as she paced.

"And have you looked up the definition of the word *love* in the dictionary lately?" Jaclyn asked. "It's kind of a big deal."

"I know it is," Alex admitted. "But so is seeing your ex-girlfriend after a year and a half separation."

"I don't understand why he went to the airport," Sage said in a garbled voice from the kitchen, an ice cream spoon protruding from her mouth. "Seems kind of insensitive to me."

"I bet his parents are making him," Meredith chimed in. "They've made it very clear that they want Lucas to end up with Olivia. I'll bet they told him he had to come."

"What is he, three years old?" Jaclyn scoffed. "He's a grown man. If he didn't want to go, he would've just said no. I think he *wants* to be there."

"This conversation is so helpful," Alex said sarcastically, rolling her eyes. In all honesty, she was as nervous to hear from Sealey as she was to hear from Lucas. They had gone to the airport together four hours earlier to meet Olivia's plane, and she hadn't received so much as a text from either.

Alex was squarely in Sage's camp. She didn't think a trip to the airport was necessary to greet Olivia, but naturally, she hadn't told Lucas that. And really, wasn't four hours plenty of time to greet an old girl-friend and get back to your current one?

"I just wish I knew what was *taking* so long," Alex growled.

"Well, like you said, they haven't seen each other for a year and a half," Jaclyn pointed out. "They probably have a lot to catch up on."

"That's what I'm afraid of," Alex whined. "All right. That's it, I'm checking my phone again." She stomped toward her bedroom where she had banished her phone after one too many digs from her room-mates. Maybe she had placed it on silent and forgotten. Maybe she had received twelve texts from Lucas and Sealey and she just couldn't hear the notifications from the living room. Never mind that she never put her phone on silent. Ever.

She heard her roommates discussing the topic as she waded through her messy room to the bed where she had chucked her phone. No mes-sages. No calls. Alex sighed and collapsed onto her mattress. In the living room, she heard the front door to the apartment slam. Kacey must be home from her new job at Angie's. Like any self-respecting theater major, Kacey now worked in the food industry to try to make ends meet as she attempted to get some semblance of an acting career off the ground. Alex didn't have the heart to tell her that a successful acting career was not likely to begin in Logan, Utah.

Alex heard Kacey's voice in the living room and suddenly the entire apartment seemed to be encompassed within a cone of silence. No sound. Anywhere. Curious about what Kacey must have said to elicit such stillness from her roommates, Alex rose to her feet and headed for the living room. It wasn't like she had reason to hang out with her phone anyway.

As she entered the living room, every eye fixed on her, making her stop. "What?" she asked.

"Oh man," said Jaclyn.

"Nothing!" said Sage.

"Well . . . ," said Meredith.

Every face had the same look of mixed panic and pity on it.

"What is going on?" Alex demanded. Her eyes flitted from face to face, and she felt a strange feeling of dread overwhelm her.

"Maybe you should take a seat," Kacey said, her voice much softer than usual. Alex didn't argue, but immediately made for the couch. Once she was seated, she turned back to Kacey.

"Okay, I'm seated. Now, spill. What do you know?"

"Well, I just came from Angie's," Kacey explained needlessly. "And right before I left, a couple came in."

Alex didn't even need her to finish. "Lucas and a girl radiating the glow of recent missionary work, I presume?"

"Lucas and Olivia," Kacey affirmed. "I actually went up and introduced myself, just so I could give you accurate information." She nodded dutifully.

"So . . . is she . . . pretty?" Sage asked while Alex processed. Lucas was out, on a date it sounded like, with Olivia. Already.

"Unfortunately, she's very prett—" Kacey was saying until Alex cut her off.

"Wait a second, how could they possibly be out on a date already?" Alex fumed. "Isn't she still a missionary? Doesn't she have to be released first?"

"According to Lucas, her parents set it up with her stake president so she could be released immediately. She went straight from the airport to the stake president's office and I'm guessing from there, Lucas's parents nudged them out to dinner together."

Alex sat dumbly on the couch, staring at her hands. "And she's pretty?" she repeated Sage's question, almost wincing up at Kacey.

"Yeah," Kacey confirmed but didn't elaborate. Alex could hear a note of compassion in her voice.

Without another word, Alex rose to her feet and went back to her bedroom, shutting the door behind her. She sat on her bed and played idly with her phone. Olivia had only been home for four hours and already she was coming between Lucas and Alex. Unable to bear not knowing any longer, Alex sent a text to Sealey.

So . . . how was it? she texted. She saw him begin to reply almost immediately.

Fine. Olivia looks great. It was good to see her again.

Are you still with her? Alex pressed, hoping that his response would clear up how Lucas had ended up at a restaurant alone with the newly returned missionary.

No, Luke and Olivia took off together almost immediately after she was released, he texted back. *I think his parents suggested that he take her out to dinner.*

Oh, Alex texted back. She took a second to gather her dignity and then sent a second text. *Are you as worried as I am?*

He never replied.

* * * * *

Alex didn't hear from Lucas until nearly two days later. In that time, she managed to talk herself into an almost manic depressive state, sure that, when he did finally speak to her again, it would be to tell her that he wasn't sure if he could live without Olivia. The thought of competing against not just the memory of Olivia, but the physical embodiment herself was almost too much for Alex. She had spent so much time scheming and planning and worrying to get Lucas to notice her. She felt like she'd filled her quota of competition already, before Olivia even returned home.

But the truth turned out to be even worse than her fears.

"Hey, Alex," Lucas stood on her doorstep, his hands clenched into fists in his pockets.

"Lucas," Alex sighed in relief. "I was starting to get worried. I haven't heard from you since Oliv—uh, since Monday."

"Yeah, it's been a little nuts," Lucas replied, smiling weakly. "I've had some thinking to do about things."

"Things? What things?" Alex said, hating how panicked she sounded. She was pretty dang sure she already knew the answer to her own question.

"Well, Olivia, mostly," Lucas said, looking at the ground. "See, the thing is, I . . . I don't think I can . . ." He let his breath out all in one whoosh and bit his lip.

"You don't think you can tell her that you want to break things off?" Alex prompted, praying she could keep the searing pain out of her voice and off her face, at least until he left. "You don't think you can tell her that you're in love with someone else?"

"No," Lucas said, looking up at her. "I don't think I can tell her those things."

Alex nodded, looking down at her bare feet and chewed on her lip.

She chanted the words *you will not cry, you will not cry* in her head as she pulled her breathing and expression back into composure. "So what does that mean for us?"

"Alex, I'm so sorry," Lucas said, reaching out to lay a hand on her arm. "I really have no excuse. I just forgot. Being separated from Olivia, I forgot that, well, there will never be anyone else for me. Just her."

Alex's eyes flew from her feet to his face. He wasn't even going to give her a chance to fight for him?

"You mean, this," she gestured between the two of them. "Us. We're just . . . over? That's it?"

"I'm so sorry," Lucas said again, and Alex thought *he* actually might cry, given the look on his face. "I've said so many things that I regret, but nothing more than telling you I loved you this past weekend. That was unforgivable."

Alex had to hold on to the doorframe to keep from sinking to her knees. "You . . . *regret* telling me you love me?" she choked.

"I thought I did," Lucas said desperately. "I promise, Alex. I really thought what I was feeling was love. But then Olivia came home, and we've spent a few days getting reacquainted and spending time with each other, reliving memories, and it's dawned on me over that time that I've always loved her. She's everything I've ever wanted and I let myself forget that when she was gone. But she's . . . *home* for me."

"Excuse me," Alex said. She reached down and grabbed the ballet flats she kept by the door. Then, pushing past him, she strode out the door and down the sidewalk. She needed to move, to have some kind of outlet. And she needed to get away from him.

"Please, Alex, don't hate me," Lucas cried, following her down the sidewalk. "I don't expect you to forgive me, but please don't hate me. I really do care about you."

"Go away, Lucas," she answered through white lips. "I can't talk to you right now."

Immediately she heard his footsteps halt behind her. He stood quietly on the sidewalk, watching her walk away. But in reality, she knew it was the other way around. She was the one left standing alone, watching him walk happily away with Olivia.

* * * * *

Alex walked to the park and sat on the bench overlooking the playground. It was near freezing outside, and Alex had no more than a light jacket on, but she couldn't even feel the frosty air as it dusted across her cheeks. At first, she felt lifeless and petrified inside, like old wood. As though emotion were something her body had no concept of. But as what had just happened began to sink into her consciousness, she found herself doubled up and sobbing, the ache and disappointment seeming too great to reside in one person.

He was gone. Lucas was gone, and he wasn't coming back.

She wasn't sure how long she cried, but soon she became aware of an arm resting warmly over her shoulders. She didn't know how long it had been there, but the moment she realized it, she jerked up and away.

"Hey, it's just me," Sealey said. And without waiting for her to respond, he pulled her firmly back into his arms, her head on his shoulder. Without waiting for permission, she allowed herself to cry into his sweater.

He held her and comforted her as she soaked his shoulder, stroking her back and whispering soft words into her ear until she was able to calm down.

"S-s-sorry," she sniffled, gesturing to his sweater. "I've probably ruined that."

"The shirt doesn't matter," he replied, studying her closely. "I'm just worried about you. I've never seen anyone cry like that."

"I'm not sure I have either," Alex replied, with a weak lift at the corner of her mouth. "How did you find me?"

"Luke came home and told me what he'd done," Sealey said, his voice sounding flinty. "He said that he left you walking down the sidewalk toward the park. It wasn't hard to locate you after that."

"Well, thanks for coming, even though I almost wish you hadn't," Alex said, sniffing. "I'm embarrassed for you to see me like this. How pathetic."

"Oh, come on," he responded. "Everybody cries."

"That's almost hilarious, coming from you," Alex returned pointedly. "I doubt you've cried since you were two."

"I was at least three," Sealey teased, winking at her. Suddenly his voice rang with sincerity. "Actually, today was probably the closest

I've come in a long time." He ran his hand up and down her arm as he said it.

Alex gasped. "Oh, Sealey! Olivia! I'm so sorry!"

Sealey looked startled for a second and then realization dawned in his eyes. "It's no big deal," he said. "I'll get over it, just like you will."

"But here I am, sobbing like an idiot, and there you are, just holding me and comforting me, when you're probably hurting just as much as I am! More!"

"Alex, it's really not that bad," he began, but Alex rode right over him.

"I'm so selfish! Always so selfish!" she cried. "Do you need to talk about it? Is there anything I can do? After all, this is mainly my fault. I'm the one who couldn't distract Lucas!"

"Alex," Sealey said firmly. "Everything happened exactly as it should. Lucas had two incredible options. He chose the one that he felt was best for him. Who can blame him?"

"You're so much better than I am," Alex sighed. "All I can do is try to think of ways to get him back."

"Please don't try," Sealey pleaded. "Just let it go."

"I'm not sure I can," she said, tears filling up her eyes again. "Sealey, I love him. How can I just forget him?"

Sealey looked at her but didn't say a word.

{ *Chapter* THIRTEEN }

ALEX DIDN'T THINK she could face church the following Sunday. She had heard through the grapevine that Olivia was already settled in Logan, ready to begin grad school in January and pick up where she had left off with Lucas. The two of them had been spotted all over town together, and Alex herself had received many well-meaning condolence texts from girls in her ward who had guessed at her discarding. She wished she could unread every single one of them. Especially since Alex had finally been given the one opportunity she had never actually wanted. She had finally met Olivia.

It had all been an accident, really. Alex had been leaving swim practice right at the moment that Lucas and Olivia were entering the gym together. Never before had Alex suspected that she would grow to hate the sight of those sea-green eyes and that curly hair, but it had happened. She couldn't even bear to look at them.

She had initially just walked right past as though she hadn't seen the two of them, but Lucas had immediately turned to follow her. His hand fell heavily on her shoulder, impeding her progress toward the door.

"Alex," he had pleaded in a whisper, glancing over his shoulder at the sweet-looking blonde watching them curiously. "I really want to introduce you to her."

"Does she know who I am?" Alex asked through gritted teeth. "Does she know about us?"

"She knows that I was dating someone before she got back, yes,"

Lucas replied. "But she doesn't know that it was you. Please, Alex. I need you to know her. I don't think you'll ever understand how I could have done what I did if you don't know her."

"I doubt I'll understand anyway," Alex muttered under her breath, but she walked back with him to where the blonde was standing.

"Hi, you must be Olivia," Alex said, holding out her hand to the girl. She was determined to be in control of this situation, even though inside she felt like she was burning at the stake. "Lucas and Sealey have told me so much about you. It's great to finally meet you in person. I'm Alex Foamer."

"Oh, Alex!" Olivia replied, eagerly shaking her hand and smiling. She was short, about five feet two inches, with long, curly blonde hair to the middle of her back. She had a tiny frame, the kind that looked as though the smallest puff of wind could blow it over. Her large, expressive blue eyes were wide and sincere.

"Sealey has told me a lot about you as well!" Olivia sang.

Alex blinked at her. "He has?" she asked.

"Yes, he wrote me all about you!" Olivia smiled. "He really admires you." Goodness and authenticity absolutely radiated from her face. Despite the animosity Alex had secretly felt toward Olivia for the past few months, now that she was face-to-face with her, Alex found she couldn't maintain it. In fact, she felt almost unworthy to stand in the presence of someone so obviously angelic.

"Oh, well, that's . . . unexpected," Alex said, a corner of her mouth twitching. The words seemed to apply so aptly to both what she was hearing and what she was feeling. "So how is it being home?"

"Oh, it's been great," Olivia answered, nodding and smiling warmly. "I mean, I miss Australia like crazy, but there have been, you know, compensations." She winked up at Lucas, and Alex felt a sharp pain knife through her, somewhere in the vicinity of her heart.

"I'm sure there are," she replied, forcing a smile. She reminded herself that Olivia had no idea who she was and was not being cruel on purpose. She felt rather proud of herself for bothering to do so. "Well, welcome home. I suspect I'll see you at church on Sunday."

"Looking forward to it. Bye!" Olivia waved, and she and Lucas headed for the stairs to the weight room.

Well, Sunday had arrived, and Alex was trying to work up the motivation to actually make it to church. She was dreading all the pitying stares and whispers that she was going to have to pretend not to notice. Knowing that if she didn't go, she could add guilt to the really, really enjoyable emotional cocktail she was currently experiencing, she sighed and pulled herself out of bed. She attempted to make enough of an effort with her appearance that it wouldn't look like she was broken, but not so much that it looked like she was trying not to look like she was broken. It was a delicate balance. Still, looking in the mirror, she was pleased with how put-together she appeared.

"Gracefully done," Meredith approved when she saw her. "You look quietly dignified."

"There's something in that phrase that sounds overtly spinsterish," Alex said, sighing. "I guess I can't escape it now."

"Oh, please," Kacey scoffed. "You are twenty-four years old. You don't hit spinster status until at least twenty-five around here."

"Gee, thanks," Alex said, rolling her eyes. "Let's just get this over with, okay?"

The six roommates arrived at church together, and Alex was touched when her five pals simultaneously closed ranks around her as they entered the chapel. It was a futile effort, given that she was taller than all of them, but the sight of little Rachel taking a protective step in front of her gave Alex an undeniable feeling of warmth.

They sat in their usual sixth row of the chapel, and Alex immediately pulled out her scriptures, wanting to look occupied if anyone happened to get any funny ideas about coming over to commiserate with her. She knew the moment that Lucas entered the room with Olivia, because the noise level rose considerably. Cursing herself for the need, but needing it all the same, she glanced in his direction.

He looked as handsome as ever in a dark gray suit and green tie. His arm was around Olivia's waist, who was looking fetching in a belted royal blue dress and matching pumps, her blonde locks cascading in ringlets down her back. Alex immediately regretted looking over when she realized how many people had noticed. The pitying looks she had been expecting were pressing in on her from all sides. Feeling the tension bunching in her neck and shoulders, she turned back to her scriptures, her eyes feeling as though they might burn a hole through the page. Meredith reached out and surreptitiously squeezed her hand.

"You can do this," she assured Alex quietly. "Nobody is stronger than you are."

The words were exactly what Alex needed to hear. They filled the hole in her heart temporarily with a comforting balm, but unfortunately, the feeling of intense relief and gratitude caused the very reaction that Alex had been trying so desperately to avoid. Her eyes filled with tears. Knowing that it would only make things worse, but refusing to cry in front of Lucas, Alex rocketed to her feet, slid as fast as she could down the bench and out of the chapel, feeling hundreds of eyes following her.

* * * * *

Alex walked back to her apartment, wiping her eyes as she went. This was the very problem with dating someone in your ward. When it inevitably went pear-shaped, suddenly church was no longer the haven it used to be. She'd have to talk to the bishop about the possibility of changing wards. If only until Lucas and Olivia were married and safely moved into a family ward. She couldn't take seeing the two of them at church each week.

If she were smart, she would've walked right up to them and started talking and laughing with them as though nothing were wrong. As though she had given them her blessing or something. It would have immediately counteracted all the pity and the ward-wide rumors, and simultaneously soothed Lucas's, Sealey's, and her roommates' worries about her. And maybe it would have even helped her heal a little bit. But even if such a thing had occurred to her in the moment, Alex doubted she would have had the ability to pull it off convincingly. It was all still too close to the surface.

When Alex arrived back at the apartment, instead of going inside, she pulled her jacket more tightly around herself and sat on the front steps of the building. The air was almost cold enough to see her breath, and now and then she caught sight of a steamy puff issuing from her mouth. She allowed the chilly air slowly in and out of her lungs, her face lifted to the clear blue sky.

She had no idea what came next. Alex knew she had no choice but to move on with her life, but she didn't know how. Lucas had been her sole focus for so long, for months before he even knew who she was. She wasn't sure how to just suddenly do an about-face. And the thought of just letting him go wasn't something she felt she could do yet. But what other option did she have?

* * * * *

Alex heard her roommates return from church a few hours later, and their voices sounded intentionally soft, as though they were afraid of disturbing her. But it sounded like they were arguing about something. The tone of their conversation was intense, confrontational, even though she couldn't make out the individual words they said. Not wanting to be the kind of dumped girlfriend who cowers in her bedroom, Alex got to her feet and went to join them.

Silence enveloped the kitchen as soon as she entered. Green, blue, and brown eyes peered at her from five different faces, some wary, some pitying, and some determined.

"Alex," Meredith began, with a resolute look on her face.

"No!" Rachel interrupted. "It's not fair. It's not right to say anything."

"I'm sorry," Meredith replied, not sounding or looking sorry at all. "I don't know Olivia. But I know Alex. And I can't handle seeing her like this. So if I can fix it, I'm going to try."

Kacey nodded firmly, while Sage looked unsure and Jaclyn looked back and forth between Rachel and Meredith, apparently content to just watch.

"What are you talking about?" Alex asked, looking at Meredith curiously. "What do you mean, you can *fix* it?"

"Kacey and I overheard something today," Meredith answered. "We were sitting behind Lucas and Sealey in Sunday school and we heard them talking about you and Olivia."

"Oh?" Alex said, really trying to sound nonchalant, but at the same time wondering why she bothered. "What did they say?"

"Lucas was telling Sealey how bad he felt for leading you on like he did," Kacey answered. "He said he hated causing you so much pain and how he wasn't sure he would ever stop feeling guilty about it. Apparently seeing you run out of the chapel today really hit him hard."

"And then Sealey said Lucas better hope that Olivia didn't find out about it because she would hate the idea that people were suffering because of her," Meredith chimed in. "He said that if Olivia found out about what Lucas had said to you before she came home and how much you loved Lucas, that Olivia would step out of the picture so you and Lucas could be together."

The kitchen rang with the sound of absolute silence. Alex stared at Meredith, her mind racing. Her roommates stared back, allowing her to process the information.

"Sealey said that Olivia would step out of the picture if she knew about me and Lucas?" she restated, making sure she understood.

Meredith nodded solemnly. "That's what he said."

"But it doesn't mean anything," Rachel insisted. "First of all, you guys should never have heard that stuff. If you hadn't been eavesdropping, you never would have. Second, Alex can't go and spill everything to Olivia! It's not right! If Lucas wanted Olivia to know, he would have told her himself."

Sage was nodding, but when she opened her mouth it was to disagree. "But with that kind of information in her hands, how can Alex not do anything about it? She's in love with Lucas; how can she not fight for him?"

"But will Lucas even want her if she does something like that?" Jaclyn pointed out. "Won't that just make him mad?"

"Maybe at first," Kacey answered. "But I think in the long run he'll see the action for what it is, proof of how much she loves him. And Lucas loves Alex too—I *know* he does. If Olivia refuses to stay with him, I know he'll come back to Alex."

"So what do you say, Alex?" Meredith asked. "How would you like to get Lucas back?"

Alex stared, her thoughts racing. She'd wanted to fight back for as long as she'd been miserable but had known she was lacking the weapons. Now she had them. How could she not use them?

"Let's do it," she said.

* * * * *

Alex sat outside the institute building, waiting for Olivia to make an appearance. Sealey had been the unwitting source of her information, informing her that Olivia was taking an institute class on campus when she had asked some questions about the girl, feigning general interest. In actuality, all Alex had wanted to know was her schedule. And, of course, Olivia was already enrolled in institute within a week of returning home from her mission. Of course. The girl was a tiny, blue-eyed, blonde-haired saint. Her face seemed to almost glow with Christlike fervor. Alex wished she could resent her, but everything she'd seen from Olivia indicated that she was kind, genuine, and unselfish. Not like Alex.

Alex stared down at her shoes, biting her lip. She'd been struggling internally ever since she'd agreed to her roommates' plot. She couldn't believe she'd come to this. So desperate was she to get Lucas back, she was willing to make him miserable first. Not just him, but also a sweet, beautiful returned missionary who had done absolutely nothing to Alex, except be just a little too lovable.

In that moment, Alex hated herself.

Why couldn't she just be like Sealey and let the whole thing go? Why was she so obsessed with having Lucas? She remembered what Sealey had said weeks before about her scheming to cause heartbreak just so she could get what she wanted. Just like everyone else, all her life she'd heard classic tales of romance where lovers made the ultimate sacrifice, giving up everything they'd ever wanted for the happiness of their loved one. Why couldn't Alex manage to do it? Why was her happiness more important to her than Lucas's? Or Olivia's?

Alex nearly stood up then, determined to try to forget Lucas at least one more time before taking this drastic step, but suddenly she remembered the way he had looked the first time he had kissed her. His curly hair slightly disheveled from the 150-foot drop of the Sky Coaster. He had looked down at her with such focus, his green eyes studying her face intently before he leaned toward her. She had seen such sweet vulnerability on his face, a look that was uncommon for the confident athlete. His lips had felt perfect on hers. Her resolve faltered at the memory. How could she give him up? When would she ever find a better, kinder man? One who loved her more gently and purely?

Alex glanced around her self-consciously as tears filled her eyes. It wasn't fair. She'd waited so long for Lucas to even notice she was alive. She thought she'd reached perfect happiness the day Lucas had told her he was in love with her . . . but it had faded much too swiftly. Why? How could life be so cruel as to give her everything she wanted and then to snatch it away so quickly?

She discreetly wiped a finger under her eyes as she glanced around once more. Her gaze fell on a couple, walking hand-in-hand toward the building. Olivia's head fell back, her curly blonde hair catching the sunlight as she laughed. Lucas looked down at her, his expression captivated as he took her in. He had never looked at Alex that way. Like the only thing that mattered in the whole world was right there in front of him. They looked complete, the two of them. Right. Whole.

In that one glance, everything slid into place inside her. Alex finally made the decision that had been plaguing her for days. The right one.

She loved Lucas. Or if she didn't, it was as close to love as she'd ever felt before. But watching him now, she knew he didn't love her. At least not in the way he loved Olivia. What right did Alex have to ruin such a beautiful thing?

Despite the fact that her tears didn't seem to want to stop, Alex smiled. The knot in her stomach loosened, and relief flooded through her as she finally realized what she had to do. Pulling her purse up onto her shoulder, she quickly rose and slipped around the side of the building before either of the laughing lovers could spot her.

* * * * *

"Alex."

Alex heard her name as she walked from her car toward the apartment. Glancing up in surprise, she saw Sealey sitting on the steps to her building. "Hi," she replied, nonplussed. "What are you doing here?"

"I just came to see how you were holding up," Sealey replied. His expression was odd, as though he was attempting to x-ray her, to find some long-buried secret in her eyes.

"That was nice of you," Alex replied, eyebrows raised. "The tearful chapel escape worried you that much, huh?"

"Kacey mentioned that you had gone to see Olivia," Sealey said, ignoring her comment. His look had hardened into something steely and determined.

"I did," Alex admitted, feeling her cheeks redden slightly. Was that why he had hung around? He wanted to know if she'd managed to clear the way to Olivia after all? Her stomach seemed to turn to stone inside her. How was she going to tell him that all hope, if there ever had been any, was now completely gone? Because of her.

"You did," Sealey repeated. He continued to watch her. "And?"

"I . . . I couldn't."

Sealey stared at her, his look unreadable. "I don't understand." His blue eyes were fixed on Alex's. "You had the opportunity to get Lucas back, but you didn't take it?"

"I know I probably should have talked to you about it first," Alex said, taking a deep breath. "After all, you had as much stake in this thing as I did. But I went, and I saw them, and I . . . I couldn't do it, Sealey."

She hadn't even really had a chance to plan for this conversation, but if she had, she would have dreaded it. Not because she regretted her decision, but because she knew she was about to destroy Sealey's hopes. And despite her somewhat volatile history with Sealey, she really did care about that. A lot.

In a weird way, she felt like Sealey knew her better than almost anybody else by this point. He'd been present for some of her most helpless, embarrassing, and horrific moments. But he'd also shared her triumphs as she'd fought for Lucas's heart. And now it was all for nothing. For both of them. She had lost Lucas, and he had lost Olivia. And it was her fault.

"I'm sorry, Sealey," she said sincerely. "So sorry. I know that you were counting on me to clear your path to Olivia, but I just couldn't do it. They were just . . . right. You know?" she looked desperately up at him, praying that he would understand and forgive her for not taking the opportunity to possibly bring him all he had ever wanted.

"You mean you're just . . . giving up?" Sealey's voice sounded different. She had never heard that tone before. It was quiet, almost vulnerable. She felt her insides clench with something like nausea. Oh, why had she ever started this whole mess? She'd done nothing but cause trouble and pain for both of them, and what had changed? Nothing. Lucas was as devoted to Olivia as he'd been from the beginning. She wanted to curl up and die.

"You didn't tell Olivia because you're going to let her have Lucas?" Sealey clarified in the same defenseless tone.

"I'm sorry," Alex whispered again. "I just . . . I can't hurt him like that. Or her. They don't deserve it. They love each other. It's . . . visible. I swear, it almost illuminates the air around them. They *should* be together. Can't you see that?"

Please see that, she begged in her mind. *Please see how right I am and don't hate me for it.*

Sealey stared intently at her, saying nothing. His eyes, wide and unsure, were full of some emotion that she had never seen there before, and therefore couldn't place. Was it pain? Disappointment? Devastation? None of those seemed quite right. But what else could he be feeling? He would hate her forever, she was sure of it. The thought was awful to her.

Guilt. So much guilt. She was nearly suffocating in it.

"I . . . ," Sealey said, but then shook his head. "I need some time," he finally continued. "Some time to process." Without another word, he turned and walked away.

* * * * *

"Mom?" Alex tried not to let her voice shake as she heard the comforting sound of her mother's voice over the phone.

"Alex?" Grace Foamer said. "Honey, what's wrong?"

That was so like her mother. Alex had said only a single word and her mother already knew something was up.

"Mom, I know I told you I wasn't, but I'm coming home for Thanksgiving after all," Alex said, taking a deep breath to steady her voice. "Is that okay?"

"What a ridiculous question," Grace answered, a smile in her voice. "We'd absolutely love to see you. Do you need money for a plane ticket?"

"I think I'll just drive, if that's okay," Alex answered.

"Al, what's going on?" Grace asked, reverting to her family's old nickname for Alex. The sound sent a comforting warmth throughout Alex's body. "What's happened?"

"Nothing, I just . . ." Alex's voice dissolved into tears and she stopped talking, just sniffling into the receiver.

"Oh, honey." Grace's voice broke at the sound of her daughter's pain. "What do you need? What can I do?"

Alex said nothing, and just continued to cry into the phone.

* * * * *

"Are you ever going to tell me what happened?" Meredith demanded as Alex stuffed clothes haphazardly into her suitcase. "What did Olivia say? Why are you running away instead of staying here to claim your prize?"

"There is no prize in this game, Meredith," Alex muttered as she looked through her closet for the shoes she wanted. "Nobody wins."

"What?" Meredith said, her voice rising in pitch in her frustration. "What are you talking about? We *told* you how to win! All you had to do was tell Olivia all those things Lucas said to you. About how much he loved and wanted you and how he was going to cut Olivia loose, and that would be enough. Olivia would let him go!"

"At what price, though?" Alex said sharply, turning to face her best friend. "Sure, Olivia would let Lucas go, but does it automatically follow that Lucas would come running back to me?"

"Sealey *said* he would!" Meredith insisted. "Kacey asked him when he randomly showed up here the other day!"

"Oh, what does Sealey know?" Alex said through clenched teeth. She didn't want to talk about Sealey. She hadn't seen him for days. Not since she had told him about her decision to leave Olivia and Lucas alone. Alex was worried about him. She knew how much he had been counting on her to take Lucas out of the picture so he could finally tell Olivia how he felt about her without hurting his best friend in the process.

"What does Sealey *know*?" Meredith screeched with incredulity. "Everything, Alex! That's the whole point! That's how this whole mess started! He knows *everything*! What did you do?"

"Nothing!" Alex shouted back. "I did nothing, okay? I saw Lucas and Olivia on campus, when they didn't know I was watching. They were *glowing*, Meredith. They're so happy together. I won't ruin that. I care too much about Lucas to do that to him, and though I don't know Olivia well, I know she doesn't deserve it either. I won't do it!" She sank to the edge of bed and bit her lip fiercely, looking away.

Meredith stared at her, her eyes shocked. Without another word, she rose to her feet and enfolded Alex in her arms. "I'm so sorry," was all she said.

Alex took an unsteady breath. She had spent too much time crying about this already. "I'll survive," she said, trying to force some toughness into her voice. "To be perfectly honest, I'm more worried about Sealey than I am about myself."

"Sealey?" Meredith said, backing away and giving Alex a perplexed look. "Why should you be worried about Sealey?"

"Well . . . ," Alex said, folding her legs up to her chin as she faced Meredith. "I never told anyone this, because I thought Sealey would kill me if I did, but the whole reason he agreed to help me was because of Olivia."

"What about Olivia?" Meredith pushed. "What does Olivia have to do with Sealey?"

"He's in love with her," Alex revealed with a hopeless look. "He has been for years. But he didn't want to alienate Lucas by making an obvious play for her. He was hoping that if Lucas could fall for me, then that would leave Olivia free for him."

"Wow . . . ," Meredith said quietly. "What a tangled web."

"Tell me about it," Alex sighed. "Unfortunately, this particular spider wasn't expecting me to drop the ball like I did. I'm pretty sure he's crushed. I haven't seen him since I told him that I wasn't going to split up Lucas and Olivia. He just disappeared. It's been weird, actually. I'm so used to him checking in with me all the time."

"That's heartbreaking," Meredith said, putting a hand to her chest. "Who would've thought that beneath that rough, sarcastic exterior, there was a real romantic? Seriously, he's loved her for *years*?"

"That's what he said," Alex replied. "Well, not in those words exactly, but Sealey's not one to say things like 'I love.' . . . I don't know, I just need to get away from all of this. I feel so depressed about Lucas and so guilty about Sealey that I just need to be around people who don't know anything about it. Who love me despite the fact that I've managed to make two people miserable, myself being one of them."

"But you've allowed two people to be blissfully happy too," Meredith pointed out. "That's got to count for something."

"Maybe." Alex smiled weakly. "But, right now, all I can see is the look on Sealey's face as he walked away from me."

{ Chapter FOURTEEN }

ON THE LONG drive to Malibu, California, Alex allowed her thoughts to wander freely. Admittedly, she spent some time thinking wistfully of the heavenly hours she'd spent with Lucas, but she spent even more time thinking of ways she could make everything up to Sealey. Maybe now was the time to introduce the idea of setting him up with Kacey, like Meredith had suggested all those months ago. They were so similar. But something in that thought was distasteful to Alex. Sealey was in love with Olivia. Olivia and Kacey were about as similar as a dove and a rampaging bull. If Olivia was the kind of girl Sealey fell for, then Kacey would be absolutely repellent to him.

Besides, the thought of telling Sealey to go out with another girl made Alex squirm with discomfort. What right did she have to try to fix him? She'd broken him. The last thing he'd want to do is follow her advice.

Alex ached inside as she thought of Sealey, but she wasn't unreasonable about it. It didn't occur to her to regret her decision and she suspected that Sealey wouldn't resent her for making it, decent guy that he was. But that didn't change the fact that his hopes were now as dead as hers. And she'd caused the entire mess. She'd hurt someone she cared about.

And there it was. The realization that she cared for Sealey, despite all the blunt criticism he'd given her, was a bit of a revelation. He was her friend. She wanted him to be happy. He'd helped her when no one else could, and despite the fact that she'd lost Lucas, it was thanks to Sealey that she'd had any time with Lucas at all. She should be grateful to him.

156

She was. The thought made the disappointment she'd caused him that much more reprehensible.

Alex pressed her foot harder on the accelerator. She needed her mom. She needed to be surrounded by people who didn't know what an idiot she'd been. She needed a few days of forgetting all that she'd lost—time where she didn't have to think about all she owed to the man who would likely never speak to her again.

* * * * *

"Al!"

"Mom, Al's here!"

Alex smiled with rusty face muscles as she pulled her suitcase out of the car. The voices of her younger siblings were music to her ears.

Abby ran up and grabbed her around the waist. "I'm so glad you're here!" the nine-year-old cried. "Austin kept saying you'd probably change your mind again and not come!"

"Why would I do that?" Alex said as she wrapped her arms around her younger sister. She smiled wider as her seventeen-year-old brother jumped the three porch steps and headed in her direction.

"Oh my gosh, you're huge," she said as he squeezed her, Abby squished between them. "How tall are you now?"

"Six five," he said with pride. "An inch taller than Aaron. He hates it."

"How's Aaron doing, anyway?" Alex asked as she headed toward the house, Abby's hand in hers. Austin grabbed her suitcase and tucked it under his arm. "I haven't seen him since his wedding last year, and I've been horrible at keeping in touch. Are he and Emily coming?"

"Nah, they couldn't afford to make the trip from Florida," Austin said, opening the door for her. "That's what happens when you get married fresh off your mission to a girl straight out of high school." He smirked.

"Well, they seem happy enough," Alex said, smacking him on the shoulder.

"Oh, they are," Austin agreed. "So much so that it makes you want to puke, just being in the same room with them. Trust me, I would know. I visited them this past summer."

Alex laughed, relishing the feeling of it. She'd taken a week-long break from such things.

"Mom and Dad offered to fly them out for the holidays, but Aaron said no," Austin continued. "I think he's determined to show everyone that he and Emily can stand on their own feet. He's still smarting from all the 'you're too young to get married' comments they got."

"Good for them, wanting to be self-sufficient," Alex said, looking around the familiar living room. "It's a good quality."

"Al!" Grace Foamer's voice came from the doorway to the kitchen as she wiped her hands on a towel. "Oh, honey, it's so good to see you!" She swept forward and enveloped Alex in her arms. Encircled in warmth and love, Alex felt like she could finally breathe again.

Grace, slim, pale, and red-haired, was even taller than Alex. She had played basketball and volleyball in college, but had given up sports after marrying Alex's father, who had also played basketball for the same university.

"Al!" the deep, booming voice of Alexander Foamer immediately turned Alex's mouth up at the corners.

"Hi, Dad," she said, turning to hug him.

"It's great to have you home, kiddo," he said, setting her back on her feet. "This is the last time we allow you to take a two-year break from family holiday gatherings."

"Duly noted," Alex said, smiling up at him. She turned quickly to face her mother, knowing that the more time she spent talking to her dad, the more likely it would be that he would ask how Sealey was doing. And she really didn't want to talk about Sealey right now.

"You got here just in time," Grace said, sliding her hand up Alex's arm. "I just pulled the lasagna out of the oven. Let's eat, and then I'll let you help me get some things ready for Thanksgiving tomorrow."

"Sounds perfect," Alex replied, her smile feeling like a saving grace on her face.

* * * * *

Thanksgiving with her family was exactly what Alex needed. The warm familiarity seemed to have the combined effect of a painkiller and elective amnesia. But this only worked as long as she wasn't alone for too long. As soon as she had enough time to sit quietly and think, everything began pressing in on her again. It was during one such moment that Grace finally caught her.

A single tear was sliding down Alex's face as she sat on the couch, her knees tucked under her chin. She stared silently out the front window, thinking of her life in Logan, sans Lucas and Sealey. It kept haunting her. And she was completely out of her depth on how to make things right.

"Alex?" Grace asked, coming to sit next to her on the couch. She slid her thumb gently under Alex's eye, wiping the tear away. "Wanna tell me about it?"

Alex bit her lip, wanting more than anything to partake of her mother's wisdom, but knowing that if she did, she would have to admit all the stupid, thoughtless things she'd done over the past few months.

"Oh, Mom," she sniffed. "I've made such an idiot of myself lately."

"Well, the beauty of such situations, is that they're almost always temporary," Grace answered, waving a hand carelessly through the air. "And at least you know about it. That means there's hope of improvement."

"I'm not so sure about that," Alex said quietly. "I've burned the bridge big time on this one."

"Oh, really?" Grace said, raising an eyebrow. "The person on the other side of that bridge doesn't believe in forgiveness?"

"I doubt it. He's pretty hard core. And I don't think I've earned it."

"Ah," Grace said, as though she suddenly understood. "It's a boy. Then it's even easier than I thought."

"What?" Alex said in confusion, looking at her mother. "What difference does that make?"

"One of the truly blessed gifts given to the male gender is the ability to easily and quickly forgive," Grace explained. "Sure, there are exceptions, but the chance that you've encountered one is pretty remote."

"You think he'll forgive me, just because he's a guy?" Alex asked skeptically.

"I'd say it's highly likely," Grace responded, rubbing Alex's shoulder. "While women are apt to hold grudges, men tend to be the opposite. They take offense quickly and somewhat violently, but given some time, they let it go and move on. It's forgotten." She waved her fingers haphazardly back over her shoulder as though she were flicking away a fly.

"Seems like a pretty dangerous generalization to make," Alex commented. "What if he's not like that?"

"If I might pry a little bit," Grace began hesitantly, scooting a little closer to Alex. "Would the boy on the other side of this burned bridge be named Sealey, by chance?"

"Oh, Dad mentioned him to you, did he?" Alex said tonelessly.

"Yes, he mentioned that he met a lovely young friend of yours when he stopped by to visit you."

"I'm not sure *lovely* is the word I would use to describe him," Alex muttered, thinking of all the sarcastic remarks and looks she'd received from Sealey over the past few months. "But he is my friend. A good friend. And I definitely caused some trouble for him. Which brings me back to my conundrum. What if he's not the 'forgive and forget' type?"

Grace smiled kindly at her but didn't answer her question. "Sealey is quite an unusual name," she mentioned instead. "What does it mean?"

"I dunno," Alex shrugged, sighing. "Judging from his nature, probably something like 'overly blunt, bossy, and sarcastic; likely to hold grudges.' "

Grace chuckled. "It sounds like you have an interesting history with this one."

"You have no idea," Alex muttered.

"Well, when you see him again, my advice would be to just be kind," Grace advised. "So many problems in this world would be solved with a little kindness. It's a universal healer."

Alex wasn't sure if something as simple as kindness would be enough to solve her problem, but she was willing to give it a shot.

"Thanks, Mom."

* * * * *

Alex returned to Logan the following Sunday, feeling refreshed and ready to face a new phase of life. Although she was still nervous to encounter Sealey and officially ask him to forgive her, she knew that's what she needed to do.

But she couldn't find him. She'd tried to call him several times since her conversation with her mother, but he'd never picked up. She'd been tempted to show up at his apartment when she returned to Logan, but she was too afraid of encountering Lucas. It was true that as she more fully accepted the idea that Lucas and Olivia belonged together, the aching around the edges of her heart became easier and easier to bear.

In fact, the time spent in Malibu, away from the situation, had allowed her to have an epiphany of sorts. She had spent a lot of time thinking through the last few months, focusing specifically on all the key moments spent with Lucas. In those ponderings, Alex detected a red flag that should have alerted her to the likely doom of their relationship, even if Olivia had not been in the picture. That red flag had been a bit of a saving grace in her attempt to forgive herself for the part she'd played in destroying Sealey's hopes.

Her realization was that Lucas's hesitancy, from the beginning, to support her in her career goals and dreams was a definite indication that eventually, their relationship would have fizzled. She knew herself. She knew that eventually she would have learned to resent him for holding her back. The thought that she didn't owe her and Sealey's current states of relative misery to her choice alone made her feel much better. But that didn't necessarily mean she wanted to willfully encounter Lucas just yet. Therefore, she would avoid his apartment in her attempt to get in touch with Sealey.

She hadn't seen or heard from Sealey now for over a week, and she was becoming seriously concerned. While she had called him numerous times, she'd only left one message, and it had been pretty pathetic. She told him again that she was sorry for ruining everything and that she hoped he was okay. She then asked him to call her. He had obviously ignored it.

Now, sitting on a freezing park bench in complete dejection, wanting to get somewhere warm, but dreading the pitying looks she was still receiving from her roommates, she wondered if maybe the time had come to move on. She had thoroughly messed up in Logan, Utah, but maybe that mess was exactly the motivation she needed to do something with her life. To start working toward that dream she'd told Sealey about all those months ago.

The speaking series was the perfect answer to her conundrum. She had almost reached her deadline for getting back to Dr. Welch—she'd actually almost forgotten all about it in the wake of losing Lucas—but now, what reason did she have to stay in Logan? The idea flashed across her mind in ultra-bright neon. Without a second thought, she grabbed for her phone and dialed.

"Fiona Welch," came the voice on the other end.

"Hi, Dr. Welch," Alex said, breathlessly. "This is Alex Foamer. I'm so sorry it's taken me this long to get back to you. I'd hoped to get my answer to you long before your deadline, but I've had some personal issues these past couple of weeks that have kind of laid me flat."

"Good to hear from you, Alex," returned Dr. Welch. "Don't worry about it. I'm running a bit behind schedule myself on the symposium. I hope things are going better for you now."

"Oh, much better, thanks," Alex said honestly. Her outlook on life was about a hundred times better than it had been five minutes earlier. "I am very interested in participating in the symposium. Is it possible you might still have a place for me?" Like a fifth-grader, she crossed her fingers.

"Absolutely!" Dr. Welch cried. "Oh, I'm so happy you decided to accept. I'm having a hard time finding people due to the fact that the symposium happens over the holidays."

"Well, I'd love to take part in it," Alex replied. "If you can get me the information, I'll be wherever you need me to be whenever you need me there."

"That's what I like to hear!" Dr. Welch laughed. "I'll email you the information packet and once you have all the necessary forms filled out, we'll get your travel all scheduled. Make sure to take a look at the subjects we're planning to cover and get back to me as soon as possible on which ones you'd like to tackle. You'll need to get started on planning your presentations here in the next week or so."

"Oh, I'm so excited!" Alex squealed. "I can't wait to get started!"

After they hung up, Alex sat fidgeting on the park bench, her mind much lighter and airier than it had been in previous weeks. She had a plan, and it felt *so good*.

And then the downer hit. The series would only last three months. Twenty cities. And then she would be back in Logan. What then? Would Lucas and Olivia be married by then? Would Sealey be talking to her by that point?

"Hey."

Alex's head shot up. Sealey Witchburn was coming toward her across the frozen ground, a sheepish look on his face. She'd never seen him look sheepish. But the look seemed appropriate. He *should* be sheepish after what he'd put her through.

"Sealey!" she cried, relief and frustration filling her. "Where have you been?! I've been *worried* about you!"

Sealey looked surprised. "You have?" he questioned, brow furrowed. "Why?"

"You just disappeared!" Alex cried. Sealey seated himself next to her and leaned back casually against the bench, eyeing her strangely. "You gave me this wounded, confused look, walked away, and I haven't seen you or heard from you since! For all I knew, you were suicidal!" she shrieked.

"Really, Alex?" Sealey said, his eyebrow raised. His expression became suddenly much more recognizable. Confidence. Amusement. "Do I strike you as the suicidal sort?"

"Well, no, but next time you decide to disappear like that, just let me know where you're going, okay? Then I won't freak out so much. I called and called and I left you a message and you never called back!"

The sheepish look returned to his face. "Sorry," he apologized. "I went out of town on business and left my phone on the plane. The airline is mailing it back to me. They said I should have it back by tomorrow morning."

"And you don't understand the concept of a pay phone?" Alex said, giving him a dirty look. "Or, heck, just *borrowing* a phone? You know, 'cause it's not like every single person you come in contact with doesn't have one."

"You know what it sounds like?" Sealey asked, smiling more genuinely at her now. "It sounds like you missed me."

Alex stopped short and stared at him. "You think I missed you?" she said, her voice sounding strangled. "You think *that* is what this is about?" Her thoughts felt panicky, but she wasn't quite sure why.

"Yeah," he said, his smile widening. "But that's okay, Foamer. You can miss me. I'm okay with that. In fact, it's actually really good news."

"Oh really?" Alex asked with sarcasm, fully expecting some in return. "And why's that?"

"Because I missed you." There was no sarcasm. None. Just straightforward, wide-eyed sincerity.

Alex gawked at him. He had missed her? A strange warmth was filling her chest. She watched him, sitting there, unconcerned. There was something different in the air. Sealey was on edge. He didn't look it, but she could feel it. An odd, electric tension was emanating from him.

"You missed me?" she clarified, narrowing her eyes at him.

"Didn't I just say that?" he said, smiling teasingly at her. "Yes, I did. Very much. Because believe it or not, I've gotten pretty used to you, Foamer." He winked at her.

"Oh, well . . . that's . . ." Her mind was blank. Confusion swam in her head. *Nice? Interesting? Really, really . . .* "Unexpected," she finally finished. What was Sealey doing? Why was he sitting here next to her, perfectly composed, with a weird smile on his face? Why didn't he appear to be devastated about Olivia and Lucas?

"You look like you have something else to say," Sealey prompted at her perplexed expression. The odd, bright smile was still firmly attached to his face.

"Olivia." It was the only word Alex could get out. But she thought it would probably indicate the direction of her thoughts.

"Ah, Olivia," Sealey said. He nodded slowly, as though mulling over his next words. "I lied about Olivia," he said smoothly.

Whatever words she had been expecting, those were not the ones.

"I'm sorry, what?" she said, uncomprehending.

"I lied," Sealey said straightforwardly. "I told you I was in love with Olivia and that I wanted to take her away from Lucas. I lied." He shrugged as he dropped this bombshell, as though its impact were a sad inevitability. For some reason, the careless motion calmed Alex enough to clear her head and allow her to think. Because while he appeared to be uncaring, she knew he wasn't. Something in the taut position of his shoulders told her he was every bit as aware of the import of his words as she was.

"So . . . you never planned to take her away from Lucas?" Alex clarified.

"No," he stated. "I never planned to steal her away. I never even considered something like that to be possible."

"So then, why—" Alex began, but Sealey interrupted her.

"I was never in love with her, either," he said calmly. "Olivia is an amazing woman, but she's Lucas's amazing woman. She always has been."

Alex looked at him incredulously. She knew he was trying to tell her something beyond what he was saying. Otherwise the electricity in the air would have fizzled by now. "Okay, but . . . but . . . *why* would you do this? *Why* would you bother to tell me you were in love with Olivia if you weren't?"

"Because I needed a plausible excuse," Sealey said, looking at her earnestly. "I needed a reason for why I was helping you with the Lucas project and that was the only one I could come up with on short notice. You caught me off guard with your demands to know my reasoning, and that was the first thing I thought of."

Alex stared at him. She understood the words coming out of his mouth, but she had no idea what he was trying to tell her.

"Sealey," she said, quite impressed with her ability to keep her voice calm and regulated. "Please. *Please* tell me what's going on here. Why are you telling me this now? Why did you lie to me? And more than anything, if you weren't in love with Olivia, *why* did you spend three months attempting to bring me and Lucas together?"

Sealey smiled softly and genuinely at the confused look on her face. Again, a reaction Alex had not been expecting. He was a completely different person than the depressed, defeated, disappointed man she had been anticipating. He seemed almost . . . happy.

"Alex," he said, looking into her eyes. He moved forward, taking her hand. He raised his other hand and brushed his fingers across her face. Strange tingles and sparks raced up and down her arms and legs. She almost jerked away, so unexpected was the contact. "It was because of you. For me, it's always been you."

"*What's* always been me?" she pressed. She glanced down at their clasped hands, feeling as though she was missing something both very important and very obvious. She couldn't help thinking that if he would just *back up* and let her thoughts clear a bit, she would immediately understand what he was trying to say. But he wasn't moving and her mind remained clouded with a mixture of confusion, numbness, and sheer panic. "What are you talking about, Sealey?"

"I never intended to let Lucas have you. This entire process, the last three months," he replied, his eyes crinkling at the corners. "For me, it's all been about me and you. I only ever wanted you."

{ Chapter FIFTEEN }

HE SPOKE THE last words softly, in a tone Alex had never actually heard him use before. It was warm and sincere. Vulnerable.

Alex was holding her breath, unconsciously hoping that might aid her verbal comprehension. "How does that make any semblance of sense?" she finally asked. "The whole point of the project was to bring Lucas and me together, and you and Olivia together. It couldn't have possibly accomplished anything else."

The warmth of his hand against her cheek was muddying her thought processes. She felt her legs begin to shake slightly in response to his touch.

"That was *your* goal," Sealey said, giving her a pointed look. "It was never mine. It's difficult to explain." Sealey looked away, out into the park, taking a deep breath. He backed away, contenting himself with holding her hand in his.

"Alex, I've been interested in you . . . forever," he finished lamely. "Almost from the first time I ever saw you. But you never looked twice at me. Your eyes were only for Lucas. I know you thought your crush was a secret, but, really, it was obvious. Everyone could see it." He squeezed her hand sympathetically. "I didn't think I could manage to make you see *me* until that particular dream of yours had died. And I didn't think I would be able to convince you to just give up on Lucas. I wasn't sure exactly what to do." He gave her a wry half-smile. "But then you solved

166

that problem for me. You approached *me* on the subject. So I took my opportunity—likely the only one I'd get."

"But it still doesn't make sense!" Alex exclaimed in frustration. "How would you helping me get Lucas's attention benefit *you* in any way? If anything, it was pushing me away from you!"

"Not necessarily," Sealey answered. And now he started to look nervous. "With you taking orders from me, I had, or I *thought* I had, complete control over the situation. I could guide you where I wanted you to go. You could get to know Lucas, but you could also get to know me. And I thought that maybe you might decide that I was a better match for you."

"But I didn't," Alex stated plainly. "You must have not seen that one coming."

"No," Sealey said, smiling ruefully. "Nor did I foresee how absolutely you would captivate my best friend." He rubbed the back of his neck, his expression self-deprecating. "All this time, I was operating under the assumption that once you and Lucas got to know each other, you'd realize what a terrible match you were. He is very much a homebody, has no ambitions to leave Utah at all. You want to travel, see the world and conquer it. He is quiet and contemplative, humble and modest, and you are . . . well, not." He smiled apologetically at her. "His family is very resistant to the idea of him ending up with anyone but Olivia, his sister is a manipulative little snot, and his parents are haughty and disapproving. And I mean that in the best possible sense," Sealey tacked on to the end, looking slightly guilty. "None of those characteristics seemed calculated to attract you. So I thought I was safe."

Alex watched him as he explained, wondering how she would react once all of it sunk in. She seemed to be operating on a significant time delay, and she honestly didn't know what she would feel when she actually had a chance to process what she was hearing.

"You underestimated Lucas's charms," Alex replied simply. "And mine, apparently."

"Very much so. Especially yours," Sealey agreed. "I have to admit, I never expected you to pique Lucas's interest like you did. I was relying on his devotion to Olivia to keep your relationship platonic. But I was wrong." He shrugged helplessly. "Luke fell for you. Hard. Everything spun out of my control, and I saw how stupid I'd been to think that he would fail to see how incredible you are. A guy would have to be crazy to turn down a chance to be with you."

Alex looked at him steadily. While she had never, for one instant, considered the idea that Sealey might be interested in her like that, she found that the thought wasn't necessarily an abhorrent one. At all. In fact, she thought she might be able to get used to it with relative ease. But that didn't mean she was just going to fall into his arms. There were so many things about the situation that still didn't make sense to her.

"So when did you stop trying to control everything?" Alex asked, clearing her throat to hide her discomposure.

"About the time Luke started asking you out on his own," Sealey replied. "Once he started showing interest in you without any help from me, I knew I had miscalculated. My goal had been to simply make you realize that your chances with Luke were slim, and to show you that you two weren't a good match anyway. But I failed to take your appeal into consideration, and really, I completely disregarded Luke's side of the equation. Once he began to sit up and take notice, I realized I was in trouble."

"But you stepped back," Alex pointed out, remembering how Sealey had started refusing to take part in the project after Lucas had asked her out at the gym. "Once Lucas started asking me out by himself, you just let him! Didn't it occur to you to try to sabotage the whole thing?"

Sealey looked at her incredulously. "Well, sure, but I'd like to think I'm not a completely horrible person."

Alex raised her eyebrow at him. A vision was forming in her head, a vision of Sealey, holding various puppet strings attached to her arms, legs, and mouth, pulling one or the other to make her dance. To make her dance just like he wanted her to.

"I don't know," she answered, her voice taking on a scathing note. "Something about this whole situation smacks of a horrible person."

"Now, wait," Sealey defended, holding up a hand. "I admit, I entered into this thing with a manipulative, diabolical plan. It was wrong. I know that." He reached forward and picked up her hand again. "But, Alex, I panicked. I was desperate to get my chance with you, but I knew it would never come unless I could get you to give up on your fantasy life with Lucas. I should have just been honest. I know that now." He sighed, wincing slightly. "Isn't that pretty much always the answer?" He looked tired as he said it.

Alex bit the inside of her cheek and looked down. How was she qualified to judge him? She hadn't exactly been honest in her dealings with Lucas either.

"And once I knew that Lucas was sincerely interested in you, I did try to approach the situation honorably. You know, at first." Sealey cringed, seemingly as a memory hit him.

"Explain that, please," Alex commanded. "Because I totally missed it, if you did. You were openly competing for my affections at some point?"

"Well, kind of," he replied, rubbing his neck again. "I'm not very good at the open approach, you know?" He glanced at her, his gaze uncertain. "It's probably one of my biggest weaknesses. I sit here, crouching behind this tower of superiority and sarcasm. But, really, I'm just this pathetic excuse for a man who's terrified to be vulnerable."

His admission was proof to Alex that he was finally willing to face that particular fear. She thought back to the rough, sarcastic King of the Ice People Sealey had been before, compared to the picture of sincerity he was now. The Sealey she used to fear and the Sealey she now actually worried about (what a thought!). It was astonishing how far they'd come in a few months.

"Once I knew that Lucas sincerely wanted to date you, all I could do was try to distract you like any other guy would. I tried to make you jealous," he continued, wincing slightly as he anticipated her reaction.

The anger was immediately back, hot and fierce.

"Ashley," Alex seethed, narrowing her eyes at him. "I *knew* there was more going on there than you let on."

"Hey, before you get all over me for my cruelty in leading Ashley on, let me just head you off. She knew about it. She was in on it," Sealey replied, holding up his hands as though to protect himself.

"Really?" Alex said, surprised enough that she forgot to sound angry. "But she honestly likes you. Why would she help you make another girl jealous?"

"Well, first of all, Ashley doesn't really like me as much as you think she does, and second, she wants Lucas to end up with Olivia even more than *he* probably does," Sealey answered matter-of-factly. "Besides, Ashley knows how beautiful and smart she is. She's not worried about finding a husband. And I don't honestly think she believes she and I are right for each other. She just likes to flirt."

"So she agreed to hang all over you and you acted like you had decided to reciprocate, all to make me jealous?" Alex asked, disbelieving. She couldn't believe Sealey had gone to all this trouble, just for a chance with her. If anything, this entire debacle was proof that honesty was considerably less effort.

"It was the only thing I could think of." Sealey sighed. "Again, apparently I'm of the male variety that will do anything to avoid the horror of having to actually say how he really feels. Of course, all my brilliant plan did was make you mad, because you thought I was leading Ashley on." Sealey rolled his eyes at the memory but smiled. "Actually, that part amazed me. She was *horrible* to you, and yet all you cared about was how much she was going to be hurting once she realized I wasn't sincere." He shook his head. "It just proved to me again what an extraordinary person you are."

Alex watched him, eyebrows furrowed, still chewing on her lip determinedly. How did she feel about all this? She felt around inside for some kind of idea. She could locate the anger, the frustration, the shock, and the confusion, but what was that niggling at the edges? It felt a bit like . . . relief? Amusement? Hope, maybe?

"Look, Alex. I had pretty much come to terms with the fact I was going to lose you," Sealey said when her silence became too much for him. "When Lucas told me that he was going to break things off with Olivia when she got home, I knew I had just made everything worse. I hated myself for what I'd done, but at the same time, I loved seeing you so happy. It was probably the most conflicted, confusing state of mind I've ever been in." He grinned weakly at her. "I couldn't believe how horribly wrong my plan had gone for me. But not just for me. I mean, I wasn't the only one who was going to suffer. Not only was I losing you, but I would be the means of seriously injuring one of my oldest friends. Because as good and kind as Olivia is, and as much as she would want Lucas to be happy, losing him would have been very painful for her."

Sealey shook his head. "I couldn't believe I'd been so willing to risk so many people's happiness, just to get what I wanted."

"Hmmm, that's interesting," Alex said with a significant look. "Because I seem to remember you accusing me of exactly the same thing."

"Well, I was in the prime situation to recognize it, wasn't I?" Sealey replied with a smile. "Really, this entire thing was a lose-lose situation for you and me."

"How so?" Alex asked.

"Because if you and Lucas had ended up together, I would have lost you," Sealey explained with a shrug. "And you, in turn, would have been unhappy with him. I truly believe that. But you losing Lucas as you did wasn't any better because you've been miserable, and I've been miserable watching you be miserable." He shook his head, but a soft smile suddenly broke on his face. "Although, I have to say, I can't quite find the words to explain to you how grateful I am that you are no longer in a relationship with my best friend." He slid a little bit closer to her on the bench. The sun was going down, and the air was getting considerably colder. Sealey's nose was beginning to turn red.

Alex watched him, mulling over what he had just said. She agreed with him. She knew she would have been unhappy with Lucas . . . eventually. Everything would have played out exactly as he said, in either scenario. But Alex wasn't ready to stop asking questions yet, so she didn't acknowledge this. "So why did you *really* show up on my doorstep that day? The day I was supposed to be telling Olivia about me and Lucas?"

"I actually did come to see how you were doing," he answered. "I hoped I might be able to *help* you get over Lucas. You know." Sealey gave her another self-deprecating smile. "But when Kacey told me what you were about to do, I got to realize all over again what an idiot I am. I really thought you were going to do it. I thought you were going to tear them apart, and I had so many conflicting emotions about it. I was furious at you for even considering doing such a thing, but at the same time, I completely understood why you would do it. I was terrified for Luke, knowing that Olivia would do exactly what you wanted her to. She would just step aside. I was heartbroken for Olivia, because that's what she would be. And I was livid at myself for causing the whole mess." Sealey shook his head, his expression far away as he remembered.

"The truth is, I wasn't actually waiting for you, when you got back," he said, turning back to her. "I just hadn't been able to find the energy to leave yet. I was dreading going home and seeing Luke, knowing how devastated he was going to be."

"But I arrived before you had a chance to escape," Alex guessed.

"Right," Sealey agreed. "And then you said the most wonderful sentence I think I've ever heard. You said, 'I couldn't do it.' That one sentence fixed absolutely *everything*. I could have told you how much I loved you right then, but suddenly I realized I didn't know how. Nor did I think, as heartbroken as you still were, that you'd be receptive. So I left. Very awkwardly and ungracefully." Sealey shrugged. "And here we are."

Alex was staring at him. Yet again. "You love me?" she asked quietly. She just sat and watched him as he appeared to gather his courage.

"Yes," he said firmly, reaching out and pulling her against him, his warmth creeping into her chest, his arms encircling her. His face leaned close to hers as he whispered softly. "I love you, Alex Foamer."

* * * * *

"You know," Alex said as they walked back to her apartment twenty minutes later, hand-in-hand. "You really are so clueless about girls."

"Undoubtedly," Sealey replied, nodding seriously. "But how in particular have I made it so apparent this time?"

"I didn't want time and space, Sealey," she insisted, shaking her head. "I was worried about you. More than I was worried about *me*, I was worried about you. I thought I'd broken you beyond repair. I thought you'd never talk to me again. You'd think all the 'I'm so sorrys' I offered would have clued you in. Yes, being without Lucas hurt, but it was easier knowing I'd chosen it. But being without you . . . I didn't really choose that part. It was an unfortunate by-product of destroying all your hopes. Or what I *thought* were your hopes at the time. I spent all that time apart thinking about you."

"I played my part better than I meant to," Sealey admitted, his teeth flashing white in the darkness. "I can't believe I managed to convince you so fully that I was in love with Olivia. I hated talking about it, because I was sure I was going to give myself away each time."

"I could tell you didn't like talking about her, but I thought it was because you were big and tough and didn't like to discuss your feelings."

"You obviously know me a lot better than I know you." Sealey chuckled ruefully. "I need to work on that."

"Well, you'll have plenty of time to work on it," Alex said straightfowardly. "But it will have to be over the phone for a little while."

"Are you banishing me or something?" Sealey asked, his face uncertain. "Where am I going?"

"You're not going anywhere." Alex laughed, rolling her eyes. "But I am. I accepted that traveling speaker series job earlier today. Right before you showed up, actually."

"Really?" Sealey's face broke into a brilliant smile and he stopped in his tracks, beaming at her. "I didn't even know that you got the job! Alex, I'm so proud of you!" He immediately swept her into a tight hug. "This is everything you've ever wanted and worked for. This is fantastic!"

"Thank you," Alex replied softly, her heart warming even further as she contemplated Sealey's reaction to her news as opposed to what Lucas's had been. That told her everything she needed to know. That was love.

* * * * *

Alex walked into her living room, a sappy smile on her face as she thought of her conversation with Sealey. She floated blissfully through the apartment and into the kitchen, opening the fridge and staring dreamily into it for a few seconds before shutting it again. She wasn't hungry. Just happy.

She turned to head for her bedroom and nearly ran straight into Meredith, who had Kacey, Sage, Jaclyn, and Rachel trailing close behind her. All of them appeared to have followed her into the kitchen with confused expressions on their faces.

"What the heck is going on with you?" Kacey asked, shaking her head. "What's with that schmaltzy perma-grin on your face?"

"Wait, I know, I know!" Sage cried. "Lucas called, right? He and Olivia have broken up and he wants you back!"

Meredith shrieked and grabbed Alex by the shoulders. "Is it true? Did Lucas call?!"

Alex felt disoriented for a second. She'd completely forgotten about Lucas Riley for possibly the first time in an entire year.

"Huh?" she asked, shaking her head slightly to clear it. "Oh, uh, no. Lucas didn't call."

Her roommates seemed to deflate before her very eyes. Each face once again took on the look of pity it had been wearing for the past couple of weeks. She was really learning to hate those sympathetic expressions.

"It's something much better than that," she said quickly.

"Something better," Kacey repeated, her look doubtful. "Better than Lucas Riley?" She narrowed her eyes. "You certainly *look* like Alex Foamer, but, seriously, who are you?"

"Alex Foamer has been remade," Alex replied, her voice dreamy.

"Oh no," Jaclyn groaned, putting a hand to her face in despair. "I recognize that look. Here we go again. Who's captured your fancy this time?"

"You'll never guess," Alex said slyly.

Her roommates continued to look at her strangely in silence.

"Seriously, Al, what is going on with you?" Meredith finally asked, starting to look truly concerned. "You were approaching zombie status when you left for Thanksgiving, and now you're . . . just . . . freaking me out."

Alex smiled warmly at her best friend. "I think I found my fish, Mer," she said, and her voice sounded so warm and so happy that it almost seemed to heat her from the inside as she spoke.

"You found your what?" Jaclyn demanded, confused, but Meredith caught on immediately.

"And . . . I take it that fish isn't named Lucas Riley?" Meredith clarified, her mouth turning up at the corners. Relief and excitement mingled on her face.

Alex shook her head slowly with a sly grin.

"Then it must be . . ." Meredith trailed off, looking at Alex with an expression of horror.

Alex nodded.

"*Who?*" Sage demanded, looking frantically between them. "*Who is the gosh dang fish?*"

"Sealey," Meredith whispered incredulously. "You and *Sealey?*" The expression of disbelief appeared to be permanently cemented on her face.

Alex nodded again, her smile widening even further. "Me and Sealey," she confirmed.

Her roommates stared at her in stunned silence.

"She's joking," Kacey finally muttered to Rachel, who stood beside her. "I mean, she's totally joking . . . right?"

Rachel just looked at Alex, eyes wide and blinking. Sage looked horrified; Jaclyn looked amused.

But Meredith was pensive. She stood there, biting her lip and considering. Finally, a soft smile began to creep across her face, shining forth in all its glory until she was beaming up at Alex.

"You found your fish!" she exclaimed and stepped forward, throwing her arms around Alex. "I *told* you there were other fish in the sea! I knew there was someone else out there for you! You finally found your fish and it's Sealey Witchburn!"

* * * * *

Alex called Sealey the minute she received her symposium information packet from Dr. Welch and practically read him the entire thing.

"Okay, now go over the cities you're visiting again and the dates you'll be there. Slowly," Sealey instructed her.

"Okay, why?" Alex asked, laughing.

"I may or may not be calendaring them," Sealey said, clearing his throat. "No judgment, please."

"None whatsoever." Alex laughed again. She couldn't believe that just a few days before she'd been a mopey, depressed head case. It was amazing what a little bit of romance could do for a person.

Alex slowly read all the cities and dates disclosed in the packet.

"Hey!" Sealey cried enthusiastically. She'd never heard him so cheerful, but instead of making her want to tease him, it just made her want to sync her mood with his. In the last few days, he had become her happy pill. "Houston, we have intersection!"

"What?" Alex asked, confused.

"You're in Phoenix and then Salt Lake the third week of February and in LA the second week of March!" Sealey informed her.

"I know I am," she replied, still confused.

"Well, turns out I will be in those cities at the exact same time you are."

Suddenly it dawned on Alex why he had been calendaring her travel schedule. He had been looking for opportunities to see her during the three months she was gone. The thought turned her into a melty, soppy puddle on the floor.

"Can I request a date for those weeks right now?" she asked. "Or do you have a waiting list?"

Sealey was quiet for a minute, but when he did speak, his voice was full of so much affection that Alex could nearly feel it shining down on her. "I'm all yours."

{ Chapter SIXTEEN }

ALEX LEFT FOR her first symposium location, Boston, in the second week of December. The conference began on the East Coast and would work its way west over the next three months. Sealey insisted on dropping her off at the airport in Salt Lake City, saying he had business in the city anyway. Alex suspected he just wanted the extra couple of hours together before their long separation. She knew she did.

"Knock 'em dead, knockout," Sealey said, leaning against his black Lexus after pulling her bags out of the backseat. "Call me when you land, okay?"

"I will," Alex replied nervously. Butterflies danced in her middle, but it wasn't because of the impending trip. Before she could talk herself out of it, she stepped quickly forward, pressed up against Sealey's relaxed form, and planted a kiss directly on his lips. Their first kiss.

Whatever he had been about to say died immediately in his throat. After she backed away, he blinked silently at her for a moment before reaching out and pulling her in for a much more substantial kiss. A few minutes later, Alex stumbled into the airport, doubting she would even need the airplane to get to Boston. The way she was feeling, she could probably just float there all by herself.

* * * * *

In the two weeks before Christmas, Alex spent four days each in Boston, New York, and Philadelphia. She spent a prodigious amount of time on the phone with Sealey between her presentations, and it wasn't uncommon to feel her phone vibrate in her pocket while she stood at the front of an auditorium, lecturing on plant-based diets and nutritional labeling. After her stint in Philadelphia, Alex flew to Malibu to spend the holidays with her family, wishing that she had time to stop off in Utah for a quick Sealey fix.

She exasperated her relatives for three full days, gushing about how much she loved her new job, Sealey, the East Coast, Sealey, her coworkers, and Sealey. Everything about her life felt white-hot shiny bright, and she couldn't help but bask in the reflected glow. And then, as if things couldn't get any better, the day after Christmas, Sealey himself showed up.

"What's up, Foamer?" he asked when she opened the door to see him standing on the porch, hands in his jeans pockets.

She screeched in surprise and threw her arms around his neck. "I've really, really, really missed you!" she cried as she squeezed the life out of him.

Sealey laughed and kissed her hard. "Likewise," he said quietly, his eyes earnest as he stared into hers. And despite her very best efforts, Alex giggled.

The week spent with Sealey and her family was celestial for Alex. Being the enthusiastic golfer that he was, Sealey succeeded in even further impressing Alexander, and his amazing free-throw abilities completely stunned her brother Austin. But it was Sealey's loving treatment of Alex that forever endeared him to her mother. When the two of them left Malibu on the day after New Years, he for Logan and she for Washington, DC, Alex's depression was tempered only slightly by the excitement of seeing a new city and presenting on her favorite topic.

Over the next several weeks, Alex also experienced Atlanta, Miami, Nashville, Detroit, Chicago, St. Louis, New Orleans, Houston, Kansas City, and Denver. She met remarkable people with fascinating life stories, and it wasn't uncommon for her nightly conversations with Sealey to begin with, "I have so much to tell you! You will *not* believe the amazing woman I met today!" Her soul felt constantly drunk with joy as she shared her passion, contributed to a cause she loved, and continually shared her new experiences with her favorite guy. A guy who ended nearly every conversation with, "I love you, Alex. I'm so proud of you."

By the time Alex arrived in Phoenix in mid-February, she felt as though she had earned the title of "Professional Business Traveler." While she still loved being able to speak and influence so many people on childhood nutrition, she was beginning to grow tired of living out of her suitcase. She longed to be settled back in her little apartment with her friends. And more than anything, she longed to see Sealey, to speak to him face-to-face and see the emotions flit across his face as they spoke.

As Alex watched the auditorium empty after finishing her class on healthy school lunches her first day in Phoenix, she did a double-take as she saw the white blond head sitting in the back row. He stood up when he saw her looking at him and offered a wide smile. Disregarding everyone in the vicinity, she ran immediately into his arms, thoroughly entertaining everybody in the room.

"I can't believe you came to my class! I'm glad I didn't know you were there, or it would have significantly hindered my coherency," she joked.

Sealey laughed and pulled her close, his lips pressed to her forehead. "That would have been a real shame, because you were fantastic. You're quite the dynamic speaker, Foamer."

Alex blushed with pleasure, the now-familiar feeling of being filled to the brim with warmth flooding through her.

They spent each of the four evenings they were both in Phoenix together and Sealey actually changed his flight to match hers when she left for the next leg of the symposium in Salt Lake City.

Her first evening in town, Sealey picked her up at the hotel and drove her to Logan so she could spend some time with her roommates. His willingness to sacrifice time with her endeared him to her more than ever.

Meredith let out possibly the highest-pitched noise that Alex had ever heard when she walked into the apartment. Alex was immediately accosted by five girls of varying heights and strengths, all vying to squeeze a part of her.

"Come baaaaack!" whined Sage. "I have no idea how many cities you've been to by this point, but I'm pretty sure that number is plenty. We miss you!"

"It's really good to see you," Kacey said sincerely, surprising Alex. While Kacey was a softie underneath the tough exterior, she rarely let her cushy side actually show through.

"The symposium ended early, right?" Meredith said hopefully. "That's why you're here?"

"No." Alex laughed, hugging her. "The symposium is in Salt Lake for the next few days. Then it's off to Seattle."

"Seattle's really cold this time of year," Jaclyn claimed. "Why don't you just skip that one and stay a bit longer?"

"*Seattle* is cold?" Alex repeated. "You mean colder than the sub-zero temperatures you people are currently experiencing?"

"But our company will warm you right up!" Rachel chirped. "We're worth thirty degrees, at least. That puts us about on par with Seattle."

Alex laughed and hugged them all again. "I've missed you guys!"

"So . . . not to pry, but . . . ," Jaclyn said, looking significantly at the door that Sealey had exited through after dropping Alex off. "How are things going with Sealey? You two gave each other about the soppiest look I've ever seen before he left."

"I know," Alex said with a blissful smile at her. "Isn't it great?"

"So, you're completely over Lucas then?" Rachel asked with a careful expression.

"Completely over Lucas," Alex replied emphatically. "We had so much fun together and he's a great guy, but I didn't really know what it meant to be in love until Sealey."

"You're in love with Sealey?" Meredith squealed. "Why is this the first time I'm hearing about this?"

"Because I haven't actually told anyone yet," Alex said, cringing at Meredith's persistent high-pitch. "Not even him."

"Wow, you've strung him along for a while, haven't you?" Kacey said, eyebrow raised. "Didn't he tell you he was in love with you like months ago?"

"I know," Alex said defensively. "But I haven't wanted to say it until I knew for sure that it was true. But I do now. So I will."

"When?" Sage asked, clapping her hands. "We'll help you!"

"That's okay," Alex returned before the words were even all the way out of Sage's mouth. "I really appreciate it, guys, but I think I'd rather tell him on my own. It's kind of an important chat."

"Seriously, Sage, who wants their roommates listening in on a conversation like that?" Kacey reprimanded. "But I do echo your question of *when*?" She turned back to Alex as she spoke the last word of her sentence.

"I'm not sure," Alex admitted.

"Well, Valentine's Day was last week so you've royally screwed up that opportunity," Jaclyn pointed out.

"Well, I didn't want to make a production out of it, and Valentine's Day seems to be a day of productions," Alex defended and sighed. "When the time is right, I'll just know."

Alex could tell Kacey was refraining from rolling her eyes with great difficulty, but she didn't care. It was too important a conversation to worry about what her roommates thought of her methods.

She spent the evening catching her roommates up on her travels, and nearly all of them were asleep by the time Sealey showed up at ten to return her to her Salt Lake City hotel. She and Meredith were sitting on the couch talking quietly when his soft knock sounded on the door.

"That's my cue," Alex sighed. "I'll see you in a few weeks, Mer, okay?"

"Okay," Meredith said glumly. But she brightened almost immediately. "Hey, make sure and call me after the big moment with Sealey. I want to hear all about it."

"I promise," Alex said, smiling. "Bye," she whispered as she quietly left the apartment.

Sealey immediately grabbed her hand as she closed the door behind her.

"So how was it?" Sealey asked. "Good to know they didn't squeeze you to death after I left. I was afraid I might be picking up a corpse."

Alex laughed. "It was so great to see everyone. Thank you for doing this. Even though you won't get home until well after midnight. You're a gem."

"Well, actually, I've decided to stay with my parents while you're in town. They're living just south of Salt Lake these days. And, if it's okay with you, I'd like you to meet them while you're here."

Alex bit her lip nervously. "I'd love to," she said, but her voice sounded like she was dreading it more than anything.

"Trust me, my parents do not have any expectations of me marrying *anyone*," Sealey soothed her. "This will not be a repeat of your last 'meet the parents' experience."

"Good to hear," Alex replied, feeling better already.

In truth, meeting Sealey's parents was simply a joy. They were not just gracious, welcoming, and kind, but downright hilarious. If she had met them in the old days of Sealey, she would have wondered how two such bright, happy, and amusing people could have produced such a grumpy cuss. But now, having experienced the lighter side of Sealey, she could see how similar they were. The evening she spent with the three of them was so much fun that when she and Sealey finally left their South Jordan residence, she was already trying to think of excuses that would require her to visit them again.

"What fantastic people," she said to Sealey as she climbed into the car. "I can't remember the last time I laughed so hard."

"Yeah, they're pretty incredible," Sealey agreed, putting his car into gear. "And they seemed to like you more than they like me."

"And they're just so *smart*."

He laughed and reached over to take her hand. "It's so great to have you home for a little bit. I've missed you."

"I've missed you too, Sealey," she said, squeezing his hand. And then, it was out, as naturally as if she said it every day. "I love you, you know."

The car jolted a bit as Sealey's foot jerked on the pedal. He swiveled his head to look hard at her. "You do?" he said, his voice intense.

"Very much," she replied, smiling. "I just thought you should know."

Sealey pulled over immediately, shoving the car into park. Without another word, he pulled Alex across the center console and kissed her with all the fervor he could muster.

* * * * *

Alex left for Seattle the next evening. From there she went to Portland, then to Las Vegas, and finally to Los Angeles, her final destination. She had been looking forward to Los Angeles, not just because she was sick to death of getting on a plane every few days, but also because Sealey was planning to meet her there. He was in LA for an advertising conference and had called her the day before to ask her to dinner for her first evening in town.

Alex was ready for him a full thirty minutes before he actually showed up. She might have been a little overeager.

"Hey, beautiful," he said when she opened the door to her hotel room to find him standing there. He stepped forward to kiss her sweetly on the mouth. "You look fantastic, as always. Ready to go?"

She nodded excitedly. "Where are we going?"

"Oh, I have something kind of special planned," Sealey said with a cryptic air. "Some guy took you on a romantic picnic once, and I'd kind of like to one-up him." He winked at her. "And because I know you better than he did, I happen to know that the most appropriate place for a romantic picnic with someone like you is not a canyon."

They drove in relative silence. Mostly they just held hands and smiled to themselves. When Sealey finally pulled off the road into the parking lot for Venice Beach, Alex's suspicions were confirmed.

"A picnic by the water?" Alex asked delightedly. "You really *do* know me!"

Sealey smiled at her and opened the trunk to grab the goodies. The beach was nearly deserted, as March was still a little too chilly for most beachgoers. But to Alex, everything felt perfect. They sat side-by-side on the picnic blanket, talking and slowly working their way through the food that Sealey had brought. Alex was so absorbed in him that she didn't even really register what she was eating.

After they ate, they walked along the water's edge, laughing and gasping when the cold water hit their toes. As Alex stood with her feet submerged in the bubbly sea foam, she felt Sealey place something cold on the third finger of her left hand.

"So what do you think?" Sealey asked, his voice strained and nervous. "Do you think you can stand to put up with me on a permanent basis?"

Alex stared at the sparkling diamond on her finger. It was the ring design she had always wanted, given to her by the man she loved more than anything.

"How did you . . . ?" she asked breathlessly, but couldn't finish. She gestured to the perfect ring on her finger.

"Your mom." He shrugged with a crooked smile. "She told me what engagement ring to buy when I was at your house over Christmas. I asked for your parents' permission to marry you while I was there."

"You . . ." she gasped. "You've been wanting to propose since *Christmas?*"

"I was waiting for you to fall in love with me, Alex." Sealey smiled. "I already knew what I wanted, but I've learned my lesson about trying to scheme my way into happiness. From now on, your happiness comes first, and I'm pretty sure mine will follow faithfully behind. After all, I've learned that all that it takes for me to be happy is you."

Alex reached up to comb her fingers through his white blond hair. He slid his hands under her jacket and around her waist, drawing her close to him. She felt the cold water swirling around her toes and the contrasting heat of Sealey's embrace. It was an absolutely perfect moment.

"Meredith used to tell me all the time how many other fish there were in the sea when I would complain about how Lucas refused to notice me," Alex said, smiling softly. "She said that I was much better off finding a fish who loved me all by himself, without me tricking or prodding him into it." She ran her fingers softly over Sealey's face, and watched as he closed his eyes, relishing the feeling. "And you are proof that Meredith was right," she said, her voice sweetly amused. "I just needed to keep fishing." She kissed him softly on the lips and pulled back to study his handsome face.

"I'm choosing to interpret that as a yes," Sealey said, not bothering to open his eyes, but skimming his lips over her face. "Although in this scenario, I'd like to point out that I was actually the one doing the fishing."

Alex grinned as tingles spread over her arms and legs. "My apologies, master fisherman." She laughed, but it died quickly in her throat as he opened his eyes and the deep blue met the dark brown. "Thank you for not giving up on me," she whispered.

As he leaned forward to press his lips to hers, the sea foam tickling her feet became as warm as bathwater on her skin. She felt the sweet confirmation that the one she had was the one she should hold on to. And she intended to hold on tight. Forever.

{ *Discussion* QUESTIONS }

1. Why do you think Alex chose to enter into a scheme with Sealey to win Lucas's heart instead of approaching the task honestly? When have you been in a situation where you had to choose between the easy road and the honest road?

2. Why do you think Alex felt as though she couldn't win Lucas's heart on her own? Was Sealey right to encourage her in this view?

3. How does the theme of honesty (or the lack thereof) cause problems throughout the story? Are there points where characters illustrated too much honesty? How did that contribute to the problem?

4. Sealey's decision to guide Alex through her romance with Lucas resulted from a lack of confidence and an unwillingness to be vulnerable. When have you been in a situation where a lack of confidence severely contributed to the problem?

5. Was it reasonable for Alex to be so conflicted between her job offer and Lucas? When the possibility of true love presents itself, should there ever be any other options?

6. If you had been in Alex's situation, would you have forgiven Sealey so readily for his deception? Why or why not?

{ About the AUTHOR }

LAUREN WINDER FARNSWORTH was born and raised in Salt Lake City, Utah. She is an avid reader, a chocolate enthusiast, and a CPA with a slight alternative music obsession and dreams of one day becoming a gourmet chef. She obtained bachelor's and master's degrees in accounting from the University of Utah, went to work as a financial statement auditor, and then decided that since creative accounting wasn't an option, creative writing would have to do. As a nice compromise, accountants tend to crop up in her stories (because she firmly believes they're underutilized in literature anyway). Having obtained two degrees from the same institution has made Lauren somewhat of a compound collegiate fan, and the only entity that holds more of her heart than the University of Utah is her hunky husband, Bryan. Lauren currently lives in South Jordan, Utah, where she spends entirely too much time watching *Gilmore Girls* and looking for excuses not to clean.

SCAN TO VISIT

0 26575 17918 7

WWW.LAURENWINDER
FARNSWORTH.COM